Best Wishes

from

Peter Wood

In the summer of 1994, a play opened in London for a remarkable season. Called *The Strike Of 1889*, remarkable is an apposite description as it played for only twenty-six performances, all of which were sold out and ended with a prolonged standing ovation. In spite of its widespread acclaim from both press and public alike, this play has never subsequently been performed.

Conceived by Steve Rogers, and written by Steve and Robert Hamilton, my involvement with *The Strike Of 1889* was as co-producer. *The Price Of A Cigar* is a development of that play and my gratitude and acknowledgement go to both Rob and Steve. Their contribution has been considerable and without it there would have been no book.

Peter Wood

THE PRICE
OF A
CIGAR

First published November 1996 by Anchor Books

Copyright © Peter Wood & Steve Rogers

ISBN 0 9528167 0 9

Peter Wood is hereby identified as author of this work

A Cataloguing in Publication record of this title is available from the British Library

Typeset by Anchor Books
Jacket design by Peter Wood & Steve Rogers
Jacket illustration by Ben Wolstenholme
Printed and bound in Great Britain by Page Bros, Norwich

Anchor Books, Anchor House, 54 Whiteadder Way, London E14 9UR

Although a small number of the characters in this book are, for the purpose of simplifying a complex issue, composites or imaginary, the events took place much as they are described.

Although a great number of the photographs in this book are, for the purposes of amplifying a particular point, enlargements or miniatures, the correct leaf shape can in each case be ascertained.

Peter Wood

THE PRICE OF A CIGAR

ANCHOR BOOKS

London in the late 1880s was the prosperous heart of a seemingly eternal Empire. The largest city of earth, it was an example to the world of all that was stable and to be admired. But it was a story of two cities.

The East End of London is a starving, hell of poverty which lies in lurking silence to threaten the life and wealth of both the City and the West End. Manifestly, this is poverty as a way of life. These people have nothing else to do but be poor.

Home Office report, May 1889.
(withheld from the public)

The events here presented occurred in London
during August and September 1889.

Chapter One

"Dad, look what I found." Shaun Lamb woke to find nine-year-old Jimmy dangling a dead rat six inches from his face. "It was in the food cupboard."

Shaun showed only passing interest. Rats, dead or alive, were hardly unprecedented in the house. The walls and floor-boards were home to dozens of the beasts and in an often fruit-less effort to discourage them from biting the family as they slept, four of his six children were delegated to sit up each night in hourly shifts. Only the two infants were excused the responsibility. "Food cupboard? No wonder it was dead. Been nothing in there for days. Go to bed, Jimmy. I'll watch for the beggars."

Jimmy tossed the rat onto the communal rubbish pile on the landing outside and clambered into bed with his brothers. In-cluding himself there were four, the two eldest granted the privilege of sleeping at the top while the youngest lay inverted at the foot. Two sisters shared the small adjacent bed, while stuffed into what once held potatoes, Shaun and his wife Mary lay stretched out on the floor. More sacking adorned the beds, improvising as bed-linen for the children, for there were nei-ther blankets nor sheets.

Apart from the beds, a small table standing beside the window, and a battered tin bathtub filled close to overflowing with grimy water, there was little else of consequence in the room. Beneath the table crouched a ragged, black and white cat of rather sad appearance that seemed ashamed to be seen in such a place. A knife, four forks, a bent teaspoon, a pair of cups estranged from their own saucers and mated with others which did not match, some half-a-dozen cracked plates, and a tin teapot, were the only indications of eating or sitting down to meals. Sitting down, indeed, would have been difficult except in Turkish fashion for there was but one chair which was in grave need of repair. In the corner stood a porcelain poodle, hideous to behold, and perched on the narrow, stone mantelpiece, a tiny clock which unlike most in the neighbourhood seemed capable of working, for it actually ticked. Eight of them, living, eating and sleeping in a room so small as to make the description all but an exaggeration.

This was 7c, Shadwell Gardens. But with nothing horticultural about it save its name. No hyacinths grew here, nor any sprig of green. Just a block of twelve dark, bleak houses with a wall at the end of the street and, beyond, a canal. But the family clung to it as the drowning man to a log, for in the East End of London there was a depth even lower than the slum – the streets.

Shaun gazed up at the ceiling. It was his birthday, his thirtieth. But a day unlikely to differ from yesterday, the one before, or, indeed, any other. In an hour he would be at the dock gates along with more than a thousand others fighting for maybe a hundred jobs. An army of the desperate, men quietly talking together – until the bell sounds. And then the wild charge as they fling themselves towards the foreman, the god who decides whose children will eat that night. The strongest will swarm around his pulpit as from behind a protecting chain he casually selects the most ravenous, and therefore the cheapest, to receive the precious tin ticket that will mean work for a day. Encircled with the chain, they will then be held for an hour until the gangers register their names. Held like rats in a cage: like frenzied human rats who see only food in the ticket. Meanwhile, the vanquished will limp away to another dock, cursing fate, to repeat their degradation, or give up for the day in despair to buy or beg themselves solace at the nearest tavern. And all this for what? Just fivepence an hour.

Work had been regular when Shaun had started at the docks some sixteen years before. But now there were more dock labourers than available jobs and even by the diminished standards of the East End, they were the most poorly paid of all the unskilled workers. Consequently, reality, if he was lucky, was two days employment and maybe eight shillings a week. Mary did all she could. With assistance from the children, she toiled at home long into the nights fitting the bristles into scrubbing-brushes. But it was a slow way to get rich. They earned just a penny for every three hundred holes filled and their fingers and eyes suffered from the effort. Lizzie, at ten the eldest of the children, worked eleven hours a day at the nearby Bryant and May factory, and Jimmy, together with two of his brothers, would gather horse manure in a bucket from the roads and sell it as fertiliser for a halfpenny a time; or, for a penny, hold a cart driver's horse while he drank at the tavern. Four of the children were meant to attend school, but neither Shaun, nor indeed anyone he knew, could afford either the fees, or to forgo their children's earnings and assistance around the home.

Between them all, the family earned about eighteen shillings a week, barely sufficient to survive. Only three of the children had shoes and none of them had tasted meat for nearly a month, their meals, if they could be described as such, concocted from the cheapest bread, margarine, tea, sugar and, on the rare occasions fortune smiled on the home, a few eggs. Once a week the neighbourhood clergy would deliver soup to families in their street, which helped, especially when it contained vegetables and scraps of fish. But they always rose from the table wanting and able to eat more.

Each week they somehow contrived to raise the four shillings rent, as for them it was pay the landlord or join the ranks of the homeless. And desperate as it was for a single man to confront life in the streets, how much more of an agony for a husband to find himself and his family but one step from the final humiliation of even the impoverished – the dreaded workhouse. Overhearing his parents discussing the prospect recently had alarmed young Jimmy. "They'd probably wash us to death."

It was now five days since Shaun had secured a ticket. Five times Mary and the children had waited for the evening when he would bring back the price of the day's work he had gone to seek. And five times before mid-day they had heard the sound of Shaun's footsteps on the stairs, footsteps which told their sad, painful tale in a single creak. No work at the docks. Another day of despair, and another night when they must go hungry to bed. How Mary had cried that previous morning when he arrived home. Today he had to get work.

For a few minutes Shaun lay listening to the foghorns on the Thames, waiting for the ships to answer each other. It was strange, but as long as they responded, he felt all must be well with the world. Carefully he drew himself from the sack and extinguished the candle. It was dawn, but the single, curtainless window, broken and repaired with paper and rags, served as much for ventilation as it did for light and the room became gloomier than before. He glanced in the direction of the children, their hunger interrupted for a few hours by sleep, and thoughts strayed to his own childhood in Eire.

His father, an honest man, had toiled as a hall porter in a Dublin hotel. Despite suffering from poor eyesight since infancy, he had, through hard work and thrift, somehow succeeded in keeping the wolf from the hearth – if not the door. Year by year his sight deteriorated and the moment of truth came at noon one Christmas Eve when, groping his way along a corridor as if it were dusk, he stumbled over a suitcase and plunged down a short flight of stairs. Faces he should have recognised were suddenly unfamiliar to him. "What's the matter?" they said. What's the matter! The porter was blind.

Into the breadwinner's shoes stepped his wife, taking in washing and sewing, while the blind man passed each day, and long into the evening, sitting in the streets, a tin cup dangling round his neck. But soon, crippled by illness, the brave woman could labour no longer and overhauled by debt, the family was evicted. How well Shaun remembered that night: only seven years old and perched astride their possessions piled up in the street. On guard, with six younger brothers and sisters crouching, bewildered, by his side, while his mother, infant in arms, hobbled away to beg shelter from a compassionate relative.

Shaun shivered involuntarily at the memory. Overnight, the *Lady Armstrong* was due to berth at West India Dock. He had to get work. Today, he had to get work.

A pebble lobbed through the open window, bounced across the floor and struck the stove with a sharp clang. "Christ! Is it time already? It's alright, Clare. It's Shaun Lamb."

Jim and Clare Harris lay on the floor separated from the bare boards by the heap of coarse sacking that comprised their bed. The tiny room, or home, for it was one and the same, differed little in its ugliness from the dull, dreary district of Limehouse that surrounded it. Wide cracks in the walls, plaster peeling from the ceiling, rotting floorboards, some of which were loose and threatening to descend to the room below. But they knew better than to complain; if they didn't like it they could go. There were dozens of others who would jump at the accommodation and the landlord was well aware of the fact.

Little more than eight feet square and six feet in height, the room could scarcely be said to be furnished for there was no bedstead, nor table, nor chair. But it was scrupulously clean and the floorboards appeared as though a scrubbing-brush was a far from chance acquaintance. A piece or two of crockery lay in a corner, but with no sign of cookery past, present, or to come. The furniture had been surrendered two months before to pay the funeral costs of Jim and Clare's two little girls who had died within six hours of each other of scarlatina. Taken to the infirmary for treatment one afternoon in the 'fever van'. They never returned. "Poor little souls," Clare had cried. "Maybe they're happy now they're dead. Lord knows, while they lived I know they hadn't much to make 'em happy."

Neighbours had assisted where they could, but the benefits of mutual help were limited when a whole district was destitute. Now, after two years of marriage, Jim and Clare had only themselves to maintain as they strived to retrieve their debts.

Born almost thirty-two years before in Wapping in East London, Jim Harris had been a labourer since he was fourteen. As a child he endured being crammed into a couple of rooms with numerous younger brothers and sisters, all living on poorer and less regular food than he could ordinarily secure for himself by petty pilfering and begging. Thus, come the age of ten, his home was the streets and docks and he had acquired considerable skill at feigning the role of the blind beggar, who could actually see; the dumb beggar, who could actually speak; and the lame beggar, who promptly dispensed with his crutch at the cessation of business hours. So skilled did he become that only rarely did he need to return home to procure meals for himself.

Almost from birth, the forces of Jim's environment had tended to harden him. He was twenty before he had learned either to read or write, scant disadvantage he thought, at least for a man of his station in life. Now, after labouring at the docks for sixteen years, his station was worse than when he had started and increasingly his greatest happiness was to be found in the oblivion of alcohol. He was not a bad man. Not inherently vicious or evil. He had normal mentality and more than average physique. But sober, how could he be anything but wretched? Jim pulled himself from the sack. It was now five days since he had secured a ticket. Today he had to get work. "Down in a minute, Shaun," he called from the window.

Clare was asleep once more. Before their marriage she had often sold herself on the dingy streets of neighbouring Hackney, streets which afforded if not the prospect of wealth and comfort, then at least an existence free from the level of poverty in which they now found themselves. Clare wanted children again, as did Jim. But not in these miserable surroundings. Overnight, the *Lady Armstrong* was due to berth at West India Dock. He had to get work. Today, he had to get work.

From Limehouse to West India Dock, the largest and busiest in the Port of London, was almost a mile. Shaun and Jim spoke little as they walked through streets of dismal monotony. Past the lamp-lighter crossing to and fro to extinguish the flaming gas lights, past the factories, smoke endlessly rising from their chimneys before blending with the receding dawn fog, past the children, perhaps fifty in number, already queuing outside the Limehouse Mission for nine o'clock breakfast. And past the open slaughterhouse where blood and animal innards splattered the pavement to provide a feast for the famished cats. No need for them to queue hours for a meal. As they walked, a babble of voices could be heard, barely perceptibly at first, but strengthening with every step as more and more men in their flat caps and loose trousers, worn jackets and collarless shirts, converged from the dark, cavernous streets and headed towards the objective common to every one of them – work for a day.

Six o'clock. Shaun and Jim reached the entrance to West India Dock where the huge wooden gates remained closed. Already gathered around were about five hundred men from throughout East London. Most stood motionless with hands thrust deep into their trouser pockets and all, with hope in their hearts, were facing in the same direction – towards the dock gates. There was an hour to wait.

The Dockers Arms opposite was full and doing a heavy trade. Outside, entertainers were already vying for business. An ex-sailor was allowing himself to be tied with four ropes, and any number of knots, and guaranteeing to free himself within a minute. Nearby, a small girl turned the handle of an organ to keep the audience amused until a man without arms appeared. He could shave himself, play the violin, and perform numerous other deeds by employing his toes instead of his fingers. Such freak shows had become popular since the emergence in Whitechapel some five years earlier of a man who had gained some local notoriety and been labelled as The Elephant Man by the London press.

Half-past six. From all directions a constant stream of men swelled the numbers at the gate. A cheerful fair-haired lad engaged Shaun and Jim in conversation. "What's the chances of work today you reckon? Stood here every day last week, but for nothin'. Me Dad's ill, see. Need the money for me Mum." No more than fourteen years of age, the boy looked frail and in no condition either to battle for a ticket or to undertake the arduous work even if he got one. He received a predictable response.

"We all need the work, son," said Harris indifferently.

Twenty minutes to seven. Six dock policemen under the supervision of a grave-looking sergeant, pushed their way through the crowd and entered the dock through a side gate, dragging a pair of heavy chains and four iron posts. "The *Lady Armstrong* berthed last night, lads," the sergeant reported. "Frozen meat. Should be work today, and for a few more to come I shouldn't wonder."

Jim Harris considered the irony. "Meat!" he growled. "Some of us might get to unload it . . . if we're lucky. But I bet none of us here has eaten any for a month."

Ten minutes to seven. From inside the gate the clanking of metal and the ringing of a mallet signalled the positioning of the chain and the erecting of the posts in their sockets. Drawn by the sound, the waiting crowd edged ever forward towards the gate, watching the hand of the clock on the dock office tower creep slowly upwards.

Five minutes to seven. The silence was unbroken save for the hoot of a steamer's whistle from the river and a brief dispute at the rear of the crowd as a latecomer endeavoured to push his way forward. Motionless cranes thrust their long, skeletal arms from the deserted quay. Large, empty wagons stood horseless and idle. It began to rain.

Seven o'clock. The clang of a bell resounded among the lofty warehouses, a low murmur rose from the crowd like a field of wheat stirred by the wind, and the great gates creaked open. Instantly, a menacing change swept over the throng. Amidst a tumult of noise, a thousand men surged wildly towards the chain, fighting and kicking for position. Then, momentarily, the uproar subsided. The foreman was nowhere to be seen. But suddenly he was there, attired in a bowler hat and black coat – and he was holding a bundle of tickets.

All self-control seemed to disappear in a moment. The whole crowd surged forward. Simultaneously, a forest of arms with hands outstretched, reached up to the air. With wild faces, and crushed against the chain, the men at the front craned forward, snatching desperately at the foreman as he sauntered along the line, eyeing them with a hard, searching glance, taunting them, evading their reach, relishing the savage struggle for survival. Then he pointed his finger. "You – and you – and you – and you."

Shouting their joy, the chosen men dived beneath the chain to claim their tickets. Again the foreman pointed. "You – and you – and you – and you."

Harris was through, but not Lamb. Separated during the initial charge, he was anonymous in the crowd. "You – and you – and you – and you."

For several minutes the foreman paced back and forth along the line, dealing out the tickets. The bundle was dwindling fast, but there was still hope and the clamour and struggle grew fiercer. "You – and you – and you – and you." Then he stopped. Just one remained.

The chain seemed stretched to snapping point as the foreman stepped back to survey the crowd, casually fingering the ticket. The noise swelled to a roar as hundreds of desperate voices pleaded for work. Lamb, now at the front, leant over the chain his arms held out. With a cruel leer, the foreman strolled leisurely along the line past clawing hands. Then he turned and repeated the torment. Finally he stopped and pointed. "You." It was Lamb.

A cry of despair ran through the crowd; the hope that had welled in their hearts was destroyed in a moment. A hundred men given work, but ten times that number denied. With hunched shoulders and downcast faces the men prepared to move back towards the gate. As they turned, a slight figure, blooded and bruised by the battle, vaulted the chain. He ran to the foreman and grabbed his arm. But the man struck out and the intruder fell to his knees. It was the young, fair-haired lad. "What the hell do you want?" demanded the foreman indignantly.

"Work. I wanna work. I'm willing to wait . . . wait in the yard with the others."

"You don't look fit for shit, boy. Clear off. Go and get yourself cleaned up."

"I'm alright," said the lad, looking up in despair at the man. "I can work, really. They're just cuts and bruises. I've gotta work. You don't understand."

The man stared down making no effort to conceal his contempt and spat within an inch of the boy. "Listen. *You* don't understand. We've got enough for today. Clear off home."

Still on his knees, the young lad gripped desperately at the man's leg. "One more, that's all, just one more. I wanna work, please..." With a blast on his whistle, the foreman summoned the dock gate police. They seized the lad and dragged him away to a cell, there to await judgement by the local magistrate.

Meanwhile, most of the men trailed slowly through the gate, although some chose to wait, perhaps until noon, on the slender chance of being taken on for a few hours in the afternoon. Outside the Dockers Arms a one-man band performed a jaunty music hall tune, achieving the apparently impossible by employing his elbows to beat a big drum which he carried on his back, while simultaneously, his right foot pulled a strap connected to a pair of cymbals fastened precariously to the drum. When he shook his head, bells tinkled merrily, and all the while he both operated a concertina and blew a harmonica, ingeniously secured to his bowler hat by a wire support. Predictably, his inventive talents earned scant reward.

A few men entered the tavern to buy consolation with what little money they possessed, but most drifted away, weary and dejected. A day's story that in docks throughout the East End was the story of yesterday and would be the story of tomorrow.

Chapter Two

A few minutes' walk from the Dockers Arms at the point where West India Dock Road encounters Commercial Road, stood the Limehouse Mission, its cheerful white brick frontage a welcome contrast to its dismal surroundings. Annie Tillett worked at both, and although she was unaware of the fact, so, quite soon, would Eleanor Marx. This was to be a surprise to the elegant Miss Marx who had not previously ventured inside a tavern in the East End, or, indeed, anywhere else.

The Limehouse Mission was administered by Reverend Adderley, a scholar and Christian socialist with unconventional manners and interests, and one of the finest amateur actors in London. It had been founded a year earlier under the patronage of Lady Hallow, left a widow following the death of her husband, his neck broken in a horse-riding accident in Epping. It had been Reverend Adderley who performed the funeral service. To diminish her grief, Lady Hallow was determined to devote herself and her modest fortune to charity and when the conditions in the East End were brought to her attention, she founded the Mission.

Apart from Sundays and Christmas Day, the Mission served small groups with a free breakfast or an evening meal. Small, that is, in respect to the size of the guests, but hardly in numbers. The attendance was a hundred and fifty at each session, of which there were two in the morning for a meal of bread, cheese and porridge, and two in the evening for a serving of Irish stew. Tickets were allocated to families on a rotation basis, street by street, by the Poplar Parish Council and local clergy, a process which provided most of the half-starved children of the area under ten years of age with at least one adequate meal a week, and for an hour transformed the wretched youngsters into a noisy, high-spirited congregation.

Once the first hundred and fifty had been fed and gone chattering away – more if ticketless street orphans had succeeded in begging a meal – they were followed immediately by the second batch which would troop impatiently into the space. In accordance with the rule printed in block letters on the ticket, each child had to come provided with both a plate – or more commonly a basin as it accommodated a larger helping – and also a spoon. These were often of varying dimensions and only rarely in proportion to the mouths they had to feed. Many of the bigger children arrived clasping nothing more than a battered teaspoon, while some of the smaller ones had the forethought to come furnished with an implement so large that they seemed prepared for a feast.

It was almost nine o'clock. Annie Tillett went outside to count in the first hundred and fifty breakfast guests of the day – those with bare feet allowed through first to lessen the risk of injury. As always, most of the morning's visitors were already queuing. Cook rarely had cause for complaint that her meals were spoilt while awaiting the arrival of late-comers. "Fill up the back seats first," instructed Annie. As they filed in, marching in quick time to music of their own making, she doubted if there were more than fifty pairs of boots or shoes between them.

A small group of children dashed along the street and stopped in their tracks as they spotted Annie at the Mission door. "Any food?" called out a little girl with long, unruly, ginger hair.

"Bit early ain't yer, Emily? See me later at the tavern and I'll see what I can do." The children raced off and vanished noisily into a back alley. Glancing after them, Annie noticed that a large ship had berthed at West India Dock, its stern visible through the open dock gates. Must be the one the men were talking about in the tavern last night, she thought. The *Lady Armstrong*. And she wondered if her brother had managed to beat the chain.

Inside the Mission, to a prolonged, high-pitched cheer, Reverend Adderley and Annie appeared amongst the trestle-tables bearing two enormous vats of porridge, one to each end of the hall. Then the Reverend blew a shrill blast on his whistle, silence was proclaimed and the children rose and sang *All People That On Earth Do Dwell.* A discerning music critic might have detected that the words became a trifle hurried towards the close, due most likely not to any vocal tuition received by the singers, but the awaiting delights of breakfast.

Twenty-five gallons of porridge later it was time for them to leave. "Mind you brush up a bit before you come next time," Annie instructed a boy whose hair looked excessively dishevelled. It was Jimmy Lamb, mysteriously, making his second appearance at the Mission on consecutive days.

He looked at her in astonishment. "Ain't got no comb, Miss."

Annie spotted a tiny, sweet-faced girl in a large Mother Hubbard bonnet, whose dress pockets looked suspiciously crammed. "Oi. What you got there?"

"Please, Miss. Bread and cheese, Miss." The child smiled apprehensively and performed a modest curtsy.

"But you know you ought not to take food away. Who's it for?"

"Please, me six little brothers, Miss." Annie suppressed a smile. The girl herself looked no more than four years old.

"And how old is the youngest?"

"Please, two days, Miss."

"Well, go along. But you mustn't take food away next time."

"Thank you, Miss. Goodbye, Miss." And away she trudged, well satisfied with the outcome.

As the second group filed boisterously into the hall, Eleanor

Marx sighed as she collected the tickets. "It's like those lines of Emerson. 'More and more, more and more, always more to follow.' "

Annie knew nothing of Emerson, or his lines, and had no intention of betraying her ignorance by enquiring about them. But she understood what Eleanor meant, and not for the first time envied her intellect.

Even the most hardened dock labourer considered Annie Tillett to be a fearsome woman. And not without justification, for although it was not an entirely accurate assessment, any misconceptions were primarily of her own making. As a ten-year-old, someone had likened her to Boadicea. Not that Annie understood the comparison, although some time later she asked her local minister and declared herself more than satisfied with the reply. As a child, she had attended Sunday school where she worked hard and taught herself most of the knowledge she possessed. Her assurance and occasional arrogance were due both to this industry which put her at an educational advantage over most people with whom she now came into contact – she could both read and write – and also the fact that physically, Annie was generally considered the most attractive woman in the neighbourhood.

Thirty-three years old, and born in Bristol, she was the eldest of five children. Her mother had died while giving birth to a sixth child when Annie was eight, and for the following three years, her father, a stevedore at Bristol docks, fought impossible odds to maintain his family. Stricken by increasingly frequent bouts of ill-health, he finally chose to settle his problems by taking the only option he knew, and one morning Annie found him hanging behind the kitchen door. And so at the age of eleven she had lost the liberty of childhood and for the next fifteen years was never free of the responsibility of a mother to her family.

In 1882, her brother Ben, three years her junior, who had left home at the age of twelve to enlist in the Merchant Navy, returned to Bristol. With Annie now free of her maternal commitments, they moved to London, finding their natural environment in the East End. Ben became a dock labourer and married at Bow Church in 1888. It was the only wedding Annie had ever attended.

For the past five years she had lived and worked in the Dockers Arms. Her authority over the often rowdy dockers who comprised the majority of the customers, was so valued by the landlady, Mrs Fish, that she allowed her to spend several hours each day assisting at the Mission. She also averted her eyes when bread and cheese disappeared from the tavern kitchen to end up in the stomachs of the street orphans who roamed the area and to whom Annie had become almost a replacement mother, a relationship, so she claimed, entirely contrary to her intention.

However, if Annie Tillett could have been considered a ubiquitous and even complex character, then Eleanor Marx, brilliant, devout, and beautiful, would surely have mesmerised a symposium of psychologists. Born in Soho in London, and the youngest and favourite daughter of Karl Marx, most of her thirty-four years had been lived in an atmosphere of social revolution and devotion to the causes of the working class. Trained as an actress, in her early twenties she travelled the country performing and giving lectures on Shakespeare. Later, both as a researcher and translator of French and German history, she worked for the British Museum, learning Norwegian in order to translate Ibsen. Unmarried, and now an author, journalist, and advisor to many of the new trade unions being established in London, she had, after years of resistance from the conservative British establishment, succeeded in publishing an English edition of *Das Kapital*, her late father's book.

Four days a week, Eleanor left the comfortable surroundings of her home in Hampstead to help the Mission, both with administration, and by teaching the local children to read and write. She would also assist Annie and Reverend Adderley with the meals, although her refusal, irrespective of the task to be performed, to wear anything but fine lace and frills, frequently proved to be ill-advised. Whenever she visited the East End,

[29]

Eleanor Marx was guaranteed to stand in conflict with her surroundings and although her attire represented everything Annie despised in respect to the inequity of life, it was, as the Reverend had observed, preposterous to imagine her dressed in any other way. Annie Tillett and Eleanor Marx were a perfect example of two people so diametrically opposed in background, education, and personality, that it would have been easy for the casual eye to overlook the fact that ideologically they were as one.

Once the morning's three hundred breakfasts had been devoured, Cook made off in the direction of the local primary school to prepare the lunches, but returned a few minutes later, this time in the company of Constable Boydell from Poplar police station. "Annie. The officer says a friend of yours has been arrested . . . for stealing from Stewart's the baker's. A roll weren't it, officer?"

"That's right, missus," confirmed the constable. "Says her name's Hemley. Gave us your name. 'Annie,' she said. Reckoned you'd be here at the Mission. Longish red hair . . . about eight years of age."

"Oh, God!" said Annie. "That's Emily."

"Ah. You knows her then, miss. She'll be up in front of the magistrate any time now if you wants to speak up for her."

Emily was one of the street orphans. "Your mummy and daddy have gone away to paradise," Annie had explained to the enquiring child some years before.

"Hmm. Gone to paradise. I'd rather they'd come to see me," had been her wistful reply.

If Annie had a favourite amongst the hundred or so orphans that roamed around Limehouse, then it was Emily. She was a constant reminder to Annie of herself, as many of the things she would say and do, seemed, to an uncanny degree, to mirror her own behaviour as a child.

The Magistrate's Court was located behind the police station and next to the baker's shop where the crime had apparently been committed. There was not long to wait. "Next," bawled the Clerk of the Court.

Escorted by a constable who towered above her, Emily entered the courtroom from a side door, and for a young, bare-footed child, climbed inordinately noisily up the steps to the dock. Once inside, only the top of her tiny head was visible above the rail. Facing the elderly, bespectacled magistrate perched imperiously on an elevated bench, lay the crucial evidence in the proceedings – minus a large bite.

"What is your name, child?" said the magistrate.

"Emily, sir," she replied breezily, with a face which in other circumstances would have lit up a room.

"Emily what?"

"Just Emily, sir. I'm a norphan."

"And how old are you?"

Tossing the hair from her face, she sniffed and thought for a moment. "Don't know, sir. Never asked no-one."

"Clerk," snapped the magistrate. "I can't see the child. Get a box for her to stand on." Hurriedly an old tea-chest was produced of sufficient size for Emily's head to emerge into open court. "Ah, good. There you are. Constable Green tells me that you stole a bread roll from Stewart's the baker's in the High Street. Is this true?"

"Yes, sir."

"And why did you steal the roll?"

Emily looked puzzled at the purpose of the man's question and wiped her nose with the back of her hand. " 'Cos I's 'ungry, sir."

"Yes, that's as maybe," snapped the magistrate, before his stern expression softened slightly and he continued in a more benevolent tone. "But don't you know it is wrong to take something that does not belong to you? Why didn't you ask the woman in the shop for the roll if you were hungry? She would surely have given you something to eat."

"Well, sir," explained Emily, studying his face intently. "If I'd asked 'er, I'd 've got locked up for beggin'. An' that's twenty-eight days. But it's only fourteen days for takin' a roll."

The magistrate ignored her apparent intimacy with the law. "Is there anyone here to represent the child?"

Annie stood up and walked a little apprehensively towards the bench. "Yes, sir. Annie Tillett. I work at the Dockers Arms and help out at the Limehouse Mission, sir."

"Ah, yes. I am acquainted with the Reverend Adderley, Miss Tillett. A fine man." The magistrate turned towards the Clerk. "Is this the child's first offence?"

"Oh, yes, sir," declared Emily quickly, and with the expression of a saint. "Def'nitely first hoffence."

"I'm not addressing you child. Stay quiet. Clerk?"

"Yes, sir. Nothing known."

The magistrate returned his attention to Emily and his words were accompanied by a look of due severity. "If I see you here again, child, you will go to prison. Do you understand?"

"Yes, sir."

"I hope you can keep her away from trouble, Miss Tillett. You may go, child."

"Thank you, sir. Goodbye, sir." Emily paused for a moment, her fingers twiddling with the hem of her dress. "Sir."

"Yes?" said the magistrate, surprised still to see her in the court.

"Can I keep the roll ?"

"Quiet," hissed Annie, "or you'll feel the back of my hand." She grabbed Emily by the arm and hauled her unceremoniously outside on to the pavement. "Now look here, Emily. Don't you ever..." But she was gone.

Jimmy Lamb looked bored. Using a piece of broken timber, he was digging a hole in a patch of waste ground outside his home. *"Jimmy!"* As ever, he paid scant attention to his mother's call, choosing instead to extract a long, wriggling worm from the earth. *"Jimmy!"* Moments later a harassed Mary Lamb appeared at the door. "Jimmy. Get out the dirt and come in . . . we're goin' shopping." Shoving the worm into the depths of his trouser-pocket, he dashed indoors where his brothers and sisters were already dressed and waiting. "Come on, we're late," said Mary, jamming an old cap onto Jimmy's head. The instant she turned away, the cap was slung idly beneath the bed.

It took them five minutes to reach the High Street and the tiny cobbler's shop on the corner with its simple message painstakingly inscribed in white paint on the window: 'If you think your boots are ended, bring them here and get them mended.' Outside, a cluster of boys were disputing with a measure of energy and unsavoury language disproportionate to the small number involved, the outcome of a game of marbles. Mary hauled Jimmy past by his collar. "And where's yer cap?"

He clutched his head in surprise. "It's gone, mum," he said simply, as if that explained everything.

"What d'yer mean it's gone? You're not getting another one." She ushered her children hurriedly into the butcher's shop. "Mornin', Mr Griffin. Any left-overs?"

The shopkeeper showed her the fat recently trimmed from a joint of meat. "This do yer?"

The fat looked tempting. "This is all I got," said Mary, staring awkwardly at the coins in her hand.

The man glanced at the money and then briefly at the children. "Hang on a minute. I'll see if there's any scraps out the back."

Two boys peered in through the open shop doorway. "What yer doin', Jimmy?"

"Nothin'," he said.

"You wanna come wiv us?"

"No, he doesn't," said Mary quickly. "Clear off!"

"Yeah, I do. I wanna go wiv 'em, mum."

"Well you can't."

"Why can't he come wiv us, Mrs Lamb?" asked one of the boys.

" 'Cos he can't, that's all."

The boy looked baffled. "That's no reason."

Mary glared at him. "He's got things to do."

"What sort of things?" demanded Jimmy.

"Just things," she said, smiling with embarrassment at another customer.

"See yer later then, Jimmy," called one of the boys.

"Don't know why he can't come wiv us," said the other.

" 'Cos he's got things to do," his friend explained.

"Yeah, but what sort of things?"

"Dunno . . . 'things', she said. Didn't say what sort of things . . . just said 'things'."

The two boys raced off down the street, singing as they went. "Mary 'ad a little lamb, 'is name is Jimmy, Jimmy the Lamb." Jimmy broke from his mother's grasp and tore off after them.

"Jimmy. Jimmy, you come back 'ere . . . you little sod."

Hands clasped around her knees, Emily was sitting on the pavement chatting confidentially to a purring cat almost as ginger and large as herself, when the three boys dashed up. "I know you," said Jimmy. "Seen you before . . . at the Mission."

"Is that yer girlfriend?" sniggered one of the boys.

"No, it ain't."

"Yeah it is, I reckon."

"No it ain't, stoopid," said Jimmy scornfully, screwing up his face and sticking his tongue out at his friends. They responded in kind and quickly he returned his attention to Emily. "Where d'yer live?"

"Don't live nowhere. I'm a norphan."

"What's a norphan?"

"Means I don't live in no 'ouse."

"So where's yer mum and dad live then?"

"Ain't got no mum and dad."

"Cor. Wish I didn't 'ave no mum and dad . . . 'specially no mum. 'Ere, I've got somefing for yer. Shut yer eyes."

Emily covered her face with both hands. As she did so, Jimmy pulled the still wriggling worm from his pocket and dropped it inside her dress. She screamed and the three boys ran off laughing as she struggled to retrieve it. After a dozen or so paces, Jimmy spotted a filthy, rotting apple core in the roadway and picking it up, hurled it at Emily, striking her forcefully on the arm. Now free of the worm, she grabbed the core from the gutter and crammed it quickly into her mouth.

Chapter Three

Lord Caldrick crammed most of a smoked salmon sandwich into his mouth and threw the remainder into a receptacle on the floor. In appearance and manner he was the very embodiment of success. Chairman of the Board of the London Dock Employers, and its largest shareholder, he had accumulated his considerable wealth during thirty years of prosperous trade through the Port of London.

From his imposing office at Dock House in Leadenhall Street, the headquarters of the London Dock Employers, Lord Caldrick was presiding over the weekly meeting of directors. Seated around the shining, mahogany table were his close colleague George Hyde and the ten other dock company owners. Together, the twelve men comprised the board. Also present was C.M.Norwood. He was a man of Herculean proportions, well in excess of six feet tall and weighing almost eighteen stone. Norwood was the Chairman of the Docks Management Committee and responsible directly to Lord Caldrick.

The agenda that morning was not a routine one. During each of the past six years, Lord Caldrick had been able to announce increased annual profits for the London Dock Employers; profits that were generally in excess of those produced by the other principal dock companies around the country. For 1888 this increase had been seven per cent. However, that morning, the Merseyside Dock Company, second in prominence only to the London Dock Employers, had declared an interim increase in profits for the first half of 1889 of nine per cent. This itself was sufficient cause for disquiet to the board and the fact that two hours hence all twelve men were due at the Mansion House for a reception hosted by Sir James Whitehead, the Lord Mayor of London, in recognition of their pre-eminent role in generating sustained wealth for the City of London, further deepened the concern in the room that morning.

"If a provincial port like Merseyside can reach nine per cent," declared Lord Caldrick, "then our objective must be greater. So what do you propose, Mr Norwood, to further increase our margins?" Before Norwood could reply, Caldrick proceeded to outline his own solution. "Prior to your arrival here this morning, the board has discussed the matter most carefully and we have concluded that there is only one avenue available to us – stop the bonus payment."

Norwood raised his eyebrows questioningly. "But sirs. That could be counter-productive. Without the bonus, the cargo would not be unloaded in good time. It is to our benefit that the dock labourers perceive some incentive to work in an expeditious fashion."

"Of course, you are correct, Norwood," agreed George Hyde. "We merely question whether the bonus is being paid when perhaps it is not always justified."

Norwood looked concerned. "I can assure you, gentlemen, that I maintain the strictest attention to the time it takes..."

"No, no, no," declared Hyde. "You misunderstand. No-one is implying that you are being negligent in your duties. You are paid to operate the docks, and this you do most efficiently. We are simply suggesting that you are perhaps a little over-generous in paying the bonus and if..."

But Caldrick was becoming impatient. "To spell it out, Norwood, the dockers are desperate for work. They are only too grateful for a wage – any wage. Some will argue I'm sure. But when it becomes a matter of being paid something, or not being paid at all, they will bite their lips and take what they are given."

"But Lord Caldrick. One aspect of your plan does concern me," questioned Sir Stuart Wallingford, another of the dock owners. "Can we get away with it?"

Norwood conceded the point. "Well, certainly they will have no-one to complain to, Sir Stuart," he declared. "Except myself, of course."

For a moment the room fell silent. Then Caldrick strolled to the window, a smile creeping its way slowly across his face. "The question is, gentlemen, not can we get away with it, but why have we not thought of it before?" There was a murmur of agreement from around the table. "Any further thoughts, Mr Norwood?"

Norwood was beginning to warm to the proposal and selected his words with due circumspection. "I could certainly foresee situations where a discrepancy might exist. An error in calculation perhaps. An unfortunate misunderstanding. Leave it to me, gentlemen. I have the *Lady Armstrong* discharging at West India Dock as we speak, and with your permission I will pass a message to the foreman immediately. And, of course, to the foremen at all of your docks in London."

Lord Caldrick selected a six-inch *Romeo y Julieta* from a silver cigar case on the table. "Excellent," he beamed. "Tea, Mr Norwood?"

James Donnelly was born in 1862 in Boston, Massachusetts. His grandparents had emigrated from Cork in Eire at the beginning of the century and through a combination of good fortune and their own endeavours, established what by the 1850s had become the largest association of cotton mills in the state. Thus the Donnelly family became one of the most affluent in Boston.

Educated at Harvard, James worked as a journalist for Reuters in New York before being posted to London in 1888 to report the Jack the Ripper murders to America. Soon his descriptive accounts came to the attention of George Buckle, the editor of *The Times*, who offered him a position as senior reporter. Donnelly was flattered. A career with the most prestigious newspaper in the world. And any doubts he may have harboured in respect to being parted from his homeland, became irrelevant when he married Charlotte Pemberton at St Paul's Cathedral on New Year's Eve, a ceremony reported in his employer's newspaper. Charlotte was the only daughter of Sir Alfred Pemberton the proprietor of the National British Bank. Seven months on, James Donnelly was finding his assimilation into British upper-class society a most comfortable one.

"Off to meet the Queen, are we, James?"

"The Queen?" Donnelly glanced down at his clothes. "Ah, yes, er, no – off to a luncheon, Mr Buckle. At the Mansion House with the Lord Mayor and some prominent businessmen."

"Including your father-in-law no doubt. And of what interest would this luncheon be to *The Times*?"

"Lord Caldrick will be receiving a commendation from the City of London for the London Dock Employers. Not the most exciting of afternoons I agree."

"No. Maybe we need Jack the Ripper back on the streets. Our circulation increased three-fold towards the end of his activities."

Donnelly smiled. "We could all do with Jack back out there. Oh, and the luncheon. No doubt you heard that the Merseyside Dock Company has just announced a nine per cent increase in profitability. Caldrick is bound to have something up his sleeve to improve on that and keep his shareholders swimming in champagne. It may be worth a question or two."

"We will see," said Buckle. "Enjoy the meal, James. And convey my regards to your father-in-law."

"Mr Home Secretary, Lord Caldrick, Gentlemen. First I would ask you to drink a toast to our beloved Queen. Throughout the world we see examples of the instability of many thrones. But not here in Great Britain. Everywhere I travel, people remark on how stable the British throne..."

As the Lord Mayor proceeded with his address, James Donnelly sat with his father-in-law, Sir Alfred Pemberton, and Dr Edwin Clarke. Dr Clarke was the Pemberton family physician and had become a firm friend of James during the past months. Just a week short of his fiftieth birthday, the doctor's staid and traditionally British disposition, contrasted significantly with the more irreverent individuality of the young American. "Remind me again, Edwin," whispered James with a grin. "Who is that man in fancy dress?"

"Very droll, old boy," replied the doctor. "You mean to tell me that you colonials don't get dressed up for special occasions and ceremonies? You are being obtuse."

"Me, Edwin? And who is the one sitting next to the mayor?"

Dr Clarke frowned. "Lord Mayor, James. He is not any old mayor. Next to him is Henry Matthews, the Home Secretary."

"The Home Secretary, eh," exclaimed Donnelly, raising his eyebrows in mock reverence. "Can I wave to him?"

"James, please. Have some respect. And next to the Home Secretary is Lord Caldrick."

"Ah. So that's him," said James, his expression adopting a more sober appearance.

"He is a very powerful man. Extremely wealthy and with close connections with senior members of the government. And next to Lord Caldrick is George Hyde, another powerful dock owner."

"Even though he isn't a lord?"

"You are being obtuse again, James."

"Forgive me, Edwin," came the reply, delivered on this occasion with extravagant remorse. "I'm just a Yankee who knows no better."

Pemberton glanced reprovingly at the two men. "Sssh!" he hissed. "For heaven's sake remember where you are."

It was ten minutes before the Lord Mayor's address drew towards a conclusion. "...and as you are aware, gentlemen, the City of London has recently passed through a period of great prosperity. In 1888, no port in the world could show such a trade as the Port of London – seventy-nine thousand sea-going vessels entered and cleared the Port, being two hundred and sixteen for every day of the year, including Sundays. You will recall that six months ago I was able to report of the increased profits made by the London Dock Employers and I ventured to add that unless we had a European war or some other event which no-one could predict, I looked forward to continuing improvement year by year and for many years to come. I have no doubt that this improvement continues and that the London Dock Employers will retain its position as the most profitable dock company in the land. Thank you all for your attention."

To loud applause and cries of 'hear, hear', the Lord Mayor resumed his seat and numerous waiters appeared in the hall to replenish plates and glasses at the tables. James watched as Sir Alfred Pemberton entered into discussion with the Home Secretary and Lord Caldrick at the head table. "Excuse me, Edwin. Duty calls."

He strolled through the brandies and cigars towards the three men. "Ah, James. Mr Home Secretary. May I take the liberty of introducing my son-in-law, Mr James Donnelly."

"Most pleased to meet you, sir."

"And, James. This is Lord Caldrick."

"And to meet you, sir."

"Ah. An American," observed the Home Secretary, exhaling a cloud of cigar smoke. "And what has brought you to our country?"

"I was sent here last year to report the Ripper murders, sir."

"Ah, Yes. The Ripper. Days best forgotten."

"Quite," said Pemberton. "James works for *The Times*."

"Oh, really. And how is Mr Buckle?"

"Fine, thank you, sir."

"An excellent newspaper *The Times*. In my experience your country could benefit from newspapers of that quality. Only last week I was reading – now what was it? The *San Francisco...*"

"*Examiner*, sir?"

"Yes, that's it. The *San Francisco Examiner*. It was questioning the right of Great Britain to govern its colonies."

"Yes. I know the publication. In fact the owner is noted back home for his views on the subject. Hearst. William Randolph Hearst. Actually he's a good friend of mine. We were at Harvard together. He was always something of an isolationist."

"Harvard! An excellent university I hear. Now you must excuse me, Mr... er ..."

"Donnelly, sir. It was a pleasure to have met you."

With the Home Secretary now deep in conversation with the Lord Mayor, James turned his attention to the Chairman of the London Dock Employers. His first question was instinctive. "Lord Caldrick. With your shareholders' meeting due next month, do you anticipate being in a position to announce a higher profit margin than the nine per cent achieved by the Merseyside Dock Company?"

"You have an interest in shipping, Mr Donnelly?"

"As a journalist I have an interest in everything, Lord Caldrick."

"Naturally. Well, you should know better, Mr Donnelly. I am certainly not at liberty to discuss such matters with the press, not even *The Times*, until such time as I have had the opportunity to address my shareholders."

"Of course, I understand. But even so, the nine per cent must have placed a great deal of pressure on you. After all, your shareholders will be anticipating an increase at least equal, if not greater..."

The tone of Lord Caldrick's voice changed perceptibly and his expression hardened. "Good day, Mr Donnelly."

It was a little past seven o'clock and the evening sun was beginning to angle across the bridge of the *Lady Armstrong*. One hundred dock labourers were gathered, waiting inside the gates of West India Dock for the foreman to appear with their day's pay. All were exhausted after eleven hours of backbreaking toil, much of it in temperatures that had exceeded eighty degrees, and few words were spoken. Soon the foreman arrived, flanked by two gangers staggering under the weight of a metal box brimming with coins. Reading from a ledger held up towards him by one of the gangers, the foreman began to deliver the pay into bruised and battered hands. "Atwell – Brewer – Carter – Chapman – Godby – Harris..."

One after another, the men grabbed at the precious coins. "Hawkins – Hunt – Jonson – Lamb – Lewis..."

Harris examined his pay. "Here. Hang on a minute. This ain't right."

"McNamara – Morton – O'Connell – O'Leary..."

"Yeah, it's short," confirmed Lamb. "Eightpence short. Where's the bonus?"

"You didn't earn it," barked the foreman, his eyes not leaving the ledger. "Pollock – Rowell – Smith – Tillett..."

"Didn't bloody earn it?' said Harris indignantly. "We got the job done quicker than you asked. The company owes us eightpence."

"The company owes you nothing, friend. You did the job in your usual time at your usual pace."

"Usual pace? Bleeding gangers worked us to the bone."

The foreman was rapidly becoming surrounded by angry men. "Oi, mate. You've made a mistake. There's no bonus. You owe us eightpence."

"And how do you work that out?" he said, surveying them with disdain. A man pushed his way forward to the front. His slight, delicate physique contrasted with many of those around him but concealed an ability to match the efforts of any of his colleagues. It was Ben Tillett. "We did a fourteen hour job in under twelve hours. Company policy states that when..." He got no further.

"Company policy states that you get the bonus if you shift the freight at a certain rate of profit to the company. You did the job in the usual time, at your usual pace. Therefore no bonus money. Are you arguing with company policy?"

Tillett shook his head. "No. I'm merely pointing out to you that according to the terms laid down by the company we have earned that bonus." There was a mumble of agreement from the men.

"You timed it, did you?" sneered the foreman.

Tillett persisted. "We all know it took less than twelve hours."

"That's right," agreed Harris. "So you gonna give us the extra eightpence or...?"

"Or what, my eloquent friend?" enquired the foreman contemptuously, jabbing his finger into Harris's chest and pushing him backwards. "I advise you – all of you – to keep your mouths shut and take what you are given. I know the ones among you that work and take the weight, and I know the ones who are happy just to slack and mouth off. I've got your names marked down in my little book, see, and tomorrow morning I may be inclined to tear your page out and throw it away. You understand?"

"I ain't trying to cause no trouble," insisted Harris. "I'm just saying we worked and earned that money. If yer didn't wanna pay it, you should have hired more men to get the job done quicker. You're obliged to pay us that bonus."

The foreman spat his reply with a venom that startled the men into silence. "I ain't obliged to do shit by anyone except the man who pays my wages. And you are in the same position. All of you. Just count yourselves lucky you got what you did." Without even a glance in their direction, the foreman then strode swiftly back to his office leaving the men to ponder the inevitability of the outcome. Most drifted disconsolately away, while a small group remained outside the dock gates to bemoan their fate.

"Bastard," growled Harris.

Lamb looked apprehensive. "I dunno. Think we've just cut off our balls. You expect to work tomorrow, now, Jim?"

"I'll try another dock."

"We earned that bonus," Lamb muttered dejectedly. "Ain't fair. Bloody back's killing me."

Harris turned towards Tillett. "Thanks for trying, mate. Not seen you around before. Where you from?"

"All over," came the reply. "I've travelled a bit." And the man was scarcely exaggerating.

Ben Tillett had always possessed a taste for knowledge and adventure. Three times as a nine-year-old in Bristol he had run away from home to the local circus, only to be dragged back on each occasion by Annie. Not that being dragged off against his wishes by his sister was an uncommon experience – as his regular attendance at Sunday school had demonstrated. It was there he had learned to read, and during his eleven years of roaming the world in numerous ships of the Merchant Navy, he had saved his money, often half-starving himself to buy books which had become as important to him as his friends. "Name's Tillett. Lately been working the East India Dock. Came this morning for the *Lady Armstrong*. You probably know my sister, Annie – works in the tavern across the road."

"Yeah," said Lamb, smiling at the thought. "Everyone round here knows Annie Tillett." He paused a moment before his face quickly became sombre once more. "It's gonna happen again, y'know."

"Because they know they can get away with it," nodded Tillett.

Harris kicked the dock wall in frustration. "Course they can get away with it," he shouted angrily. " 'Cos we stand here and let them."

"There's nothing we can do," sighed Jonson. He had been listening gloomily to the exchanges. "Nobody wants to be out of work."

Harris turned on the man. "But if they ain't gonna pay what's rightfully ours, why should we work?"

"Tell that to yer wife and kids when they ain't eaten for three days," snapped Jonson.

As the men wandered away in the direction of the Dockers Arms, Shaun Lamb shrugged his shoulders and stared down at the ground. "My wife and kids have hardly eaten for three days anyway," he muttered.

Leaning against the bar, Annie Tillett was listening to her brother talking with the men. There was a mood of dejection in the room. "How many days could you last without work?"

Around twenty dockers had congregated in the tavern, taking consolation in the ale and pursuing their earlier conversation at the dock gates. "Not many," said Lamb. "Can't afford not to work."

"Yes," questioned Tillett. "But how many days in the past have you gone without work?"

"Until today, I hadn't worked for a week."

"Exactly. Now how long do you think the company could last without workers?"

"It couldn't," replied Harris. "They'd have to give in."

Tillett nodded. Although his voice was low there was no doubting his determination. "Yes. If every man joined a strike it would be over – what – in less than a week."

"A strike?" exclaimed Lamb, suddenly alarmed as he realised what was being proposed. "You're talking as if they're idiots."

"No, friend. Not idiots. But they know that if we get unified, then there's nothing they can do to stop us."

"Reckon you're talking bollocks, Tillett," scoffed Jonson.

Harris glared at him. "Why don't you shut up and let the man speak?"

Jonson turned on Harris. "And why don't...?" But Tillett had heard enough.

"Friends, friends," he said quickly. "Let's not fight. Let's save our anger for the employers. Listen to me. Ever since the one man has hired the many, he has known that without the labour of the many, he is nothing. His money is nothing and his so-called power is nothing."

"And you're nothing . . . nothing except words," sneered Jonson, his eyes hurriedly searching the room for support. "You're not all falling for this, are yer? Why the hell should the employers listen to your words, Tillett? They don't have to listen to any of us."

Tillett looked dispirited by Jonson's remark and fell silent. Inclined to stutter, especially when he became excited, he had never been an instinctive orator and his impassioned thoughts would often remain unspoken.

But not so his sister. "So why shouldn't they listen to you? They'd have to if there was no-one to shift their goods. Think about it. Ben's right. If you got yourselves unified, you could bring the employers to their knees."

Jonson laughed. "Christ, you've started her off now, Tillett.

[45]

Annie, it's got nothing to do with you. You don't know what you're talking about."

"Must run in the family," scoffed Brewer, allying himself with Jonson.

Not known for her patience or self-restraint, Annie flung an ale-soaked cloth into Brewer's face. "Look at you all," she mocked, making no effort to disguise her scorn at their indecision. "Sitting around, getting drunk, whining about your problems. And what are you all doing about them – nothing. Call yourselves men! Why don't you just have another drink, and another, and another. That'll sort things out nicely. That'll solve all your problems. Christ, you're a liability to yourselves. Your bosses must be laughing themselves silly in their boardrooms. Pay you just enough to get you drunk and to keep you right where you are."

"No, it ain't good," admitted Lamb, shrugging his shoulders as if accepting their plight as beyond retrieval. "But it's better than nothing."

"But is it?" said Annie sceptically. "Is that what you want? Is that how you want things to go on? Day after day, week after week. Being treated like the scum of the earth? So that when you go home tonight and your wife asks you if you've got any money for food, all you can say is 'the foreman cut short our wages'. Is that how you want it to be? So when your sons and grandsons take your place in years to come, they're treated in the same degrading way. Their life worth no more than a rat. 'Cos like the rats, if they drop dead from exhaustion there's always another dumb, stupid animal to take their place."

"But no-one wants to risk losing what we got," reflected Lamb quietly.

"So what have you got?" challenged Annie. "Tell me that. What have you got that's worth holding on to?"

"We've got something," sighed Brewer. "Talk like that and we'll end up with nothing."

Not for the first time in his life, Ben Tillett was feeling himself both heartened and eclipsed by his sister. "No. All you've got is what they have given you. Like Annie said, that image they have of you, like a rat, like a frightened rat in a hole."

Harris banged his fist bitterly on the bench. "Bastards! That's all we are to them. Rats in a hole." Most of the dockers nodded solemnly in agreement.

"Makes you angry, Jim, does it?" urged Annie, her voice becoming louder as she sensed a developing resolve amongst the men. "Course it does, 'cos it's true. I'll tell you for nothing. If it was me, I couldn't bear them to have that image . . . that false image they've kept going to keep you in your hole. And I don't believe for a second any of you really want it." Annie paused. But none of the men spoke. "So isn't it time for you to tear down that image? Isn't it time for you to take it in your hands and once and for all break it over the bastard's backs?"

She swept away to her office at the back of the tavern and for fully a minute there was silence. Then Harris spoke. "So what we gonna do then? We gotta do something."

Most agreed although Lamb still battled with the instinctive caution that had always influenced his judgement. "It's easy for Annie to talk. We're the ones who have to face 'em every day."

"But that's the point," insisted Tillett. "We don't face them. Don't you understand that? But we can do nothing, not without strong support. First we must get everyone together. Tomorrow, after the shift, we'll meet here. Tell everyone on the docks. Here, tomorrow night. Then we'll decide."

There was little fresh talk as none of the men seemed inclined to pursue the matter further. "I'd best be getting home," said Lamb. "See yer tomorrow."

Tillett also withdrew from the group. Frustrated with himself at his lack of command, he wanted to see his sister; he needed her help. She was sprawled on the floor feeding a litter of half-a-dozen mewing kittens when he entered the office. "Thanks for what you said, Annie. If only I could speak like you."

"You can speak," she said firmly. "The problem with you is you expect them all to agree with you straight away. Soon as you get shouted down you start slipping. The advantage I've got is having had people disagree with me all my life. If I go into a fight I reckon on getting bloody."

Ben smiled. "Somehow I don't think it's quite that simple.

You've always been able to – I don't know, people seem to listen to you."

"Maybe I just shout louder than you."

"Well, there's no escaping that. You can shout louder than anyone I know."

It was Annie's turn to smile. "About the only thing I got from father," she said, picking up one of the kittens. "When I had to nurse you lot. I thought that was the best way to do it – shout louder than any of you. And you usually did what I said."

Ben shook his head. "No. There was more to it than that. People listened to you – we listened to you. Remember the circus? Dragged me away by the scruff of my neck like I was a little child."

"You were a little child."

He sat down on the floor beside his sister. "I need your help, Annie."

She resisted the urge to put her arm round him and instead smiled reassuringly. "You don't need my help," she replied firmly. "Just use that fire that's already in you and get out there and finish what you started tonight. You can do it. There's no doubt in my mind."

Ben felt heartened by her words. "Break it over the bastards' backs?"

"Yeah," she said, eyeing him solemnly. "Break it over the bastards' backs."

Chapter Four

As he trudged home from the Dockers Arms, hands thrust deep into his trouser-pockets, Shaun Lamb passed an old woman. She was a tramp. Like a snail she carried her home balanced on her back, all she possessed stuffed into a meagre bundle of sacking and secured with a length of cord. "Spare a few coppers, sir? I ain't eaten all day."

"Sorry, I can't . . . don't have much . . . sorry." Lamb continued a few paces and then glanced back at the tavern. He then turned and lengthened his stride, hurrying towards the hunched figure shuffling away in the direction of the West India Dock gates and the deserted police-box outside, her dormitory for the night. He held out a few coins. "Here. Sorry it ain't much."

"Bless you kindly, sir."

Mary was still assembling brushes when Shaun arrived home, the completed heap on the floor evidence of her hours of toil. The children were asleep, as was the cat curled awkwardly across a small packet of bristles lying unopened on the table. "You're late. Where've you bin? I was worried."

"We got a full day's work."

"How much you get paid?"

"Four-and-sevenpence. But they held back the bonus."

Shaun placed the coins on the table, the cause of his lateness exposed by a lingering smell of ale. "Four-and-sevenpence?" queried Mary. "There's only four-and-a-penny here. You spent the rest in the tavern?"

"Only had one jug of ale, that's all."

"So where's the rest?" Casually, he told his wife about the old woman. "But we need it," she protested. "We need it as much as others. They pays you next to nothing as it is. I can't believe you'd give it away . . . and to a stranger." Her incomprehension was obvious in her face. "Next time close your eyes . . . walk past. You've got a family here, remember. Your family comes first. What made you go to the tavern anyway? You don't normally go. This gonna be a regular thing?"

Shaun shook his head firmly. "No. Course not. But we were all talking . . . about them not paying the bonus. I think something's gonna happen, Mary. I can feel it. The men . . . they're getting restless. Met this bloke today. Tillett . . . Ben Tillett. Didn't speak like us. Like he was educated or something. Things been said tonight in the tavern. Made me think."

"What sort of things?" said Mary, looking puzzled.

Shaun reflected for a moment. "He said if we wanted things to change . . . make things better, we could. If we all got together."

"Change? Change what? What things?" she questioned, still seeming confused.

"Dunno. We're gonna meet again tomorrow night. Figure out what we're gonna do. Maybe form a union. Some are talking about striking. This bloke Tillett reckoned if we stay out they'll have to pay us what's right." The words were almost casually delivered, but their effect on Mary could hardly have been more immediate.

"Striking!" she exclaimed, her voice edged with unaccustomed anger. "And you're going along with this? If you're thinking about striking, Shaun Lamb, you can forget it . . . and forget it right now. You just remember one thing. You've got a family that needs feeding. You need to work or your family goes hungry. I can't support us on the money I bring in. How we gonna pay the rent? I s'pose that Jim Harris has talked you into this?"

"No-one's talked me into nothing. I can think for meself."

"This ain't like you. You've never been one for no trouble before. Always kept your head low . . . worked hard . . . minded your own business."

"I know," said Shaun, shaking his head in a gesture of frustration. "But I'm sick of it. And if the men decide to do something, there's such a thing as loyalty."

"Loyalty?" echoed Mary. "What loyalty? You just remember where your loyalties lie. With your family."

"I know that. I know where my loyalties lie."

"With your family. What about us? If you go on a lost cause it's not only you who gets betrayed. You can't just hope that things work out. Hope we all get fed. You've got to think about us, Shaun. Me and the kids. It's no good pretending we're not here while you go off and do whatever it is you're gonna do."

Shaun looked affectionately at his wife's shocked and angry face. He was frightened himself. "But I am thinking of you, Mary. I always do. Why do you think I go to work every morning? Why do you think I hang around that dock day after day waiting for work? I do it for you . . . you and the kids."

There was a lengthy silence before Mary replied – as ever, her own loyalty to her husband unfailing. "I'd have to take in more washing. Do more brushes. The kids would help."

Shaun shook his head. "You do a full day already. You can't do no more. But there's a lot of talk down at the docks. About the way them employers treat us. Like rats, Tillett said. And I want it to change. I'm sick of it. And the only way it's gonna change is if we get off the floor and fight back."

She looked at him anxiously across the room and spoke with a sense of foreboding plain in her voice. "But would it really change anything? A few dockers marching round the streets of East London . . . waving a few banners . . . chanting slogans. You really believe that's gonna change anything?"

"I have to Mary. I have to believe it. This ain't no life for a man. The bonus money . . . it made us angry, but that's not what it's about. It's much more than that."

As its name implies, the *East London Advertiser* had little in common with *The Times*, catering, as it did, for an area not noted as teeming with newspaper readers. For the most part, this was due to the inability of the bulk of its potential customers to read, or, indeed, to afford the halfpenny purchase price even if they could. Nonetheless, the paper was respected in East London and its words reached appreciably more people than its circulation figures suggested, as news and articles of interest would be read aloud by the better educated, and subsequently retold in taverns, shops, and meeting places throughout the area. Like all good local newspapers it encouraged an exchange of information between itself and its supporters, the most recent example of which had, quite incidentally, just been brought to the attention of *The Times* itself. For there was, indeed, one notable connection between the two newspapers. The editor of the *East London Advertiser* was Henry Buckle, the younger brother of the head of its more illustrious counterpart. "So, Henry. There are mutterings of discontent amongst some of the dock labourers in your domain," said George. "But not yet a story, I think – even for the *Advertiser.*" And George Buckle smiled, for, potential story or not, he knew the very man who would profit from a day's excursion into the depths of the East End.

James Donnelly looked astonished and for a moment scarcely seemed to know how to respond. "What? A dockers' meeting – to discuss forming a union? But surely one of the junior reporters is more suited to an assignment of this nature, Mr Buckle. If it can be described as an assignment?"

Buckle smiled. "Firstly, James, we do not have such things on *The Times* as junior reporters – just varying degrees of seniority. Secondly, I am somewhat short of available staff at the present time due to holiday commitments. And thirdly, in the light of your new friendship with Lord Caldrick and your blossoming command of the subject, I supposed that you would be eager to attend. Granted the food will not be as sumptuous as at the Lord Mayor's luncheon, but you cannot expect all the best assignments. People might suspect favouritism." Buckle tactfully declined to reveal that his principal motive was to indicate to his sometimes presumptuous reporter that working for *The Times* entailed more than just a series of social occasions.

"But dock workers?"

"Just go, James. Meet the leaders, troublemakers, whatever they are. Establish the general mood. You know what is required."

James smiled ruefully and threw up his hands in a gesture of surrender. "Thanks, Mr Buckle. I'll let you know if I find The Ripper."

Upwards of a thousand men were swarming outside the Dockers Arms with half as many, or so it seemed, waiting restlessly inside. When he arrived, Ben Tillett was both astonished and excited by the numbers. Pushing his way through the crowd, he located Annie. She was taking refuge behind the bar. "I've n-n-never seen so many p-people," he stammered, "l-least of all addressed them. I p-pray I can find the right words out there."

She touched him reassuringly on the shoulder and smiled. "You'll need a bench . . . outside . . . to stand on so they can all see you."

Harris spoke first. "Men. Keep it down now. Men . . . it's good to see so many of you here. There's been enough delay, so let's get on with it. On my left here is Ben Tillett who some of you may know. We're all fed up with the way we're being treated and I for one ain't gonna put up with it no more. I'm sick of them cheating us . . . breaking our backs for their own profit . . . paying us a wage barely enough to survive. We've called this meeting to see if you're with us and I'd like you to listen to what this man Ben Tillett has to say."

Harris stepped down to heartening applause. A hansom-cab drew up and James Donnelly leaned out from the window. "You sure this is where you wanna be, sir?" asked the driver doubtfully.

James alighted. "Sure, wait here. I'll not be long." His arrival in West India Dock Road amidst the ragged looking dockers was greeted with curiosity and some suspicion, being far from suitably dressed for either the occasion or the locality, looking more like a dock employer than a dock labourer. Quickly realising his ill-judgement, he grinned sheepishly at the legion of turned heads and swiftly and elaborately produced a notebook and pencil to indicate his purpose. Watching from a first-floor window, Annie Tillett wished she could have tipped a bucket of swill over the fancy intruder.

Ben Tillett took a deep breath. He began hesitantly, but his voice gathered in confidence as the resolve of the men became clear. "Friends, friends and fellow workers. For too long we have been brutally and inhumanely treated by the dock owners who are interested only in dividends – dividends for their shareholders. I believe that nowhere in Europe have men had to endure such terrible conditions as those under which the dockers now work. But we will get no alteration in our wages, and no alteration in our conditions, unless we are one voice and organise ourselves into a union – a union of dockers. Are you with me?" A cheer of confirmation swept through the crowd, and in the moment's pause before Ben could resume, Annie's eyes sought out the uninvited guest who stood so conspicuously among the men. During that same pause, James looked up from his notebook and observed a woman glowering at him from the tavern window. An interesting looking lady, he thought.

Tillett reached into his jacket pocket and withdrew a crumpled sheet of paper. There was now a firm authority in his voice. "I propose to put the following demands to the Dock Employers. For an increase in wages from fivepence an hour to sixpence an hour, and sixpence an hour overtime to eightpence an hour." The men cheered in approval. "For the bonus payment to be guaranteed when it is honestly earned, and for the abolition of all inhumane work selection procedures at the dock gates." Again Tillett was halted by an ovation and he raised his arm to silence the men. "Tomorrow I will put these demands to the employers and if they are not met I propose we take action by implementing a strike." For a moment he paused, glancing round at the throng assembled expectantly before him. "Friends. People say that nothing can be done to help the dock labourer. But what if the dock labourer should do something to help himself?"

Amid overwhelming support Tillett stepped down. The hour and the man had come. But the man knew that he had not come alone as he edged his way slowly through the excited crowd towards the tavern, acknowledging the nods and calls of approval. As James entered his cab, he glanced up once more at the window. But it was empty. Annie was already downstairs in the bar with her brother.

As he spoke, Ben knew from her expression that she felt proud of him. "My tongue, at first it was dry in my mouth. And my throat, it almost refused to function. But I was driven on by the feeling of the men." As they were speaking, a man wearing a blue reefer suit, a white straw hat, a coal-black beard, and carrying a wooden cane, pushed his way through the crowd and into the tavern. By the manner in which he was received he was plainly a celebrity of sorts. Hearing the disturbance, Ben looked around and saw the commanding figure of John Burns bearing down upon him. "John. John Burns. I'm pleased, but surprised, to see you here."

"Hello, Ben. Sorry I missed your meeting. What are you up to then? Eleanor Marx tells me you want to form a union of dockers."

Unlike Tillett, John Burns had all the qualities of a born showman. A member of the Executive of the Amalgamated Society of Engineers, the largest trade union in the world, and a long-time champion of the working class, his impudent recklessness appealed to the masses. During a demonstration the previous year for the unemployed, he had climbed onto a window ledge of the Ministry of Defence building in Whitehall to give an impromptu address, while officials in frock-coats attempted to dislodge him with broom handles. He was subsequently arrested for his indiscretion and served six weeks in prison. With a voice like a megaphone, his wealth of picturesque language was derived in no small measure from extensive reading in his library at home in South London. One of a family of eighteen children, and thirty-two years old, he had first come to public attention eight years before when, as a senior engineer, he had produced and then driven the first tramcar on the roads of Britain. So alarmed were the onlookers at the sight of this contraption traversing the streets of Crystal Palace, that not a single one could be persuaded to become a passenger. Recently elected to the London County Council, in addition to his working class support, John Burns also enjoyed the respect, if not the outright approval, of the middle and even the upper classes of London.

"Yes, someone has to do something, John," said Tillett. "We can't go on like this. You know how they treat us."

"Well, if you need help, Ben. And of course Eleanor with her experience with the unions would be a great asset."

"Thanks, John. Now come and have a drink." Tillett knew he might soon need all the assistance he could get.

James and Charlotte Donnelly lived in an imposing residence in Belgrave Square, a few minutes' stroll from the delights of Hyde Park. It had been their wedding present from Charlotte's parents, a gift owing less to generosity than their desire that Charlotte should continue to live in a manner befitting that of the Pemberton family. It was mid-evening and the Donnellys were dressing for a dinner engagement with friends. James, late home from the East End, still had the dockers' meeting on his mind. "It was the feeling of unity."

"What?"

"It's hard to describe. A sort of Alamo spirit. Sure, I've seen poverty before, of course. Seen the faces of men with no future. But this. They appeared to see no alternative for themselves but to fight back, and there wasn't a decent set of clothing between any of them."

"Pearl or sapphire?"

"Sorry?"

"What do you think I should wear?" asked Charlotte, her words delivered with a contrived patience. "The pearl necklace or the sapphire."

"You are definitely wearing that dress?"

"It has taken me half an hour, James. I am not changing now."

A broad smile extended across his face. "That's never stopped you before, dear. The pearl."

Charlotte glanced philosophically towards her husband. "I am so fortunate to have married a man with taste."

Mrs Fish had agreed to give Ben Tillett use of a room above the Dockers Arms and an hour before a second meeting of dockers was due to begin, Ben was waiting inside, together with Eleanor Marx, John Burns, Will Thorne, and Tom Mc-Carthy. The latter two men were the respective General Secretaries of the Gasworkers' and the Stevedores' Unions, both of which had their headquarters, and the majority of their members, in the East End. Both had been invited by Eleanor. With a dearth of trained organisers at Tillett's command, she knew the advantage of securing the assistance of experienced union officials, notably Thorne, who, against all expectations, a few months earlier had won an eight-hour working day for his gasworkers. Eleanor sat down at the table, and almost as if she were royalty, the four men followed suit. "Will your men definitely vote for a strike, Ben?" she enquired, brushing a smudge of dust from the cuff of her dress.

Tillett nodded. "As the employers have ignored our demands, it now seems the only step we can take."

"Then I can assure you," announced McCarthy with a broad grin, "that my four thousand stevedores will come out on strike in support."

Tillett was the only one in the room not to appear heartened by this unexpected announcement. "Tom. Have you spoken to your executive about this?"

"No. But I am the Secretary of the Amalgamated Stevedores."

"But you can't state that the stevedores are implementing a strike when you haven't even spoken to them about it."

McCarthy looked puzzled. "Which takes time, Ben. Which you don't have. I'm trying to help you here. As soon as your men hear that the stevedores are supporting them and prepared to take action, any dockers who are still worried will be mightily encouraged and you'll have everyone out in no time. And when I go out there and make the statement, the stevedores will believe their union is involved and come out anyway. It saves all the nonsense of clearing it with my executive."

"But you can't do it, Tom," insisted Tillett. "It's immoral – and unlawful. We should proceed through the correct channels. Will, John, what do you think?"

Thorne considered for a moment. "He has a point, Ben. In all likelihood the stevedores would eventually come out in support anyway. So surely it can only assist you if they do so right away?"

Eleanor Marx tapped her pencil emphatically on the table and the four men turned in her direction. "So who do you agree with, Eleanor?" asked Burns.

"It is an interesting situation, gentlemen." As ever, she wished to be in possession of all the facts before committing herself to an opinion. "Please correct me if I am wrong, but Mr McCarthy is offering the dockers the support of his union."

"This is entirely correct, ma'am," confirmed McCarthy.

"Please, Tom. It's Eleanor. I have told you before, I am not the Queen."

"But he is offering their support without any reference to them or their leaders," said Tillett.

Eleanor looked confused. "But Mr McCarthy is himself one of the leaders of the Stevedores' Union."

"Agreed." said Ben. "But this is not the issue at present. A union is a union of men – not just one man acting on his own."

Eleanor smiled. "Yes, gentlemen, Mr Tillett is correct. It is not the issue at present. But what should be of more concern, Ben, is the plight of your men. And it seems to me that Mr McCarthy has addressed that issue and suggested a rather constructive idea."

"But it's immoral," insisted Tillett. "We would be deceiving fellow workers."

Eleanor looked unimpressed. "I can think of far worse acts of immorality which have been practised by your employers for many years now," she replied sharply. "Or have you forgotten that fact?"

Tillett shook his head. "No. I haven't forgotten that fact. But I am determined not to stoop as low as my enemies in order to beat them. Gross immorality does not justify the use of petty immorality."

"Ben. Please," said Eleanor, still puzzled by his reaction. "If you are at all nervous about being responsible, whether directly or indirectly, for immoral acts, then I suggest that you look again at the path you have chosen for your men and their families. Let us suppose this proposed strike lasts longer than you expect. Will your conscience be able to cope with the immorality that such action will most definitely bring in its wake? You hesitate to deceive fellow workers, and yet you have no qualms in plunging thousands of men, women and children into a time of intense suffering. I have had the advantage – if one may call it that – of seeing starving children wandering through the street like ghosts, begging for food, collapsing where they beg, to be pushed into the gutter by a passing gentleman. And I have seen men fighting in the street over food scraps – men who only a few days earlier would have called one another neighbour and friend. And I have even known parents reduced to such hopelessness that they have sold their children – a baby sold off to a stranger for a few shillings. Such things, and worse, you may expect in the weeks to come – immorality, as a direct result of a strike you have engendered. Mr Tillett, one's 'conscience' may remain unstained, but one's hands will almost certainly be drenched in blood."

Ben considered his reply for an uncomfortably long time. "Firstly, Eleanor, I must congratulate you on delivering such a moving speech. You should perhaps speak to the men sometime. Secondly, I feel obliged to point out that the benefits of your experience in no way put me at a disadvantage. You may have seen starving children wandering in the streets in search of food – but I have *been* a starving child searching for food."

"Yes, yes, Ben," said Thorne, with a hint of impatience. "You don't need to tell us that. We know. We know where we've all come from."

Tillett glanced briefly towards Eleanor. "It seems to have slipped the minds of some," he muttered.

"No, Ben," she responded, shaking her head. "I did not intend to underestimate your personal experience of these things. I merely wished to ensure that the image of them was firmly planted in your mind, and then to show by comparison how little the action suggested by Mr McCarthy could be called immoral."

"I've heard Cardinal Manning preach that it's right for a starving man to steal a loaf of bread if that's what he's been reduced to," laughed Thorne, seeking to lessen the tension.

Eleanor walked across to the window and smiled. "So. A member of the church who speaks sense – how rare. I propose, Mr McCarthy, that you make no statement today concerning strike action by your members. Mr Tillett is the leader of the dockers and the matter is for him to decide. I also suggest that if you speak with your executive and they are in agreement with your views, then Ben will be more than pleased to accept your support for his men." Eleanor glanced through the window and down at the crowd gathered below. "And now, gentlemen, I see that your audience impatiently awaits you."

The numbers outside the tavern were similar to those of the previous meeting. James Donnelly, less elegantly dressed than before, stood at the front in conversation with a reporter from the *East London Advertiser*. Tillett had decided to speak first and while he clambered onto the bench, James noticed the same woman standing beside the tavern door, that he had seen during his previous visit. Catching her eye, he smiled politely, but quickly, and with a firm sweep of her head, she turned away.

"Friends and fellow workers. Two days ago our demands were given to the Dock Employers. It grieves me to inform you that those demands have been ignored. There has been no response." Briefly, Tillett's words were lost in a roar of abuse aimed at the employers. "The gauntlet has been thrown down and I know that all of you to a man will accept the challenge. At this very moment the dock owners are sitting back in their leather chairs, drinking brandy and smoking cigars, laughing and thinking to themselves – that's the end of that little problem. Tell me, friends," he yelled, asking a question to which he already knew their answer. "Is it the end? Is it the end of their little problem?" The cries of 'no' echoed along West India Dock Road. "From this moment, let not a man among you set foot on their property." For more than a minute the crowd cheered before Tillett brought them abruptly to silence with a wave of his arm. "Friends. Mr John Burns."

Burns performed at his blazing best, his straw hat inevitably perched upon his head, his cane brandished and pointed to emphasise his every word. "Up until now your heads have been filled not with revolutionary strategy; not with justice and fair treatment, but with thoughts of survival. Will I get picked to-morrow? How much will I get paid? Will I get the bonus? And you dreamt those thoughts, and you woke up with those thoughts. And if you got hired by the man, you were so bloody grateful all day, you'd be touching your cap to him and calling him 'sir'. That is the genius of their method. Because in doing so, they washed your brains of any inkling that you can have power over them. But now, the one thing that the man feared has happened. Now, you have got yourselves together. Now, you are fighting back."

As the ovation for the people's hero subsided, with a slightly self-conscious smile, Tillett stepped quickly back onto the bench. He had omitted to put the strike resolution to a vote. "Friends. Yes, our demands have been ignored. But this is just the beginning. I pledge my word that if you stand firm and waver not, we will claim and win the sixpence an hour; we will claim and win the right to the bonus; and we will claim and win the abolition of all slave-driving methods currently in use, not only here in the East End of London, but throughout the country. All in favour of strike action please show." Every man's hand was held aloft for the proposal. "Friends," said Tillett, pointing dramatically towards the gates of West India Dock, "as from midnight tonight, let the docks of London be silent."

With a final flourish of his arm, Ben Tillett stepped down

amid a display of great hope and enthusiasm. James Donnelly fought his way towards the bench in an attempt to speak to him, but both Tillett and Burns had dissolved into the crowd amid a welter of handshakes, back-slapping and cries of support. As he approached, Thorne was conducting an animated conversation with McCarthy and Eleanor, while Annie looked on. "James Donnelly from *The Times*."

"That'll be the *New York Times*?" asked McCarthy. "You're a long way from home."

"No, no, the London *Times*." smiled James, amused by the Irishman's assumption, reasonable though it was. "I wonder if I might speak with Mr Tillett? I have a few questions I'd like to ask."

"As you have doubtless observed, Mr Donnelly, Mr Tillett is somewhat engaged at present," said Eleanor. "But I will certainly attempt to locate him. Tom, Will, come with me please. I cannot penetrate that throng on my own."

The three vanished in search of Ben and for a few moments James and Annie surveyed each other. Annie spoke first and her words were delivered with more than a trace of sarcasm. "I saw you before. Bit of a campaigner are we, Mr Donnelly?"

James looked a little disconcerted. "Campaigner? I'm sorry. You appear to have the advantage, Mrs..."

"Tillett."

"Ah, Tillett. Yes, I see." He bowed slightly in acknowledgement. "Well, Mrs Tillett. I just report what I see and hear."

"Really!" she replied coldly. "And how much do you get paid for that?"

"I'm not sure. I could work it out, of course. If it's of interest to you."

Conveniently, at that moment Eleanor returned with Tillett. "Ben, this is Mr James Donnelly from *The Times* – *The Times* in London."

The two men shook hands. "Mr Donnelly. Yes." Tillett offered no smile, but his tone was cordial. "Your newspaper published our demands yesterday. Only a small column, around a hundred words, I think – but most appreciated nevertheless. I had anticipated publicity in the local press, but not in such an august publication as yours. Do you know this area well?"

"It was a hundred and two words actually, Mr Tillett," corrected James with a smile. "I reported the Ripper murders, but I'm not familiar with this part of the East End."

"Well, Mr Donnelly. Then I should perhaps educate you as to the world we live in, far removed from that of the City or the West End. If you will do me the honour at your convenience of being my guest, I will show you what needs to be reported."

"That could be an interesting idea and I will certainly discuss your invitation with my editor." He looked towards Annie and smiled graciously. "And naturally I would also discuss with him my salary for such an assignment, Mrs Tillett."

"*Mrs* Tillett?" grinned Ben. "Is there something you haven't told me, Annie?"

James looked confused. "You assumed, Mr Donnelly," she said. "Actually, it's Miss. I'm Ben's sister."

James smiled and turned back towards Tillett. "Tell me. What are your immediate priorities now that the strike has been confirmed?"

"To organise funds to buy food for the men and their families," said Ben firmly. "We need to plan marches, rallies and other fund-raising endeavours to draw the plight of the dockers to the attention of the public."

"And if these activities do not raise sufficient funds?"

Tillett frowned at the question and thought for a few seconds. And the thought disturbed him. "Then we must pray, Mr Donnelly. Pray to God for charity."

At that moment there was a roar from the distance. It was John Burns. "Ben. We need to draw up a manifesto."

Tillett acknowledged the call with a brief flourish of his cap. "Mr Donnelly – James. I hope I can call you that. My apologies." He extended his hand and this time smiled with a warmth that belied the fact that they had met less than five minutes before. "Thank you for coming, and do not forget my invitation."

Annie felt irritated by her brother's familiarity and made little effort to conceal it. "Don't thank him. He's only doing his job . . . reporting what he sees and hears. I must get back to the tavern. See you tomorrow, Eleanor."

Eleanor Marx smiled as Annie and Ben vanished into the swirling crowd. "You have met Annie Tillett then, Mr Donnelly?"

"Yes. She sure seems upset about something – or someone. Me for example."

Eleanor nodded diplomatically. "She has a natural distrust of strangers. A suspicion of anyone from another world – as have many of these people. Perhaps Annie exhibits this just a little more obviously than most. Now, we have not been formally introduced. I am Eleanor Marx – and to avoid confusion it is Miss Marx."

"Pleased to meet you, Miss Marx," said James, bowing slightly. "Would that be spelled MARX?" Eleanor smiled and nodded by way of a reply. "Then should I perhaps make the obvious assumption?" Again she smiled and again he proffered a slight bow. "Your father, Miss Marx. You must have been proud of him. It's only since my arrival in England that the extent of his influence on European politics during the past twenty years has become apparent to me. Now, tell me: the background to this strike; the obvious discontent felt by the dockers? Is it just about the sixpence an hour and the withholding of their bonus, or are there other unspoken causes?"

For a moment Eleanor remained in thought. "An interesting question, Mr Donnelly. I saw you arrive earlier in a hansom-cab and you are obviously well familiar with this form of conveyance. So let me answer your question this way. When a cab horse trips and falls and lies stretched out in the street amidst the traffic, there is no question of debating how it came to stumble. The priority for the driver is to drag the poor beast back on to its legs. And the cab horse is a very real illustration of the plight of the dockers. When it falls, it is usually because it is overworked, and if you return it to its feet without addressing its condition, then it will be only to repeat its agony. The horse may have fallen through overwork, or it may have been its own fault – through stupidity or carelessness. But that does not matter. If not for its own sake, then merely to prevent an obstruction to the traffic, all attention should be concentrated upon the question of how to get it off the ground and back on to its legs. The load is removed, the harness is unbuckled, and everything is done to assist it up. Then it is returned to the shaft and once more restored to its regular work." Eleanor paused momentarily. "And that, Mr Donnelly," she declared sternly, "is the first point. The second is that every cab horse in London has three things. Food in its stomach, adequate shelter for the night, and work allotted to it by which it can earn its keep. And that humble standard is at present unattainable by both the dockers, and by tens of thousands of men, yes, and women, of all trades here in the East End. When they are down, they should be helped up, and whilst they live, they should have food, shelter and work. And it is for this reason, Mr Donnelly, that we are here today."

As midnight approached, silence reigned over the world's greatest port. Ships lay at rest, cranes and jibs remained still. It was the thirteenth of August and fifteen hundred men were on strike.

Chapter Five

Clare Harris stood re-heating the remains of the previous morning's porridge on the stove. "Does this mean I'm gonna have to go out and work again?"

Jim glared at his wife. "What's wrong, been missing it?"

"Miss the money, that's for sure. What's it gonna be like now?"

"We'll manage."

"Is this what you call the way we've been living . . . managing? I could earn in a night what it takes you a week to bring in."

Clare's seemingly deliberate attempt to provoke her husband succeeded and he lashed angrily at the wall with his belt. "I told you. If you wanna stay married to me, I'm the only man you're gonna sleep with."

"Make you feel bad does it?" she said, continuing to taunt him. "That I can earn more than you. That you could live off my earnings if you'd let me back out there. I'm tired of living like this. Tired of eating like a beggar . . . bits of bread . . . cheese that's gone hard. We could do so much better . . . move outa here . . . get something nice . . . eat meat occasionally, for Christ's sake. And with you on strike it's gonna get worse."

Jim shook his head firmly. "But this is gonna change everything, Clare. A few days. That's all it's gonna take. Then those
bastards'll have to listen to us. Then things'll get better."

"And what does better mean to you?" she asked sceptically.

His face shone with conviction. "Regular work . . . an increase in pay . . . no getting cheated by the employers."

"How much of an increase?"

"We're asking for a penny an hour."

She laughed at him with disdain. "A penny? I'm sorry, but a
penny. It's slave labour. You break your back for nothing. The
only ones who benefit from what you do are the employers.
And I should know. That's where most of my money came
from."

Jim kicked violently at the heap of bed sacking on the floor.
"I don't want you talking about it, Clare. Not here . . . not in
our home. I'm your bloody husband, for God's sake. You listening to me?"

Clare's voice rose in anger. "Oh, I'm listening," she said sarcastically. "I'm listening alright. That's all I ever bloody-well
do. And where's it got me?"

"You could take in more washing."

"Take in more washing?" she shouted in astonishment. "Is
that the answer . . . the answer to all our problems. Take in
more washing. Listen to me. It's about time you swallowed
your pride. About time you faced up to the fact that I could
support you and get both of us out of this pigsty. I've got no
problems sleeping with other men. Don't care what they're
like. And it's my bloody body. What you so worried about? It's
me who'll have to do it. You can bugger off out with your
mates."

Clare ducked too late to avoid his hand which struck her
heavily across the left side of her face. "I ain't gonna be no
pimp," he yelled. Slowly she sank to the floor and for several
seconds there was silence as Jim paced the room. "I gotta go. I
got work to do. Everyone's been given something to do. We'll
be alright. Don't you be thinking about it no more."

He snatched his jacket from the floor and hurried away,
slamming the door behind him so loudly that a horse-shoe

which hung from a nail above the doorway, dropped to the bare floor with a clang. Although this was far from the first occasion on which he had struck her, she doubted it would be the last. Her eyes were closed and she made no effort to raise herself from the floor. Be so easy, she thought: just a few a week. How can he expect me to go on living like this. No food, no security, no chance of more children. And now this strike. Be so easy. With Jim always out at nights, it would be so easy.

As Clare Harris sat silently absorbed in her thoughts, less than a mile away only the contrasting temperament of Shaun and Mary Lamb moderated the exchanges.

"I've already told you, Mary," he said with a confidence that belied his feelings. "It should be over in a few days."

"A few days, you reckon? So how we gonna survive? Me and the kids."

Shaun had expected the question and his answer was prepared. "I've gone days without work before. So how's this gonna be any different? Anyway, there's talk of funds being available."

"Funds? What funds?" she asked sceptically. "They gonna give you money...while you stay out of work?"

"That's what was said."

"By who?"

"This Ben Tillett."

Mary looked unconvinced. "Oh! This Ben Tillett! So that makes everything fine then. This bloke you hardly knows comes up and says, 'don't worry mate, you just strike and we'll give your family money'. You heard him say that, did you?"

"Jim Harris heard it."

"And you believed it? You believe they're gonna give you money. That there's gonna be enough for all of you. Enough to keep all the families from starving?"

He looked at her with all the reassurance he could manage. "They're talking about marching . . . to get funds. Nothing's been decided yet. We'll find out soon." He glanced at the clock on the mantelpiece. "I gotta go. We've all been given something to do. Don't worry, Mary. We'll be alright. We'll get by."

Shaun kissed his wife fondly on the cheek. She forced a smile to her lips and squeezed his hand, but she said nothing. For once, his gesture of affection gave her no comfort and she stood there long after he had left the room.

George Buckle called Donnelly into his office. "So they are on strike now. When is the next meeting?"

"Tillett informs me that meetings, rallies and suchlike should soon be organised for every day."

"Right. You obviously have a feel for this, James. I would like you to follow it through. Get down to the docks and talk to anyone there. Get to know the leaders – the families. Yes, what about the families of the men? See if you can speak to the wives. Find out how these people are living down in the East End."

"Sure, Mr Buckle," he said, exhibiting none of the indifference apparent during their conversation of a few days before. "In fact, Tillett has asked me to meet him for a tour of the area – to be educated as he called it."

That evening, James and Charlotte Donnelly were entertaining Sir Alfred Pemberton and Dr Edwin Clarke who, together with their respective wives, were guests at their residence. Having concluded the meal, the men retired to the smoking room. "Brandy, father-in-law? Edwin?" James filled three glasses from the decanter. "...No, I was there. I saw what happened."

Dr Clarke smiled sceptically. "They may have felt unified at the time, James. It is all part of the mob psychology. But as soon as they are alone with their wives and families, away from the crowd, that excitement will fade and they will get on with their lives."

"Hey, come on, Edwin. Don't you think you're being a touch cynical? What do you think, father-in-law?"

Pemberton considered for a moment. "Whether Edwin's analysis of mob psychology is correct or not is hardly the issue. When all is said and done their demands have been and will certainly continue to be rejected by the dock owners."

"But what about the call for a strike? You think they are bluffing?"

"James," said Pemberton emphatically. "I know they are bluffing."

Dr Clarke nodded in agreement. "You have to understand these people, James. They work, they eat, they sleep. That is all their lives consist of. Now, give them a charismatic figure, a man with leadership qualities, like John Burns, or perhaps this Tillett fellow – someone who offers them the Kingdom of Heaven. Then as likely as not they will follow him right through the gates of Hell. Until, of course, it's time for the next meal, and they find that the next meal isn't there."

"Exactly," confirmed Pemberton. "Lord Caldrick tells me that the Dock Employers are not over-concerned. There may be one or two who will stay out for a few days. But this will not jeopardise the work that needs to be discharged at the docks. There are plenty of others who will be only too grateful to fill their places. As Edwin says, the whole thing will be over in a matter of days and the troublemakers, the so-called leaders, will move on elsewhere."

Charlotte, and Laura Clarke, appeared at the door. "Excuse me, gentlemen, but Laura is about to sing for us, and I shall accompany her. Shall we adjourn to the music room?"

As the three men withdrew, Pemberton spoke quietly to his son-in-law. "To be honest, James, I am surprised you bothered to attend these meetings. And I am even more surprised that Buckle considered the details sufficiently newsworthy to print. It is inflaming a potentially volatile situation."

A broad smile spread rapidly across James's face. "Volatile, father-in-law? But I thought you said it would be all over in a few days."

Meeting in their newly established committee room above the Dockers Arms, Tillett, Burns, Thorne and McCarthy, together with Eleanor Marx, had several priorities. It was the second morning of the strike and with hunger the main ally of the employers, it was essential to keep the men and their families fed. But first the new Dockers' Union had to be established and union cards issued to allow the leaders both to identify and control their members. Then pickets had to be organised. Marshalled by Harris, some of the men had already formed themselves into a watching band at the various dock gates. Tillett feared that the employers would introduce labour from outside the area, a manoeuvre which, should it prove successful, would have a disastrous affect on the strike. Only when these two matters had been addressed could the committee then apply itself to the question of funds – the foremost issue to the men. Tillett was convinced that marches and rallies would soon need to be orchestrated, as the sight of an army of half-starved marching men might touch the public conscience – and public conscience could keep the men from starving.

Meanwhile, Eleanor had already begun to make contact with local clergy and charity groups, and that afternoon was meeting her long-time friend William Booth. Some twenty years earlier he had inaugurated a religious philanthropic organisation then called the Christian Mission operating from a small hostel in Limehouse. Holding its early meetings in streets, music halls, and tents, it began to expand throughout Britain and in 1880 became known as the Salvation Army. It was Eleanor who had suggested the name. And Reverend Adderley had arranged for Thomas Barnardo, who had recently opened three small orphanages in the East End, to meet Eleanor later that week to discuss plans for the collection and distribution of food.

But one act of fund-raising had already been accomplished. Travelling from home that morning, John Burns had interrupted his journey at Limehouse Railway Station. For nearly an hour he walked the platform, cajoling City commuters both there and on waiting trains, gathering coppers into his famous hat. This collection was bolstered just prior to the meeting by the arrival of a cheque from Lady Hallow for ten pounds. Thus the official Strike Relief Fund was inaugurated with the modest sum of fourteen pounds, six shillings and fourpence. It was evident that for the next few days, at least fifteen hundred men

[71]

and their families, would, for the most part, need to rely on their traditional allies of patience and the pawnshop.

It was soon after midday when James Donnelly arrived outside the Dockers Arms for his appointment with Ben Tillett. On entering, he was immediately approached by a poorly dressed young woman. "Buy me a drink, sir?"

"Er, yes. Yes, of course. What would you like?"

Before she could reply they were joined by a second and older woman. "Clear off, Janie. This one's a bit too cultured for you."

"Oi. I can 'andle 'im, Beth. I was 'ere first."

James tried to conceal his embarrassment. He had not immediately realised the profession of the women. "I'm sorry – I didn't... Actually, I'm looking for someone. A man."

"A man?" exclaimed Beth.

Janie giggled. "Don't know any blokes round 'ere as does that sorta thing. You wanna try the west side of town for that."

James was looking increasingly self-conscious. "Ben Tillett. Do you know him?"

"Lord," said Beth. "I'll put some trousers on if it'll help . . . and you can call me Ben. Won't cost you no extra."

"Steady on, girls. This man's a reporter. Best leave him alone." It was Annie Tillett. "Come on," she instructed tersely, leading him to the office behind the bar.

"Didn't know this was your game as well, Annie," Beth called after them. And both she and Janie collapsed into laughter.

"It's sure nice to see you again, Miss Tillett," said James, giving a sigh of relief. Coincidence or not, he appreciated her timing. "It is still Miss Tillett, I assume?"

She ignored his question. "Ben's going to be late. He had to go out. Told me to ask you to wait."

There was an uneasy pause which had lengthened into a silence before James pursued the conversation. "How old was that girl out there?"

"I thought you had such places in America."

"Sure we do, but..."

"Of course. You've never been to one. She's eleven."

"My God," he exclaimed.

"She's been working here for nearly a month. Honour's easy enough when a girl has plenty to eat, Mr Donnelly. But it's quite different when she's starving. Don't feel sorry for her. She's one of the lucky ones. She's well paid by the way of things around here. In her profession the youngest get paid the most."

"And her parents? Do they know – do they know what she's doing?"

"Her mother does. Beth. You met her just now." Annie was enjoying his discomfort. "She has five children. Janie's the eldest. Her husband died last year and she was faced with a choice . . . like so many others. Watch her children starve, or go out to work. What would you do, Mr Donnelly? What would your wife do? Your sister? Your daughter? Now Janie's learning the trade for when she needs to take over and support her mother and the others. Which she'll have to, when Beth's crippled by disease . . . dreadful diseases the hospital will refuse to treat. Morality is for the wealthy, Mr Donnelly. For the types you mix with."

Just then Ben burst through the door. "Mr Donnelly – James. I do apologise. I've had a distressing morning. I hope Annie has kept you entertained."

The two men shook hands. "Yes, well," replied James diplomatically, "she has certainly kept me interested. But I've not been waiting long. And your morning. Distressing, you say?"

Tillett nodded. "A funeral – the wife and young child of a docker. I didn't know him. A respected man driven to such despair by his circumstances that he gave strychnine to his child and then cut his own throat. At the same time his wife also cut hers. Fortuitously, if such a word can be used in this sad situation, the attempt on his own life failed. Now he is in Newgate prison awaiting trial for murder. At the graveside this morning the man's brother showed me a letter – a letter the poor wretch had written before attempting his life. I sought his agreement to show it to you."

"May I see?" said James curiously. Ben handed him two

[73]

crumpled sheets of notepaper and straining to decipher the often faltering script, he slowly read aloud.

" 'My Dearest George, Twelve months have I now passed of a most miserable and struggling existence and I cannot really stand it any more. I am completely worn out and our father who could assist me won't do any more, for such was his last message. Never mind, he can't take his money and comfort with him and will one day probably find himself in the same boat as me. He never enquires whether I am starving or not. Three pounds, a mere flea-bite to him, would have put us straight. I can face the poverty and shame no longer and would sooner die than go to the work-house. We have, God forgive us, taken our darling Billy with us out of pure love and affection so that he should never be reminded or taunted with the crime of his heartbroken parents. My poor wife has done her best at needle-work, washing, house-minding, in fact anything and everything that would bring in a shilling, but it keeps us only in starvation. There is no prospect anywhere, no ray of hope.' "

James stopped reading, visibly moved by the stark despair of the words, and after a few moments he handed the letter across the table for Ben to continue.

" 'For six weeks I have stood in the crowd at the dock gates without work. I should go there again if I could, but with scarcely nothing to eat for five days I am too weak for the fight. May God forgive our miserable, broken souls. Prayer has helped us nothing. It must be God's will or he would have ordered it differently. Dearest George, if you could sell what little furniture we have it may fetch two pounds, enough to bury us in a cheap way. Don't grieve over us for we shall not be worthy of such respect. Our clergyman has never called on us or given us the least comfort, though I called on him a month ago. We have only you in the world dear George, who cares what becomes of us.' " Tillett paused, looked up at James and then at Annie. "And the letter is signed, 'your affectionate but broken-hearted brother, Arthur.' "

For a few seconds they sat in silence. Then Ben carefully refolded the letter and returned it to his pocket. "And if you multiply that man's desperation by thousands of others, Mr

Donnelly, you will be close to the truth. Now shall we go?"

The following five hours proved deeply distressing for James Donnelly and gave him much to consider. Immersed in thought as they walked alongside the Thames on their way back to Limehouse in the evening, he noticed a group of children apparently playing on a mudbank uncovered by the receding tide. "Who are they, Ben?"

"They're orphans. Mudlarks we call them. This is where they work. While the tide is low they scatter themselves along the river bed, crawling among the barges in search of copper nails, bolts, coal, old rope – anything they can find among the rubbish to sell, or even eat."

James looked concerned. "But many of them can be no more than eight or nine years old."

Most of the children ignored the two men, but one, recognising Ben, clambered up the bank and with a broad smile, scampered towards them. It was Emily. " 'Allo, Mr Tillett," she declared enthusiastically. Before Ben could reply, she looked enquiringly at James. "Spare a few coppers, sir?"

James nodded and immediately felt for his pocket. "Careful," warned Ben. "They'll mob us."

"This your friend, Mr Tillett?"

"Yes, Emily. This is my friend James. He's a very important newspaper man."

Emily pursed her lips thoughtfully. "Newspaper man! Where's yer sell 'em, sir? Outside the station?"

Already taken by the sweet expression and infectious grin of the little girl, James looked amused by her remark. "No, no. I write for the newspaper. I don't sell them." He noticed her legs were pitted with scars – rat bites Ben told him later. And one of her feet was cut, the slow trickle of blood staining the pavement. "Where are your shoes?"

"Ain't got none, sir." She paused and screwed up her face in an effort to remember. " 'Ad some once. When I's little. You got any money for me, sir?"

James stared at her foot and crouched to examine it more closely. She drew back in caution. "It's alright, Emily. Let me see."

[75]

"I could do wiv a few coppers, sir. If you've got 'em to spare."

"Please. Sit down for a moment. If you sit down for me I'll give you all the coins in my pocket."

Emily hesitated and glanced towards Ben for reassurance. Then she allowed James to approach her once more. "What yer gonna do?" she asked.

Removing his jacket, James tore the lining into two large pieces. "Mr Donnelly!" exclaimed Tillett. "I don't think..."

"No, Ben. I live the life of a rich man. I must do this."

"But, James," said Ben quietly. "No one man's money alone, however rich he may be, can change the view."

"I know," James conceded, well understanding the reality of Tillett's words. "But let me do this." He turned back towards Emily who was sitting confused on the kerbside.

" 'Ere. What yer doing?" she said.

"Please. I'm not going to hurt you."

Slowly Emily extended her foot and James knelt and began wrapping the material carefully around it. "You making me a shoe?" she asked, studying him inquisitively.

"Yes," he smiled.

"Then yer gonna do the other one?"

"Of course."

"Then yer gonna give me some money?"

Tillett noticed the other mudlarks were becoming curious and edging towards them. "James, we ought to leave shortly."

James finished securing the material and cautiously Emily stood up. "There. How does that feel?" he asked.

" 'Urts a bit. But I likes me new shoes. Now do I get the money, sir?"

James smiled and handed her some coins, and the two men resumed their journey to Limehouse. " 'Bye, Emily," said Ben. "See you around."

" 'Bye, Mr Tillett." Emily ran off back towards the riverbank. After a short distance she stopped, turned for a moment and waved. " 'Bye, paperman."

Outside the doorway of the Dockers Arms, James sat in a cab in conversation with Ben who was talking to him through the open window. "You felt guilty because of all you have seen today. Because you can't do more, can't re-clothe and feed them all. It's been like seeing your own conscience. But you are in a position to bring their situation to the notice of the public. We need a voice – and you, James, can be our voice. You can report the horrors that the people of the East End endure just to survive. You can follow our cause and report the facts. The way things are – not the way others perceive them to be."

James nodded. "I have limited powers, Ben. But I'll do everything possible to help."

"And your editor? Will he publish the truth? Sometimes the truth can be too difficult to accept."

"Yes, he will publish it," said James. "He will publish it because he's a good editor – and because it's the truth. Goodbye, Ben. Drive on, cabby."

As the hansom drew away, Tillett turned to see his sister standing watching at the tavern doorway. "We have a convert, I think," he said.

Annie looked unimpressed. "A convert to what?"

"He can help us, Annie. You must try to hide your feelings until you get to know him better. Remember how long it took before you accepted Eleanor."

She gave a single, dismissive laugh. "There's no comparison between Eleanor and your Mr Donnelly. And anyway, why would I want to get to know him better?"

"Well, he's a handsome fellow."

"And what's that supposed to mean?"

Ben smiled.

For the second time James arrived home late from the East End, so much so on this occasion that the Donnellys' dinner guests for the evening had already departed, engulfed in Charlotte's apologies. "Everyone wanted to know where you were. I had to apologise to Captain and Helen Townsend. It was most embarrassing. Edwin brought along the Schubert *Lieder* music. Laura sang beautifully – and I played beautifully. What happened? Why are you so late home?" Deeply engrossed in his thoughts, James gave no reply. "*James*. What is the matter?"

[77]

"Oh! Sorry, Charlotte," he said hurriedly, belatedly aware of his wife's voice. "I had to – Buckle sent me to the East End. To report on the poor."

"The poor? You're too sensitive for that job, James. Why Mr Buckle is so interested in the poor, I cannot imagine. I hope that you will inform him that you were forced to miss a dinner engagement in the company of my friends." Suddenly she noticed the torn lining of his jacket. "My God! What happened? Have you been attacked?"

He shook his head. "A girl, couldn't have been more than eight. She lives on the street and didn't have any shoes. So I wrapped her feet in the lining. It will be in tatters by the morning."

"You tore your jacket for a street urchin?" she exclaimed, horrified by his explanation. "James. This has nothing to do with you. It is not your problem. You cannot get involved. They live in their world and we live in ours. That's the way it has always been."

James gazed earnestly at his wife. "Charlotte. You have no idea what it must be like for these people. They say man always gets less from life than he demands. But these people – they demand so little to begin with that what they get cannot possibly sustain them."

"We make a regular donation to the Widows and Orphans fund," she said, confused at the depth of his concern.

"And that's it? The end of the matter? A donation to the Widows and Orphans fund. My God!"

"Have you been drinking, James?"

He turned away in frustration. "You're not listening to me."

"No, because you are obviously drunk," she replied, somewhat ruffled by his manner. "I don't know what has come over you. I am going to bed now and I suggest you do the same and clear your head of all this nonsense."

With an indignant rustle of silk, Charlotte swept from the room and for fully a minute James stared after her. He poured himself a brandy. Lifting the glass to his lips he noticed a smear of blood on one of his hands. Quickly he put down the glass, gazing intently at the stain and touching it gently with his fingers. He then walked to his study to begin his report.

As James Donnelly sat typing, seven miles away Ben Tillett was receiving a message from Tom McCarthy informing him that the Stevedores' Union had voted to join the strike immediately in support of the dockers. Also that evening, all dock labourers at the neighbouring Tilbury and Surrey Commercial Docks had voted to cease work forthwith. It was the sixteenth of August and seven thousand men were now on strike.

Chapter Six

The Times   London   Saturday, August 17, 1889

There has been some talk recently in respect to the so-called plight of the working classes, notably the dock labourers who live in the East End of London. To address the accuracy of this talk, I have recently visited the locality to make myself acquainted, in some degree at least, with the poor there, and to gain knowledge of their homes and circumstances. I wished to see and inspect the actual condition of these homes; establish if they were overcrowded, or falling into decay, and if any of the inhabitants were truly half-starved. I wanted to gain some understanding of the ways and means of living of these people and to hear from their own lips what complaints they had to make about their lives. The places I shall describe are not the dens where thieves abide, or the haunts of wretched vice. They are the homes of the ordinary poor who have the privilege to live in London at the heart of the greatest, wealthiest, and most powerful empire the world has ever seen.

Being unfamiliar with the district, I considered it prudent at the outset to seek the assistance of a skilful guide to direct my progress. The gentleman I had the good fortune to procure was Mr Benjamin Tillett who is well familiar with the East End and its people, and has recently acquired a certain prominence in the East London press as a result of his position as General Secretary of the new Dockers' Union currently in dispute with the London Dock Employers.

Although the sun was shining brightly when I began my journey, as a visitor still relatively new to these shores, I deemed it prudent to carry an umbrella. In the gardens of the West End I left the roses in full bloom and the birds were singing in the elms and chestnuts. In the East, however, such summer delights as these were not to be discerned. Hardly a tree was visible nor a bird to be heard; nowhere could I escape the sight of poverty as my hansom penetrated one unending slum. The filthy streets and slimy pavements were bounded on each side by rows of dismal houses with nothing to relieve their monotony. All were thronged with ragged children making believe to play, although, it seemed, with little or nothing to play with.

Hardly a cab did we meet as we journeyed eastward, while mine was evidently like an apparition from another world from the way the children ran breathlessly alongside. Few shops were to be seen and even the public houses and taverns which were abundant had few customers at their doors. The children seemed to have the streets to themselves for scarcely a man was to be perceived and only occasionally a woman, either carrying a baby, or hurrying along as though hastening to work. Here and there a cat was crouching in a doorway or creeping along furtively in a quest for stray food.

I bade farewell to my cabby at Limehouse Station where Mr Tillett awaited. Striding our way through the sad streets, we chatted with one of the few men we came across. He was standing in his doorway and returned with enthusiasm the greetings of Mr Tillett whom he certainly recognised. A group of dirty, ragged children, perhaps twenty in number, were gathered near the gutter and performing a war-dance around two babies who were sitting bolt upright and with eyes wide open, in a dilapidated perambulator into which they were squeezed. "They're as numerous as flies," the man solemnly remarked. Indeed the simile was well chosen for the children seemed per-

[81]

petually in motion while making an incessant disturbance for little apparent result. "I've lived 'ere or 'ereabouts for nigh on thirty year and never found life 'arder than it is now. I worked down at the docks, I did. And most of me mates too. But the pay was so low and four days out of six there weren't no work I could get. I got too old to fight for a ticket, see."

We passed into a street which contained twelve houses, six on either side and each of two storeys. On the right side stood a large dust-bin, and although not above half full, it signified its presence as plainly to the nose as to the eyes. That the inhabitants were not precise marksmen in the disposal of their rubbish was clear from the accumulation around the bin which added to the unattractive odour. Each house contained four rooms and every room was home probably to a whole family, perhaps six in number. The sum of inhabitants in the street which was some twenty-five yards in length would therefore exceed two hundred and eighty and with no water supply located in the buildings, all of the families shared but a single tap positioned at some thirty yards distance. For purposes of ablution just two outside water-closets serviced the twelve dwellings.

The home we entered was the smallest I had ever seen. It measured seven feet by six and, perhaps, six in height. Fully half the bare floor was covered by a bedstead, and a strip of sacking was laid across the rest. "Me and me 'usband and three kids sleeps in 'ere," explained the mistress, a plain, solemn-looking young woman in a threadbare dress. Beneath the window stood a small table with a teapot and some unwashed cups. A kettle lay silent in the hearth beside a downcast-looking cat who appeared, like its mistress, to be saddened by the memory of departed better days. "Yes. The five of us sleeps in 'ere," she repeated. "But we've a littler one be'ind which we gets all included in the four bob a week."

Proceeding to this smaller room we found her statement of its size to be true. It measured hardly more than five feet by six. Two panes of glass were broken in the window but still the chamber had a stuffy smell. A limp and dirty pillow and a pile of sacking lay in the corner, and save for a broken chair there was no other furniture to hide the bare floor. "Me mother an' the little girl sleeps 'ere," she continued, and introduced us to a grey-haired lady diligently sewing a large sack extracted from a heap of about twenty. As an adjacent pile of sewn sacks amounted to no more than three, her labours were doubtless far from complete. "Fifty-five come November," the mother confided, and further advised that the little girl who slept with her in that tiny room was not one of the family, nor in any way related. "Mother keeps 'er 'cos she's a norphan," explained the daughter simply, as though that were a sufficient reason for housing the little mite.

As we left the building and stepped outside into the desolate passage, we spied a little, barefooted boy four or five years of age wearing ragged clothes. Beckoned to approach, he explained that he was 'playing', although this fact was not apparent as he had nothing, nor indeed anyone, to play with. On being presented with a penny and asked by Mr Tillett what he would do with it, he replied, "Give it to mother," before departing to do so. Moments later mother appeared and I asked if her son had performed his promise. "Yes, sure. 'E's a good boy is Bob an' never breaks 'is word." The woman was clean in her dress and grave in her demeanour, and indeed her gravity was not without good reason. Her husband had died suddenly when Bob was a year old and she was left with eight children to bring up. "Shure, three are livin' out now and doin' for theirselves. So besides meself and Bob 'ere, there's but three of 'em sleepin' on the floor wiv us upstairs." And what of the eighth child? "Me little girl, Rosie. Me only little girl. The fever took 'er away, not a month ago. The mission buried 'er, me 'aving no money to do it meself. I wouldn't wish 'er back though. She's better where she is, I'm sure of that, sir. And though I were main proud of 'er, poor little mite, I wouldn't wish 'er back."

"Do you ever see a clergyman?" I enquired of the four women who were now gathered around us and who, although living in the same house, were inhabitants of four separate homes. I had wondered, being mindful of the unrelenting miles of want around me, if the church was capable of coping with such an undertaking. "My clergyman comes to visit me," said one of the group, somewhat proudly, emphasising the pronoun as though she kept a priest solely for her private use. Another, an Irishwoman, sniffed at such presumption. "Sure, he'll come to any one of us," she said. "But why should we be troublin' him exceptin' when we're dead?" Bob's mother, still looking grave, signified assent. "That's true enough," she said, "that's true enough." And she seemed to look more grave.

We turned into a slimy courtway off Commercial Road to view a row of blackened tenements. There was a faint smell of cooking in the first house we visited, faint, that is, when compared with the far less savoury odours ever-present in the East End. Still, the smell was as strong as one could expect when one traced it to its source and found that it came from so very small a pot. This was slowly simmering on a fire which for its modesty must have been made to match. Despite its size it made a bright spot in a room which otherwise was sadly dull and dismal to the eye. There was no cloth on the table nor covering on the floor and signs of comfort were nowhere to be seen. There was a cat whose presence often seems to give a room a cosy look; but in this case it looked sorely thin and worn. Near the ceiling hung a palish yellow canary imprisoned in a cage so small that it could hardly hop. During our whole visit, it stood silent on its perch and neither sang nor chirped a single note, and perhaps the inference is fair that its life was no more cheerful than that of the cat – not to mention the six other inmates of the room.

I felt curious as to what was in the pot. "Two penn'orth of fish, penn'orth of potatoes and a pinch or so of salt." That was in the pot with about a quart of water, and that was the day's meal for mother and five children. Mother was a comely, bright-eyed, civil-speaking woman. "Forty-two last birthday, fifth of November. Remembers it by Guy Fawkes. Me husband's at the hospital he is, 'cos he got hurt in the back. He's a docker and now work is short there's such a crowdin' at the gates. That's how he got jammed. A strongish man he is too. But not being overfed, you see, a small hurt tells on him." Wages? "He earns three shillings a day – when he can get work. But then he goes a week idle, and p'raps more." She paused a moment to reflect. "And that's what takes the beauty off of it."

I pointed to the sad want of repair apparent in the premises and her anger blazed out at the mean greed of the landlord whom she holds to blame. "Yes, the plaster's off the walls and the floor's half in holes and the roof it lets the rain in. But he won't do nothin', bless you. Not spend a penny, he won't."

Might we see where they slept? The second room, we found, was the same size as the first, say nine feet square. There were two beds both covered with coarse sackcloth. The parents slept in one and their five children – the youngest of which was nine years old – in the other. The floor was bare, the walls were grey, the ceiling rain-discoloured; there was neither chair, nor table, nor clothes-closet. Under the window, as if half ashamed to be taking so much room and of being so little use, stood two broken teachests. I presumed there was a water pump somewhere handy in the neighbourhood but as far as I could see there was nothing in the house to serve the purpose of ablution.

I remarked upon the damp which stained the walls and one in particular. Mother led us outside the house to a small enclosure at the back where a heap of filthy rubbish lay festering against the wall whose dampness I had observed. I gave my opinion that the authorities ought to see it. "They won't do nothin'," says mother, "not if you goes on your knees to 'em. Why, yes it do smell bad at times, but it's no use us complainin'. The landlord 'ud soon turn us out if he caught us a-grumblin'." How long had it been wet and festering? "Well, mostly since last winter. When I think as how me three children were all took away so sudden, one after the other, somehow it's me belief the dampness might have done it. Yes, sir, they all died in a fortnight, they did. Me own children, all took away last April. And a jolly good cry I had when they was took. And I've had many a cry since. But there, cryin' ain't no good. Tears don't change nothin'." While she was telling us this tragedy, I saw that her eyes looked a little dim and there was a slight sob in her voice. But I could detect no other sign of sorrow, for the people of these parts can little indulge in the luxury of grief. And had she turned to prayer? "Well, yes, sir, I have. But if God's heard mine, he ain't seen fit to answer 'em, that he ain't."

As we proceeded in the direction of West India Dock on the Isle of Dogs – seemingly a misnomer for it is hardly a true

island – I observed that a number of houses in the neighbourhood had been pulled down and Mr Tillett advised that they
were deemed too decrepit to be lived in. Most of the other
homes might share that same fate, I thought. One such was in
a row of shabby tenements that seemed too small to be spoken
of as houses. We ascended a short flight of stairs, with care, for
it possessed only one sound step. There was no landing and it
led straight into a room where I saw a scene which will be en-
graved on my memory for many years to come.

The room was almost bare. There was a broken chair attempting to steady itself against a wall black with the dirt of
ages. In one corner, on a shelf, was a battered saucepan and a
piece of dry bread. On a cord hung across the room were rags
– garments of some sort. A flower-pot propped open a broken
window-frame and at one side of the room was a sack of heaven
knows what. It was a filthy sack, greasy, and black and evil-
looking. I could not have guessed what it contained, but what
was on it was a little child – a neglected, ragged, grimed, and
bare-legged girl of about four. There she sat in the stark,
squalid room, perched on the sack, erect, motionless, expres-
sionless – and on duty. For she was 'a little sentinel', left to
guard a baby that lay asleep on the bare boards behind her, its
head on its arm, the ragged remains of what had been a shawl
flung across its legs. And, indeed, that baby needed a sentinel
to guard it. Had it crawled more than a foot or two, it would
have fallen down the unprotected stairs.

The furniture of the room had been seized the week before
for rent. The little sentinel's father – this we unearthed later
from the mistress downstairs – was a military man, and away,
and her mother had gone out on 'a arrand'. If it was anything
like her usual 'arrands', the mistress below informed us, it
would bring her home about dark very much the worse for
drink. Think of that little child on that dirty sack, keeping
guard for six or eight hours at a stretch. Think of her utter
loneliness in that bare, desolate room; every childish impulse
checked, left with orders 'not to move, or I'll kill yer.' Left sitting there often until night and darkness came on, hungry,
thirsty, and tired herself, but faithful to the last minute of her
mother's absence. "Bless yer. I've known that young 'un sit

there eight hour at a stretch. I've seen her there of a mornin' and I've seen her there when I've come agin at night. Lor, that ain't nothin', that ain't." Nothing! Left with a human life in her sole charge at four. What will that little girl's life be when she grows old enough to think? I should like some of the little ones of the West End whose every wish is gratified and who live surrounded by loving, smiling faces, and tendered by gentle hands, to see the little child sitting sentinel over a sleeping baby on the floor. Budging never an inch throughout the weary day from the place that her mother had bidden her to stay.

After traversing a gloomy maze of narrow, winding streets, we came to Shadwell Gardens and the dwelling of a dock labourer known to Mr Tillett. Our meeting proved of singular interest to myself as the occupier of the home originated from Dublin in Eire, the birthplace of my own grandfather. Sadly, this ingredient was the sole variation from the familiar. In two small beds, six children somehow contrived to sleep, while the parents, Shaun and Mary, made do on the floor.

I asked Shaun about the strike. "Well, sir. If it gets bad, there's things I can pawn. Don't get much use out of me Sunday suit – not these days. Ain't been to church for ages. God's probably forgotten what I look like. Then there's me tools. Get a bob or two for them. And if it all works out like Mr Tillett says it will; if we get what we want, a decent wage, no more being cheated by the employers – then I can buy the stuff back. I say if. But I know things are gonna be alright. This time I reckon we're gonna get things done. The men leading us, Mr Tillett, John Burns. They know what they're doing. You feel you can trust them. I'm not saying I'm not worried, 'cos I am. I'm just as scared as the next man. But you have to be optimistic. And Mary, me wife. She's behind me. And that's the main thing, sir."

A cat mewed at the door and Mary smiled and let the sorely thin creature scamper into the room. "Found her in the street one night, near Wapping," she confided. "It was raining and there was an east wind blowing – enough to blow your hat off. She was mewing piteous, she was. So I wrapped her up in me apron and carried her straight home with me. And here she's lived since – though it ain't much of a living. She don't cost us nothing. I never buys no milk for her, nor meat neither. And you know, sir, she grows all her own clothing. She ain't like me lad Jimmy – she don't wear out no boots. Well yes, she ain't much of a beauty. But I'd be sorry to lose her. You see the children likes to play with her and it ain't much they get to play with, not when one's poor."

I remarked on what I mistook for mice-holes in the floor and the corners of the walls and said I thought the cat must be neglectful of her duty. "Mice-holes," said Mary, smiling at my ignorance. "They ain't mice's holes, they're rats' holes. Fast as we block up one, they make another. They're too sharp for the cat to catch. And as for setting traps, it ain't a mite of use. When the candle's out and there's nobody to see them, they come out of their holes and kicks up such a row. You can't hardly sleep at times for the squealing and squeaking. Nuisance? Well, yes, they're a slightish nuisance. They jump on the bed and we has to keep a stick handy to knock them off it. More than once they've run across me face and Shaun says he's heard them gnawing at his whiskers."

I asked Shaun why the dockers had chosen to strike, and how they expect to overcome the power of the dock owners. "We had no choice, sir. It's heart-breaking to wait at the dock all day and never get a job. And then come home without a copper and find the children crying and sobbing for their supper. It feels grievous to have children and not know how to feed them." This was said, not in a begging way, but as a sad fact. A sudden anger appeared in his voice. "And there's thousands such as us down here in the East. And if a man gets lucky and beats the chain, and gets a day's work, then them employers, up there in their big offices, sitting in their big chairs, they pays him next to nothing for his labours. Now tell me, sir. Where's the rights in that?"

Several minutes' fast walking – as fast, at least, as we could go without trampling on the children who sat anywhere and everywhere, or scampered in our way – brought us to a cellar in which some time before, a poor woman had died of starvation after bringing into life an unfortunate babe. As we departed, I observed two little figures who recalled to me the pair of wretched, abject children who were introduced by the Ghost of Christmas Present to Mr Scrooge by the names of Ignorance and Want. Stunted and half-starved, uncared for and unkempt, each with one piece of sackcloth to serve as clothing, with pale though filthy faces, and bare legs reddened with rough usage, and well-nigh black with dirt, they stared at us half savagely and then scampered to some hiding-place like two small, scared, wild beasts. Poor wretched little creatures! Who could be their keeper, these saddest specimens of civilised existence? I am not a man of sentiment but my eyes were somewhat moistened by looking at this pitiful pair.

The second and concluding report of my travels through the East End will appear in this journal on Wednesday of next week. But for the moment I beg to share with you one last reflection. As I returned westwards through the City of London, upon my instruction, my hansom halted outside St Paul's Cathedral. How lofty and how noble appeared its spacious dome compared with all the mean and wretched rooms I had been visiting. The organ was pealing forth the grandest of its tones and the choristers were sweetly singing their evensong of thanksgiving and praise. Ah, my young friends, I thought. You may well sing 'Oh, be joyful'. How many are your joys and how few can be your griefs. Well clad and well cared for as you are, what a contrast are your lives to those of the poor children of the East End who go supperless to bed tonight.

By the end of that day, seamen, firemen, lightermen, watermen, and numerous allied trades at both the Port of London, and Tilbury Docks, had voted to stop work in support of the dock labourers. It was the nineteenth of August and twenty thousand men were now on strike.

Chapter Seven

"Page four, top right-hand corner." George Hyde threw a copy of *The Times* on to Lord Caldrick's desk in his office in Dock House.

"I've seen it," said Caldrick.

"He claims to have visited some of the families of the dock labourers and virtually cites the so-called poverty as justification for the strike."

Caldrick remained less agitated than his fellow director. "There has always been poverty. Donnelly is young. This is probably the first occasion he has seen it. So he feels the need to write about the subject."

C.M.Norwood had entered the room with Hyde. "One wonders why Buckle allowed it to be published. I would have expected more responsibility from *The Times*."

Caldrick thought for a moment. "George. You are a friend of the family. What is the fellow up to?"

Hyde shrugged his shoulders. "Well, Pemberton did tell me the other evening that Donnelly expressed some sympathy for the workers. Beyond that I cannot tell you what his motives are."

"Right. There is no need for us to panic. The problem can

be easily remedied."

"What do you suggest," muttered Hyde. "Hang the upstart?"

Caldrick turned towards the Chairman of his Docks Management Committee. "Norwood. I want you to find a journalist who will report the facts with a little more objectivity and discretion than Donnelly. And while you are addressing the matter," he added, selecting his words with meticulous attention, "you might devise a situation whereby the dockers are, how shall I say, encouraged to believe that their interests would best be served by returning to work. A disagreement among themselves perhaps – tension brought on by the burden of the strike. Do whatever you have to do. You understand?"

"Yes, of course," nodded Norwood vigorously. "Leave it to me."

Lord Caldrick dismissed Norwood from the room. "Of course, George, you are right. Things would be a lot simpler if we could just hang him."

While James Donnelly might have guessed the tone of the conversation in Dock House, closer to home such speculation was unnecessary. Charlotte had already indicated her displeasure at what she perceived as his further involvement in matters best avoided by anyone connected with the Pemberton family and she continued to express her opinion during her three-monthly routine examination by Dr Clarke. "You talk to him, Edwin. Tell him it's wrong. Earlier, when he was trying to explain it all to me, he actually referred to one of these labourers as his friend. It's too much."

"I *have* had a word with him, Charlotte," responded the doctor solicitously. "But you must understand that he feels he is doing his job. But don't worry. In a few days it will all be forgotten. The striking men will return to work and James will find something more socially acceptable to report. However, I will be seeing him later this morning. We will be watching the cricket at Lords. Leave it to me. I will speak to him again."

"Thank you, Edwin. I am sure he will listen to you and appreciate my position in this situation." Suddenly, Charlotte looked concerned. "James? Watching the cricket? I trust he is not becoming ill."

Some hours later the two men were ensconced in the pavilion at Lords Cricket Ground, watching the third day's play of the match between England and the American touring side. Stirring performances with both bat and ball by W.G.Grace and the Reverend Thornton, had placed England in a dominant position. At the commencement of play, the American team was batting determinedly in an attempt to save the game – a resolve all too necessary as with the sun shining from a cloudless sky, rain was an unlikely ally. James looked bemused. "And so as I understand your analysis, Edwin, we require 148 runs to avoid defeat by an innings, and presently we are 48 runs for the loss of eight wickets, and with only two wickets to go. So in a nutshell, the situation for our team appears hopeless."

"No, no, James," smiled Dr Clarke contentedly. "Not hopeless. It is infinitely worse than that." A bellowed appeal from the pitch indicated the fall of the penultimate American wicket. Watching the dejected batsman trudge slowly towards the pavilion to a sympathetic ripple of applause from the sparse crowd, the doctor seized the opportunity to fulfil his pledge to Charlotte. "Incidentally. Might I have a word, old boy? Charlotte is a little concerned and requested that I speak with you about this report of yours. And I believe another is due in a day or so."

"Edwin, please," said James, a touch irritably. "We're trailing by God knows how many runs in this rather silly game of which only you English appear to comprehend the rules. And you want to talk to me about my wife's lack of understanding of my responsibilities?"

"I must be honest with you, James. It's not only Charlotte."

"Not you as well, Edwin?"

"No, no," the doctor said quickly. "You will always have my full support and my belief in what you are attempting to do for these people. I am merely pointing out, as a friend, that it is not simply a matter of reporting what you see and hear. I understand that the Dock Employers, Lord Caldrick, George

Hyde, and the others, are not best pleased. These are powerful men, James. Be careful. That is all I am saying."

"*How's that?* " Dr Clarke was interrupted by a roar from the pitch. "Ah. Allison is leg before wicket," he beamed.

James looked perplexed. "And what in heaven's name does that mean?"

"It means, dear boy, that England has just won the game. Another brandy?"

Above the Dockers Arms, the strike committee was now meeting daily from eight in the morning until well into the afternoon. But progress was slow. Ben Tillett was still in the process of organising the printing of union cards and with upwards of three thousand applications for membership already received, distribution was likely to be delayed for several more days. And persistent rumours that the Dock Employers would attempt to bring men in from outside the East End, meant that an effective network of pickets at every dock gate in the Port of London was essential. Fortunately, in this instance, the substantial numbers on strike were assisting the process.

The obtaining of funds was now becoming crucial. Early indications from Eleanor were that for around a penny for each person, The Salvation Army, Reverend Adderley at the Mission, and various local charities and church groups in the East End, could provide a simple meal each day for the men and their families for the duration of a short-lived strike. But this penny increased to a daunting figure when multiplied by the numbers involved and Ben knew that their very survival depended on the committee raising sufficient funds for food.

The first mass march, four miles from West India Dock to Tower Hill, had been arranged for ten o'clock the following morning. Ben believed that by exposing the City to the sight of a ragged procession of half-starved dockers, workers in the offices, banks, and places of trade and commerce, could be persuaded to contribute to the strike fund. His aim was to mobilise around three thousand men although John Burns was more optimistic and estimated that five thousand would make the journey. That morning the *East London Advertiser* had reproduced James Donnelly's article from *The Times,* and Ben later visited their office in Mile End and received assurance that details of the march would be published in the following morning's edition. News of *The Times*'s report had spread rapidly through the East End. Few had read the original, or indeed needed to, as they were familiar enough with its ingredients which they scarcely needed to be revealed to them by an outsider. Nonetheless, its message was being told and re-told in streets, taverns, and homes throughout the area, and by the following morning, so would be details of the march to Tower Hill.

C.M.Norwood was not in the habit of patronising the bawdy attractions of the Pig's Trotter tavern in Hackney, during recent years an increasingly shabby district which both in character and geographic position, cushioned the wealth of the City from the squalor and despair of the East End. However, his presence on this occasion was to fulfil two separate engagements, each of which could have been deemed clandestine in nature. The first, with Clive Redgrave of the *Daily News,* was already in progress and Norwood was indicating what he expected from his guest. "Report the disruption that could be caused. The crippling of the country's economy, the shortage of food and essential materials. Emphasise the close relationship between this and the French Revolution. Leave your readers in no doubt as to the potential of such a mass movement. The fact is that anyone who owns property, from the smallest market trader to the richest businessman, will be a target if things were to become out of control – as well they might. Is that clear?"

Redgrave nodded sternly. "I understand entirely, sir."

"Good. Now there's someone I'd like you to meet." Norwood signalled to a prostitute who was waiting close by. She approached and he handed her a shilling. "I'd like you to keep my friend company for a while, young lady." He then turned and looked penetratingly into the reporter's eyes. "It is gratifying to meet a member of the press who can see the reality of the situation."

Redgrave smiled, a little uncomfortably. "I always consider myself to be a realist, sir."

Norwood stood up. "I'll contact you in due course."

He strode from the room and Redgrave turned his attention admiringly to the woman. She leant forward towards him and smiled invitingly. "Now, sir. What can I do for you? My name's Clare."

Outside the Pig's Trotter, Norwood was seated in a cab awaiting the arrival of Harry, his second appointment of the evening. Harry was a man of neither words, nor style and the Pig's Trotter was a more lofty establishment than he would ordinarily grace. Brawn was his speciality, despite the absence of a thumb and forefinger on each of his hands: brawn, and an unerring ability to execute orders. And Norwood had the very assignment to accommodate him.

Between them, the strike committee and the *East London Advertiser* had done an effective job of publicising the march. By eight o'clock, two hours before the procession was due to begin, all along West India Dock Road as far as the eye could see, thousands of men were waiting. Old men with pinched and anxious faces; middle-aged men with a look of stern resolve; and younger men inclined more towards defiance; while intermingled amongst them were women, some with babes in arms, some with families clustered around them. Across the locked dock gates stretched a row of policemen in good-humoured conversation with the crowd, while ranged against the long, blank dock wall was such finery as the men could boast by way of flags and banners, many improvised from the most curious materials. Nearby, a brass band, particularly assertive in respect to its lead cornet and bass drum, doggedly played *We All Came Into The World With Nothing*, to general indifference.

Away from the dock, much of the East End was drained of its usual activity. Shops and public houses had but few occupants and most eating houses were closed. Only at the pawnshops was business brisk, the squeeze of poverty revealed by the continuous stream of women exchanging family possessions for a few desperately needed coppers.

By nine o'clock the crowd already exceeded the five thousand predicted by Burns. Outside the Dockers Arms, Annie Tillett was striving both to control and encourage the men, while Eleanor Marx had long since taken refuge inside the Mission. Jim Harris, Shaun Lamb and Will Thorne were talking with Mary Lamb, there with her six children to watch the proceedings. Someone had hurled a pebble at one of the police officers, knocking his helmet askew, and Jimmy Lamb was involved in a high-pitched and repetitive exchange with one of his younger brothers after being accused by him of perpetrating the crime.

"Did."

"Didn't."

"Did."

"Didn't."

"Did."

"Didn't."

"*Did.*"

"*Didn't* "

Still the numbers on the street were mounting inexorably. As the hand of the dock office clock approached ten, banners were brought from their resting place and suddenly and unaccountably, hundreds of men, many decked in old top hats bound with coloured ribbons, became possessed of flags secured to handles, pikes, or sticks. Then, equally unaccountably, for no-one appeared to be issuing orders, the procession fell in. It was a motley assembly with a grim sense of humour. Mounted on broom handles, groups carried effigies of a skinny docker's cat crouched, snarling at a fat employer's cat; an out-sized employer's baby wearing frills, and a bony docker's baby dressed in tattered rags; the employer's dinner, an enormous plate piled high with meat and vegetables, and a docker's dinner – a crust of bread and a tiny herring.

At last all was ready. The procession had by a process of evolution distinctly its own, formed from assembled chaos. As the church clock struck ten, a great cheer announced the breath-less appearance of Tillett and Burns, their arrival delayed by the huge numbers on the streets. "Right, lads. Keep your heads clear and don't do anything rash," yelled Tillett.

For a moment hardly a sound was heard. Then the band at the front launched itself into *Rule Britannia*. There was some initial difficulty in starting, but the lead cornet and bass drum were much in evidence. Fifty yards back, a rival band got un-derway. This was all fife and drum and as, with a notable spirit of independence, they declined to follow the lead of the blar-ing brass at the front, much cacophony ensued. To add to the clamour, Jimmy and his brother were squabbling once more. This time it was Jimmy's insistence that he could bang the bass drum more deafeningly even than the bandsman.

"Yeah?"
"Yeah."
"Yeah?"
"Yeah."
"Yeah?"
"Yeah."
"*Yeah?* "
"*Yeah.*"

Emily listened to the discussion with interest before it was ended abruptly by a resounding clout from their mother. Then, with a theatrical flourish well suited to the occasion, Tillett waved his arm, and fifty thousand men, their stomachs empty and their boots tied up with string, began to march.

The procession was headed by a posse of foot and mounted police. Then came Burns, waving his straw hat, Thorne and McCarthy, wearing brightly coloured scarves, and Tillett, chat-ting with the Metropolitan Police commissioner. Above the throng fluttered the banners of numerous trade and friendly societies. There were the Foresters; Doggetts prize-winners; the Sons of the Phoenix, in gaudy scarves; a stalwart battalion of watermen in scarlet coats, pink stockings and velvet caps; and East London painters, carpenters, and joiners. Soon the banners increased by one as a body of three hundred men from Millwall timber yard marched up amid general cheering.

Wagons followed, manned by ballast heavers forever winding-up and tipping out their buckets with a miniature crane; coal-men fishing for coppers with bags on the end of poles; Britannia in a Union Jack skirt and a thick moustache; a bearded Father Neptune with a tin trident; a doctor in a top-hat; and a barber with a enormous razor. There were fish heads, onions, tiny loaves, and toy dogs, carried on poles, all bearing the inscription 'Docker's Dinner'; together with stevedores, sailors, firemen, engineers, shipwrights, and most classes of workers representing the docks and shipping – and there were the dock labourers themselves.

As the column reached Poplar Hospital, a few pale faces were seen at the windows and every man in the march raised his cap as they passed. Throughout its length, Commercial Road was lined with vast crowds. Groups of collectors deployed each side of the procession with their roughly constructed wooden boxes, gathered a harvest of desperately needed pennies, often boarding buses and trams, their horses halted by the proceedings. At several points the march was joined by new contingents which emerged from the slums, alleys and hovels, to swell the forces on the move.

Towards the City, popular sympathy was demonstrated by continual bursts of cheering which Tillett acknowledged by calling out "remember the collecting boxes". At one point a woman with a haggard, anxious face ran out from the crowd. She asked him when the strike would be settled, and to think of the children at home. "Cheer up, missus," Tillett reassured her with a smile. "It will not last long and then times will be better." But he knew that hunger was playing havoc in the ranks of his men, and the women and children were thinner and paler than a week before. One by one, pieces of furniture were disappearing to the pawnbrokers' and the despair in many dockers' homes contrasted grimly with the bright banners and lively tunes of the procession.

Eleanor had composed a verse for the men which by the time they arrived at the end of Commercial Road, most had miraculously learnt. Thus prepared, and led by Burns and his thundering voice, they proceeded to bellow the words to a tune vaguely reminiscent of *My Bonnie Lies Over The Ocean.*

> I'm one of the thousands who're out in the East
> because we'll no longer be slaves,
> No more we'll be sweated or used as a beast
> and crushed into premature graves,
> We're all in this together, resolved and alert,
> to win what is right, just and true,
> We ask for no more than an honest desert,
> so give the poor docker his due.
>
> Yes, give the poor docker his due,
> the tally you never will rue,
> The rent we must meet, our children must eat,
> so give the poor docker his due.

Throughout its duration, the marchers freely exchanged jokes with the escort of police and when the procession reached the City boundary at Aldgate, the Metropolitan Police handed over to the City force to the singing of *Auld Lang Syne.* It was now almost noon and the pace slackened gradually in the narrow streets of the metropolis. Penned in the trough of offices, the music of the bands seemed louder, and the City went to lunch that day with its windows rattling to *Rule Britannia.*

After passing along Aldgate, the marchers turned off into Leadenhall Street, the location of Dock House and the Dock Employers. The streets were clogged with the procession and all traffic had been suspended. Spectators, bewildered but sympathetic, gathered at office windows and lined the pavements to see the show. Collecting boxes attracted showers of coppers thrown from windows and house tops, as well as contributions from the ground – the very jingle of the coins an encouragement to the men, a promise of a much needed meal. There was some jeering and booing as the march passed Dock House, but otherwise good humour continued to prevail. Immediately behind the first band of which there were seven at different points, Superintendent Forster of the City

[99]

police walked with Tillett and Burns, and at one stage produced a tin of cough lozenges from the recesses of his uniform when he noticed that Tillett's voice was becoming husky. Thus, early on, friendly relations were being established between the strikers and the representatives of law and order.

It was almost one o'clock as the men advanced on Tower Hill. They talked little now as the journey required all their concentration and strength. Such was the length of the procession it took nearly an hour from the time Tillett and Burns arrived at the Hill, for the men at the back to appear. Tillett took up a position on the roof of a hansom-cab, seating himself near the edge and dangling his feet over the side dangerously near the window. He looked out across the Thames and then at the ragged battalion massed before him. Everywhere there was the appearance of a great labour revolt, but nowhere had there been even a hint of disorder. In ten minutes they could have sacked every food shop in the City and satisfied their hunger and the hunger of their families. Contrast this, he thought, with the French mobs which rioted with the cry 'give us bread'. Not so the British docker, independent even in his direst plight. 'Give me work' he says, 'and pay me fairly.'

Tillett recalled uneasily that an army marches on its stomach. "It's not for a dinner of 'addocks and 'errings we grumbles about," one of his dockers had said. "No. It's when we 'as to buckle our belts and rub our stomachs for a dinner, as it gives us the 'ump." Ben Tillett wondered how long his army would be content to rub its stomach for a dinner. The bell of the Fenchurch Street Station clock chimed twice. And he wondered for whom it tolled.

On this occasion, Lord Caldrick was less composed. "Have you seen this?" he demanded, flinging that morning's copy of *The Times* on to Pemberton's desk at the National British Bank. "Read it. Read it now. All of it."

Only the sound of Caldrick angrily pacing the room broke the silence for the next few minutes as Sir Alfred Pemberton sat reading his son-in-law's words, and became increasingly concerned as he did so.

This is the second and concluding report of my recent journey to investigate the plight of the people who reside in the East End of London. As you will recall, my valued guide for the day was Mr Benjamin Tillett, the General Secretary of the new Dockers' Union.

A few minutes' brisk walk brought us to a dark court reached by a narrow passage from a shabby street within a short distance of Wapping railway station. There we came across a block of six identical dwellings which surprisingly bore the builder's name, for I imagine no-one would be proud to be identified with such a dismal looking place. Inside the lower room of one of these homes lived a widow with her family. But it is not quite so easy to make calls in the East End as it is in the West. This was so when we arrived and we were puzzled as to admittance for there was neither bell, nor knocker, nor handle on the door. Presently, however, appeared a little girl who curtsied and promptly produced the handle from its hiding-place and gave us entry to her home. She was plainly clothed in an old dress of thin material which matched her figure.

The room was so dark that it took a minute or so for our eyes to adjust to the gloom. The bed had not been made, for there was, indeed, no bed to make. It is true there was a bedstead with sacking on it, all huddled in a heap. But to have 'made' it into a bed would have bemused any housemaid. Two chairs, a small work-table, and a sack half filled with straw, were the only furniture; three shillings would have purchased everything in sight. A large bundle of new sail-cloth lay on the table and grandmother and mother were employed in making hammocks. They could earn four shillings by making ten which was all they could manage in a week, for the cloth was heavy to sew.

The little girl had hastened home to assist her mother and grandmother, a toughish job for hands so thin and weak. But did she never go to school? Oh, yes, sometimes. And which did she prefer, home work or school work? Oh, she liked home work the best, she answered rather quickly, as though there could be no doubt. But surely it was harder? Oh, yes, it was certainly that, but then it brought in something, and mother was so poor. A pleasant, sad-eyed little girl with a delicate prettiness doomed to fade quickly away like the colour from a sunset sky, she is ten next birthday although seeing her small limbs I should have guessed her two years less. There was a shy smile on her lips as she corrected my mistake in supposing that she had to sleep somewhere on the floor. Oh, no, grandmother and mother both slept on the bed, and she slept at their feet. There were three other children and they slept on the floor, all three together on a sack between the bedstead and the wall. And had they nothing for a covering? Oh yes. They had their clothes.

Clothes! Poor little child! When winter comes, their clothes will hardly give much comfort. All she wore, and indeed possessed, was the thin dress pinned at her throat, a feeble jacket, and a pair of cotton socks. Had she ever had a doll, or tasted a plum-pudding, or been taken to a pantomime? Many a query like these I felt inclined to ask this hard working little girl who had answered so prettily in a soft and gentle voice the many questions I had put. But there was sewing to be done and we were taking up her time. To compensate for the precious minutes she had lost in telling me her story, I slipped something in her hand while bidding her good-bye and from the stare it attracted and the smile that quickly followed, I came to the conclusion that a coin other than copper is not a common sight to a child in the East End.

Mother accompanied us to the front door. Her husband, a dock labourer, had died last winter at the Bow infirmary. "He worked mostly at the docks, he did. But the pay was so bad an' he couldn't get no work. An' he got weak for want o' food. An' then he catched a chill a waitin' hour after hour in the wet. So he went to the hospital an' lay there till he died. Last Christmas Day – merry Christmas as they calls it. We wasn't very merry with him there lyin' dead, an' we'd nothing much to eat."

Pemberton stopped reading and looked up uneasily at Lord Caldrick. "I see what you mean. This isn't journalism. It's propaganda for the unions."

"Of course it is," replied Caldrick tersely as he tossed a partially smoked cigar into a receptacle on the floor. "And it gets worse." Hurriedly, Pemberton turned his attention back to the page.

Our journey was all but concluded when in a narrow thoroughfare we discovered a small shed built on a tiny scrap of ground. At a rough guess the shed was a dozen feet in length, and varied in its width from three feet at one end to seven feet at the other. Its long walls were poorly constructed of brickwork, while the others were fashioned from wooden planks. These, in many places, were an inch or so apart. Seen near to a farm, the shed might have been deemed a stable or a cowhouse. But here, in this great city and centre of civilisation, it was inhabited by humans and dwelt in as a home. Three evil-eyed cats sat uneasily on the roof. Cats are as common here as the children and the kittens are the only truly pretty things we have seen since we started our exploration.

We were warmly welcomed by a pleasant woman of about fifty years of age. Business-like in manner and brisk in speech, she was poorly clothed; indeed her dress looked well-nigh threadbare, but in clothing and person she was scrupulously clean. The house, or shed, or room, was as clean as herself: although the ceiling was patched up, one window would not shut, the plaster was in places peeling from the walls, the shrunk door let in the draught, the floor showed many a small hole, and there was a rather large hole in the roof. "Yes, it do want doing up a bit," observed the woman with a smile. "But there, we're happy enough in it, though it might be a little higher." This was spoken in apology, for at the point where I was standing my bare head touched the ceiling. "Yes, it's low, there's no denyin'. But one don't need no ladders when one wants to clean the ceiling. Papered it meself I did, true as you stand there. Me an' me son helpin' me. One day, somehow or other, we mended the roof, 'cos it used to leak most terrible. Needed a humbrella to keep the rain off. I dunno how we done it hardly, but the wet don't henter not so much. Leastways exceptin' it's snowin' in winter. An' there's nothin' can't keep snow out when it comes to melt, there ain't."

A small boy was playing in the room. He had no playmate, nor plaything, and seemed to be attempting a game of hide-and-seek by himself. To vary the monotony of his playing alone, I took him by the arms and gave him some jumping in the air. He seemed to relish this new form of entertainment and when we bade goodbye, he eyed me rather wistfully, much as a dog may eye its master when it desires a walk. Chancing to look round when we were halfway down the street, I perceived my young playmate closely following at my heels and he began to cry when he was called back by the woman. Well, I thought as he left us, it is a simple thing to please a child who wants a game to play, and this little fellow can certainly have known but fleeting pleasure in his life when he finds so much enjoyment in a few jumps in the air.

And now I must stop and bid farewell to the people of the East End among whom I have recently been travelling, and talking a little when I found them so inclined. Everywhere I heard the same complaints, of high rent for wretched room, and of low wages for arduous work. The purpose of my journey was to seek foundation for the action currently being adopted by the dock labourers against what they perceive as exploitation by their employers, action widely supported by the people of East London. Did their circumstances, and those of all the inhabitants of the East End, warrant the threat of broadening disruption being imposed upon the rest of the nation? My conclusion, based on the honest evidence of my own eyes and ears, is that no strike was ever more justified.

The average age of death among the people of the West End of London is fifty-nine years. In the East End it is twenty-nine years. That is to say the person in the east has half the life expectancy of the person in the west. Talk of war! Here, in the heart of peace, is where the blood is being shed. And here not even the civilised rules of warfare apply, for the women and children and babes in arms die as frequently as the men. I am told by Thomas Barnardo that more than half of the children in the East End die before they reach the age of five. What slaughter! Even Herod scarcely managed quite so shamefully. Here, in 1889, in the West End and in the East End of London, people are living simultaneously in different centuries. No cause was ever more justified than that of the dock labourers and of the people of East London.

Chapter Eight

Pemberton lowered *The Times* and looked up uncomfortably at Lord Caldrick. "As I said. Propaganda. Nothing but propaganda that will encourage socialism into our society and all that comes with it."

Caldrick nodded brusquely. "May I be blunt, Alfred? Your son-in-law is proving to be a persistent irritant and this situation cannot be allowed to continue. If it does, the whole profitability and, indeed, future of the docks could be called into question."

"Come now. You don't seriously believe that?"

The reply was accompanied by a wry smile. "No, Alfred. I don't. But these reports are creating a false impression for those who are susceptible to untruths. This one all but accuses us of being murderers. You must speak to the man."

"I will, I promise," said Pemberton, offering his associate a fresh cigar. "And please don't worry. It's damn infuriating, I know. But starving men cannot strike indefinitely. I am certain it's but a matter of days. However, I will speak to him immediately."

"Will he listen to you though?"

Pemberton glanced across at Lord Caldrick and smiled. "He is living in a house paid for with my money." Caldrick looked reassured. Pemberton was speaking his language.

Meantime, tension was building between James and Charlotte, and her displeasure following his initial report in *The Times* was now even deeper with the publication of the second. No sooner had he arrived home than she rushed downstairs and pursued him into the lounge. "You have no right to do this. Two of our neighbours avoided me in the street this morning. I cannot believe you are being so selfish."

James sighed. "Good evening, Charlotte. How are you?"

"Didn't you even consider the affect it would have on me? This is *my* life that is being ruined."

He turned in astonishment and for a moment they looked at one another across the yards of plush carpet. "Ruined? Please explain to me, Charlotte, how your life is being ruined."

"Well, if you cannot see that..."

"No. Please. I would like you to explain. Ruined? You say your life is being ruined."

Charlotte raised her eyes in a gesture of annoyance. "You cannot see it? Then I shall go to my room until you are willing to discuss this reasonably."

"No, damn it," he said sharply, his customary geniality evaporating as he spoke. "Stay here and tell me about ruin." Startled by the manner of his response, she hesitated at the doorway. "No?" he persisted. "So I'll tell *you* then. I'll tell you what ruin is. Selling your child to a stranger for a few shillings. How does that sound? Sleeping with five different men every night. Prostituting yourself to feed your children."

Charlotte looked shaken. "I'm not going to listen to you talk like this."

"Yes you damn well are," declared James, his words harsher than he had intended. Nonetheless, he continued unrepentant. "Sleeping under a jetty and eating scraps thrown from the boats. Fighting with your friends and neighbours every morning just for a day's work. Fighting – for one lousy day's work, for God's sake. Not enough? A mother, holding a baby in her arms, watching it die because she's unable to feed it. Don't talk to me about your life being ruined, Charlotte."

"How dare you use that tone to me in my house."

"*Your* house? I'll use whatever tone I like in *our* house," he said angrily.

Charlotte's reply was spoken with both control and deliberation. "Please refrain from raising your voice. I have no wish to advertise our differences to the servants. You can use that tone with your new friends. Goodnight."

Suddenly irritated with himself for his lack of control, James poured out a brandy. But he scarcely had time to make himself comfortable in the chair, before the butler appeared. Sir Alfred Pemberton was waiting in the hall. James sighed. He knew what to expect. "Forgive me for sounding like a foolish old man. But isn't this a case of biting the hand that feeds you? You are heaping abuse and condemnation on a society which has accepted you; taken you in as one of its own."

James looked exasperated. "Why hasn't it occurred to anyone that I'm merely doing my job?"

"You are doing more than that, James. It is clear to anyone with any sense that you have taken a side. And that does not make for good journalism."

James shook his head. "I've taken a side? No, father-in-law. That's not the issue. What I've done as far as your friends are concerned, is taken the wrong side. That's what you are trying to say. It has nothing to do with good journalism."

Pemberton smiled. "Well, it's a problem that can be easily rectified. All you need to do is write a report suggesting that you were perhaps misled by the strike leaders. An error of judgement on your part and that you now see things as they really are."

"And?"

"And what?"

"And if I don't?"

"You are now a member of the long-standing Pemberton family and you owe a loyalty to its traditions and to those of London society."

James fixed his gaze firmly in the direction of his father-in-law. "And what about loyalty to the truth?"

Pemberton ignored the question and poured himself a brandy. "You know, James. Charlotte is very upset by all of this. I am sure you are aware of that. It would be a terrible shame if she were forced, by circumstances, to leave you. A scandal perhaps. Debts."

"*Debts?*" echoed James. "What debts? Are you out of your mind?"

"These are the rules of the game. And if one is not prepared to abide by these rules, then one must leave the field."

Momentarily, James remained silent before a wry smile crossed his face. "I see. Not exactly cricket, is it, father-in-law?"

"How long do you reckon it's gonna go on for, Ben?" asked Brewer. "It's already been eight – nine days. Bit longer than you said."

As he did on most days, Ben Tillett was taking his turn on the picket line. Jim Harris, Shaun Lamb and several dozen others were on duty outside the main gate of East India Dock. Ben placed his hand on Brewer's shoulder. "The campaign is starting to bring money in. Any day now we should be able to issue food tickets."

"Yeah," scoffed Harris. "How much longer d'you think them employers can last without any workers, eh? They can't, can they. They'll have to give in."

"Yes," agreed Tillett. "As long as we keep the blacklegs out. As long as every man stands firm and the docks stay empty, it should soon be over."

Lamb looked less certain. "D'you think they're that unprepared? Seems to me like we're not crediting them with much sense. More as if they're idiots."

"No, not idiots," said Tillett. "But the employers, they've played the only hand they've got. Whenever you complained – what were you threatened with?"

"No work tomorrow," growled Harris.

"Exactly," said Tillett. "No work tomorrow. And why? To show us they pay our wages and they can stop our wages; they can hire a man or they can pass a man over. And when they did that to you, what did you go home thinking about?"

"Killing the bastard foreman," snarled Harris.

"Yes, Jim. Those thoughts may have entered your head. But I'll wager they weren't foremost in your mind. When you got home, you went to bed not thinking of how to get justice – but simply 'will I get picked tomorrow'. And that is the ingenuity in their method. Because in doing so, they cleared your brains of any notion that you could have any mastery over them." Tillett glanced around at the faces of the men as he endeavoured to reassure them. "It won't be easy, of course it won't. You know that already. But now, for the first time, the odds are highly in our favour. Ever since the one man has hired the many, he's known that without the many, he is nothing. And the one thing he's been afraid of is what has happened here – a union of workers."

It was becoming dark. "I gotta go," said Lamb. "Lizzie, me eldest. She's been poorly. Promised Mary I'd not be late. See you tomorrow."

Lamb began the walk home and turned into an alleyway alongside Blackwall Iron Works. As he did so, two men, unseen by him, emerged from a doorway and followed at a short distance. It was now dark. Thinking he heard footsteps, he stopped and looked round. The men stood still. "Hello. Anyone there?" There was silence. He was becoming increasingly uneasy and continued along the alley, quickening his pace with every stride. A third man stepped out in front of him: he was holding a pickaxe handle across his chest. Lamb stopped in his tracks, his sense of unease turning to alarm. Hurriedly he spun round, only to see two men standing behind him preventing his escape. Instinctively he turned back and for an instant saw the handle of the pickaxe bearing down on him in the grip of two gloved hands. Two hands – with three fingers on each one. Then they became a blur as he was bludgeoned to the ground. Struck down by a single blow that killed him.

By mid-morning several hundred men had gathered outside the Dockers Arms, and Annie and Ben Tillett, together with

Will Thorne, were attempting to retain order. "You all knew it would be a hard fight," said Ben weakly, finding difficulty in focusing his thoughts and taking control of the situation.

"We didn't know we were gonna get murdered," called out one of the dockers. "Not only are we starving to death, the employers are now gonna knock us off one by one."

"There is no evidence of the employers being r-responsible," said Tillett defensively, stammering slightly as he strove to re-gain authority. "That sort of talk will only cause panic."

"Who was it then, Jack the Ripper?"

"Friends. I don't know who was responsible for this grievous crime. But I can tell you here and now that if the employers were in any way connected, this squabble between ourselves is exactly what they would have wished. We cannot – must not allow this to weaken our resolve."

"Weaken our resolve?" shouted one of the men angrily. "What about my family. I've got a family that's starving. We've all got families that's starving." The man's words were lost as countless calls of agreement reflected the dejection in the crowd.

"Friends, friends," said Tillett, holding his arms aloft. "As from tomorrow, every man will receive a penny food ticket each day for himself and for each member of his family. Ar-rangements have been made for local tradesmen throughout the East End to exchange these tickets for food. Or you can go to the Limehouse Mission, the Salvation Army Hostel, or sev-eral other locations where meals will be provided. A full list of shops and meal centres will be displayed on the wall here out-side the Dockers Arms. Pass the word around. Be here tomor-row morning from eight o'clock. And stay calm." As the men slowly dispersed with at least some consolation for their fami-lies, Annie and Ben left the strike committee to continue its preparations for the distribution of the food tickets. They had to see Mary Lamb.

Ben stayed only a short while. He gave Mary a batch of food tickets and an assurance of the union's support for her and the children. Once alone, the two women clung to each other, the bleak silence broken as Mary gently began to sob. It was a few

[111]

minutes before she pulled away. "Cup a tea, Annie?"

"No. Stay there. I'll do it." Annie was searching desperately for the right words. "The men . . . next weekend . . . they're marching again to Tower Hill. Ben says there'll be a tribute to Shaun . . . to show everyone there that..." Her voice trailed sadly away as she realised such details meant nothing to Mary. No words could console her. Not at that moment.

Annie prepared the tea and the two sat silently together at the table before Mary managed a bleak, distant smile. "What we gonna do, Annie . . . me and the kids?"

Annie did her best to sound reassuring. "Like Ben said. We'll look after you. See you're all alright. Ben's gonna visit your landlord . . . to fix things about the rent . . . just for a few weeks till everything gets sorted."

For several minutes Mary stared down dejectedly at the table, her heart transparent in her expression. Finally she spoke. "He was a good man, Annie. Never passed a day without thinking of me before himself . . . me and the kids. I know we ain't got much, but he always did his best for us. Deserved better than this, that's for sure. Better than having his head smashed in." Mary's eyes filled with tears and she began to cry once more. "Why'd they do it, Annie? Why Shaun? He never hurt no-one."

Annie took Mary's hand and the room again fell silent. Soon, almost to herself, Mary began to speak. As she did so the cat jumped into her lap and softly began to purr. "When I was a little girl, I saw a tightrope walker in a field not far from here. He was as high as the roof of this house, probably higher. No-one moved as we all watched. Everyone kept their eyes fixed on him. Like they were up there, taking each step with him, keeping their balance with him. But then, when he was halfway across, a terrible thing happened. A flock of birds flew past. Close enough to make him look up. The look, no more than a glance. But all that it needed. One foot slipped from the rope, the pole sprang from his hands, and then his body fell downwards – struggling all the way. The crowd below, who had held their breath and been with him every step of the way, fled as one from the falling body. And amid screaming and shouting, the man hit the ground, crumpled and broken. Dead in a few minutes."

Mary's voice wavered and she paused, dabbing her tired, reddened eyes with an apron moist from the pain of the past few hours. Startled by the movement, the cat jumped from her lap and mewed softly beside the door for a few moments before springing up and making its escape through the open window. There was a sign of despair in Mary's voice as she went on. "Now, with Shaun not here, I feel meself walking that tightrope. In me arms I carry the kids instead of a pole to keep me balance. Behind me, stretch the days we've survived. In front of me, the days still to come. And if nothing crosses our path, if nothing knocks me or forces me to lose me balance, then we'll make it to the end of the rope. But if we fall – no-one's gonna care. Don't matter what promises have been made. Or how much people want to help. If we fall, it's just gonna be us and the ground." Mary sighed and stared forlornly ahead, her eyes moist, her fingers twisting aimlessly in the folds of her skirt. Fighting her own tears, Annie gazed down at the tea, and the room again fell silent.

Well before eight o'clock the following morning, a crowd of around four thousand had gathered outside the Dockers Arms for the distribution of food tickets. Several hundred of the men, on picket duty, or on the streets or stations with the collecting boxes, had sent wives or children to represent them and it was likely that many of those present would need to be patient for some hours ahead.

Inside the committee room Eleanor Marx was seated at a small table littered with letters and telegrams, bills and manifestos. Appointed as financial secretary, on her rested the responsibility not only of organising the distribution of tickets, but also the issuing of collecting boxes, receiving and acknowledging contributions, and supervising the overall relief effort. Some gifts of tea, milk, bread, soup, and other provisions were being received daily from East End shopkeepers. These were being transferred to the Mission from where Reverend Adderley had agreed to provide two additional morning and evening meal sessions to accommodate dockers' wives and children bearing their precious penny tickets. Moreover, to cater for the ever mounting numbers, The Salvation Army hostel had offered to provide half-a-dozen standing-only meal sessions to allow up to three thousand hungry mouths to be fed each day.

It was shortly before eight when Tillett, Thorne and Mc-Carthy took their seats at three trestle-tables at one end of the committee room, each with a huge roll of tickets. Just inside the door, Annie Tillett was seated with instructions to note every recipient. With union cards still not available, no strict inspection of who actually received tickets would be possible, so people would need to be taken at face value. It was Annie's task to ensure that the same face appeared only once.

As the dock office clock struck the hour, John Burns emerged at the tavern doorway to take control of the crowd. "First, I want all the children," he yelled, and hundreds of bare-foot girls and boys broke through the pack to surround the entrance. Planting himself in the doorway, his back jammed against one side of the frame, his foot up against the other, Burns allowed the children to creep in, one at a time, under his leg. As quickly as Tillett, Thorne and McCarthy could tear the tickets apart, they were seized by little outstretched hands, the children trotting off at once to exchange them for food. The women came next, and then the men. For seven hours, Burns, stripped to the waist, remained at his post, forcing the men down as they came to him; chatting, persuading, encouraging – even remonstrating if they showed signs of losing control, until finally the street was cleared.

With most of the crowd representing not just themselves but their whole family, around thirty thousand tickets had been issued to a value of one hundred and twenty-five pounds. In one corner of the committee room stood an old chest filled with a vast quantity of coppers, the proceeds of the past four days from collecting boxes and the Tower Hill march. As, in spite of its bulk, the contents amounted to no more than three hundred pounds, Ben Tillett was aware that the day's endeavours would provide but temporary relief and contented himself with the knowledge that the tickets had boosted morale when it was sorely needed. And he was thankful that the relief organisations and most of the local tradesmen had agreed to wait before claiming their myriad of pennies. Burns dragged himself upstairs. "Will. From tomorrow we must appoint a separate committee for each of the five dock areas to handle this ticket distribution on a local basis."

Thorne smiled and nodded. "Yes. We are all very much of the same thought. Now, come and sit down. You've earned a few minutes' break." Thorne had been reading *The Times.* "I get the impression Donnelly is shying away from things. A man murdered – we all guess it was the employers and the report is just a paragraph hidden away between details of a railroad accident in Baltimore and an election in Australia, and with none of the fire we've become accustomed to."

"Maybe he's losing interest," suggested Annie. Ben glanced across the room at her and she shrugged her shoulders.

Emily and a group of her friends were tearing along Shadwell Gardens on their way to a Punch and Judy show outside the Mission, when she saw Jimmy Lamb sitting by himself on the wall beside his front door. She stopped, staring at him inquisitively. "Hello. What yer doin'?"

Jimmy looked up. "Nothin'," he replied quickly.

"Nothin'?"

"*No nothin'.* Me dad's dead."

Emily stared at Jimmy's downcast face and fiddled with the ends of her hair. "Oh." She paused a moment. "We're goin' to the Mission."

"What for?"

"Punch and Judy. Comin'?" Jimmy hesitated and glanced towards his closed front door. Then he dashed off with Emily.

The performance had just begun as they arrived at the Mission. Around two hundred children were seated in rapt attention in the roadway watching Punch, Judy, and the rest, all portrayed with admirable skill by Reverend Adderley. James Donnelly was also there and enjoying his first exposure to the rowdy proceedings. As the interval approached, Annie Tillett appeared from the Mission bearing two buckets, one laden with loaves and the other brimming with meat-bone soup. "You don't look the Punch and Judy type, Mr Donnelly."

"Oh. Hello, Miss Tillett," smiled James. "Well, you know what they say – we're all children at heart. Aggressive character isn't he, this Punch? No, actually I'm here to meet Reverend Adderley. I'm writing an article about the Mission, for *The Times*. Oh, and I'm also here to deliver a package." Annie glanced at the cardboard box stuffed under his arm, but asked no questions.

The children spotted Annie and the enticing contents of the buckets. Instantly she was besieged. "Oi. In a line. You know the rules. In a line or no-one gets nothing." Annie held out the bucket of loaves. "You can make yourself useful, Mr Donnelly. Break them into four and dish them out."

It took little more than fifteen minutes to provide every child with their quarter loaf and ladle of soup. Near the end of the queue was Emily. "Hello, paperman," she said, and she smiled at him with such delight that he had to smile too.

"Emily! Hello. How are you?"

"Look." She pointed to the lining. Only one frayed piece remained, now knotted untidily around her neck. "Still got it."

James smiled. "I'm surprised any is left. Here, I've brought you a present." He handed her the box.

"Cor. This for me? Fanks, paperman." With unexpected ferocity for a small girl, Emily ripped at the lid, her eyes gleaming with excitement and then widening as the contents were exposed. "Cor, look. Shoes!" Flinging the box aside, she perched on the kerbstone and quickly slid her bare feet into the smooth, shiny blue leather.

"Oh, heavens!" exclaimed James. "They're too goddam big. They'll need to be changed."

You won't get the chance, Mr Donnelly, thought Annie – and she was right. "No, paperman, I want 'em," yelled Emily, jumping to her feet and tearing back to the booth. Once there, she shoved her way through the waiting audience and flopped down in an ungainly heap next to Jimmy Lamb.

Smiling, James carried the empty buckets to the Mission doorway. "Is that it, Miss Tillett?"

"Yes, thanks," said Annie. They exchanged glances. "So, you know Emily then."

"She was my first encounter with the children on the riverbank," he replied, smiling at the memory.

She paused for a moment. "We thought maybe you were losing interest in the strike. I heard it was a poor report. The last one about the murdered man. Shaun Lamb. You remember? You met him when you were with Ben."

"My God! Yes, Lamb. The man from Dublin. That's right. Shaun Lamb. I didn't realise it was him. How tragic. And his wife and children. How in heaven's will they survive? The poor woman. Who is to help her – amongst all those others?" James hesitated for a moment. "Er, yes, the report. No. My editor wasn't convinced – that the employers had any connection with it."

"Common sense is enough," she declared quietly as they entered the Mission. "So what's your next story going to be?"

"How about – how about a story of a young woman who spends her time helping the starving children of the East End?"

If it was James's intention for Annie to become a trifle embarrassed, then he succeeded. "I don't think your readers would be interested in something like that," she said hurriedly.

James smiled. "Maybe not," he replied, thinking quite the opposite.

Clare Harris and Mary Lamb were sitting despondently on a pair of old tea chests in Clare's home. On a third equally dilapidated chest which served as the table, lay two shillings, proceeds from Clare's labours the previous evening in the Pig's Trotter tavern in Hackney. The two women were sisters and had just returned from Shaun's funeral. Men at the Dockers Arms, and many more besides, had contributed their precious coppers to provide Lamb with a decent burial, and Cardinal Manning, always a friend of the poor and oppressed, had led the service. "You cannot wear a crown without bearing a cross," he told a dispirited Ben Tillett afterwards.

Both women had known enough death and misfortune in life, their own and in that of those around them, to understand that they must not allow it to drag them down – that they must sustain each other. Clare placed the money on the chest and pushed it towards Mary. "Please. You must take it."

"But I won't be able to pay you back. It'll take forever. I can't earn enough."

"You can pay me back a penny a month. You can manage that, can't you?"

"But you . . . you must need it as bad as me."

"I had a few bits of jewellery," lied Clare. "One of me boyfriends gave 'em to me years ago. So I pawned 'em. We've got enough to keep us going. And Jim says the strike'll be over soon."

"I don't wanna beg. Not off me own sister."

"You ain't begging. You didn't say nothing. I'm giving it to you."

"Lending," corrected Mary quickly.

Clare gave a brief, cheerless smile. "Yeah, lending," she agreed.

Mary glanced gratefully at her sister and gathered up the coins. "Thanks. I didn't know what I was gonna do. Mr Tillett . . . he gave me some help. But I think the union's in the same boat as the rest of us. Said he'd speak to me landlord. But I don't think it'll do no good. I hope you don't think that's why I came back here?"

"You came here to talk. Same as always."

"Yeah. Same as always. But not really the same. He's in a better place now though, thank God." Mary sighed and began to pull at the wedding ring Shaun had given her thirteen years before. "Could you . . . I'd feel better if you'd take this . . . in case I can't pay you back."

Clare shook her head. "Mary, no. I can't take that."

"Please. It ain't worth much. But it'll make me feel better. We both know I won't be able to pay you back."

"No, I don't want it. A penny a month. You'll manage that."

Mary placed the money back on the chest. "Don't. A penny a month. That's stupid. Please . . . take it . . . or I won't be able to take the money."

Clare stared at the ring lying in Mary's outstretched hand. After a few moments she nodded reluctantly, taking it and pushing the coins firmly back into her sister's hand. "Now go and get some food and feed your kids."

Just then Jim Harris came in. He wasn't drunk but Clare guessed he had been drinking. "Hello, Mary. Am I interrupting something?" he said, too loudly for the stillness of the room.

"No. I was just going, Jim."

"Don't go 'cos of me. Stay and have a drink. I'm sure you could do with a drink . . . after this morning. Get the cups, Clare."

"No. It's alright. I've gotta get home to the kids. Left them with a neighbour." Slowly Mary stood up. "But thanks for what you said at the graveside today."

Jim shrugged his shoulders and swayed slightly as he threw down his jacket. "Poor bleeder deserved better than me speaking for him. Now you sure you don't wanna drink? Just a quick swig before yer go?"

"Jim," snapped Clare. "She don't want to."

"No, I can't," said Mary quickly. "Thanks anyway. I must go."

As she turned to leave, Harris saw the ring lying forlornly on the chest. "Mary. You forgot this? I take it it's yours?"

The two women exchanged glances and Mary hesitated in the doorway. There was a brief silence. "Yes. It's hers," confirmed Clare, trying to sound casual. "She asked me to try and pawn it for her. She hasn't got time to go herself. The kids, y'see."

Jim's mood suddenly changed. "You must think I'm stupid or something," he said, raising his voice and looking disbelievingly at each of them in turn. "How much did she give you, Mary? How much, eh?"

Taken aback by his manner, Mary remained silent, and it was Clare who answered. "I haven't given her nothing," she insisted.

"Do I look stupid? How much, eh?" Jim's face hardened. "Must've been difficult . . . putting a price on a wedding ring. How d'you value a thing like that? I suppose it made it easier . . . fact he's dead. But still . . . must've been hard." He swung round and glared directly into Mary's eyes. "Not too hard for my wife though. She sees things different from most of us. Only thinks in terms of money . . . what things are worth in shillings and coppers."

There was something in his tone which struck Mary as odd and, confused, she continued to hesitate uncomfortably in the doorway. "Jim. Clare didn't give me nothing," she repeated lamely, not knowing what else to say. "She's going to the pawn-brokers' with it . . . like she said."

Harris stared intently at Mary's hand, clasped so tightly her knuckles looked pale. Suddenly he grabbed out, forcing her hand open and snatching at the coins, most of which scattered noisily in various directions across the room. "Well, well. Look at this. Pawnbrokers'? Where d'you get all this money, Mary?"

It was Clare who replied. "I-I lent it to her," she stammered unconvincingly. "She gave me the ring as a deposit . . . alright?"

"That's nice, my dear," he mocked, glaring furiously at his wife. "Nice and sisterly like." Again he confronted Mary. "Gave it to you as a deposit, did she? D'you know where she got this money? Do you?" Instinctively, she could feel his eyes blazing in her direction and she dared not look towards him. "I reckon I know just where she got it. She thinks I'm stupid, but I know. I know only too well where that came from. Thing is . . . do you?"

Alarmed by his aggression, Mary could scarcely manage a whisper by way of an answer. Even so, her voice trembled. "Pawned some jewellery."

"Jewellery? Pawned some jewellery? Don't be stupid. Look at her . . . she ain't the bloody Queen."

"Jim. Please," said Clare. She glanced hurriedly towards her sister. "I'll see you tomorrow."

"No . . . no, don't leave," he insisted, moving across the room to position himself threateningly between Mary and the door. "Not without your money. Don't you want it no more?"

"Christ," shouted Clare. "Just give her the money and let her go."

"I'll give her the money, don't you worry. But not before she knows where you got it."

It was Clare's turn to look alarmed. "Please, Jim. No."

"This money, Mary . . . which you were gonna buy food with to feed your widow's belly and your fatherless kids . . . this money came from the very same men as killed your husband." Mary gasped and sank slowly down on the chest, incomprehension obvious in her face. "That's right. Oh, not directly. I'm not saying the actual men who beat the hell out of him, gave her this money. But it comes from the men who hired the bastards . . . or friends of those men . . . or someone on the same side as those men. 'Cos they're the only ones who can afford little luxuries like my wife. D'you understand? No-one round here can afford her . . . even when they've got work. Men in suits . . . men with money . . . men who don't really need to work . . . they're the ones. The ones who toss a coin to you on a street corner. Who go to church every Sunday and rut my wife during the week. *My wife in somebody else's bed.*" Mary quietly began to cry. "So d'you still want it, Mary? Do you? Still want your thirty pieces of silver? Think it's worth it? Fair exchange for a wedding ring?"

Clare erupted in fury. "*You self-righteous bastard,*" she screamed. "For the past few days you've been eating food bought with the money I earned. You've been buying gin with the money I earned. And you've been gambling with the money I earned. What gives you the right to condemn me?"

"I didn't realise. Didn't think you'd go back to it so quick."

"Where d'you think I got it?" she yelled. "Sewing sacks?"

Harris grabbed a handful of coins from the floor and flung them wildly at Mary. "Take 'em. Take 'em and go."

"She's ain't gonna want to take 'em now . . . not after that."

"*Take 'em,*" he screamed.

Mary cowered back against the wall. "She ain't like you," sneered Clare. "She won't wanna live off that kind of money. Not like you've been doing. You accuse her of being a Judas.

[121]

But it's you . . . you're the one. You're the Judas . . . you hypocritical bastard. You're the Judas."

Jim Harris grabbed a half empty bottle of gin which stood on the mantelpiece and struck his wife a fearful blow across the head. Almost before she had slumped full-length to the floor, he knew she was dead.

During the day, workers at the Tate and Lyle sugar refineries in Silvertown and Plaistow, the Bovril factory in West Ham, the South Metropolitan Gas works, R. Whites bottling plant in Southwark, the Mile End Granary, the McDougall's works in Millwall, and the armaments factory at Woolwich Arsenal, had all voted to stop work in support of the dock labourers. It was the twenty-seventh of August and fifty thousand men were now on strike.

Chapter Nine

"What you have to consider, Mr Buckle, is that if I give in to all this, they will lose their fear, fear and respect for their employers. And then there is no telling where it would end." In his capacity as Chairman of the Docks Management Committee, C.M.Norwood was in conversation with George Buckle at *The Times* office in Printing House Square, with a view to correcting the newspaper's partial reporting, as he perceived it, of the facts. Naturally, given the eminence of *The Times* and, indeed, its editor, Norwood had no intention of implying anything so imprudent as bias; emphasising the implications of the strike to the nation was more his intent.

"But Mr Norwood," said Buckle, offering his guest a drink from a selection standing on a cabinet beside his desk, "last week the dock labourers and their supporters held a demonstration at Tower Hill. Fifty thousand men were present."

"And does that not worry you? Fifty thousand men."

"All of them peaceful."

"For the time being," declared Norwood cynically.

"As I understand the situation from Mr Donnelly, they have no intention of causing civil unrest."

"But if these men are given what they want, then they will

simply ask for more."

"Maybe so. But perhaps they have a right to ask for more," responded Buckle coolly.

"Not only ask, but take. That is my concern. The working-class, you see, needs to be ruled."

"Like slaves?" suggested Buckle, raising his eyebrows questioningly.

"In a sense, yes. They don't fully understand the way things are, the way things should be: the way of the world that's apparent to educated men like ourselves."

"But I understand that some of these 'slaves', are as educated as many of us."

Norwood laughed condescendingly. "The men you speak of, the leaders, the speakers: these are men with grievances, agitators, petty revolutionaries. They are all self-educated. And what kind of tutor is the self? Simply because they can talk, and they can talk quite well particularly to the undiscerning, this does not mean they are educated. Not in the proper sense of the word."

Buckle smiled. "But surely many great men have been self-educated?"

"Perhaps so. But that depends on how one assesses greatness."

"History. History, I think, can be the only arbiter of a man's greatness. Now a question, Mr Norwood. Is it correct that men hired by yourself have been intimidating the strikers? They say they have been threatened. And in one particular case they claim a man was murdered."

Norwood laughed once more, on this occasion a little unconvincingly. "What about the howling crowds of strikers, picketing every dock and warehouse, stopping business and threatening vengeance on all who do not comply with their demands? Thousands of men are out who have no desire to strike, but were compelled to do so."

"I have heard no such reports."

"But I am telling you about them."

The two men exchanged glances. "Then I would be most interested in any evidence you may have," said Buckle sternly.

Norwood paused, then continued in more tentative fashion. "All I ask of you, Mr Buckle, is that I be given fair treatment. These reports of yours are a little disconcerting when one's only intention, and that of the Dock Employers, is to uphold the tradition of English liberty. That is the truth of the matter."

"The truth?" said Buckle, focusing his gaze questioningly in Norwood's direction. "The problem is that truth is a spinning coin. Only the winner sees the right side when it hits the ground. Which brings me back to the murdered man."

Norwood considered for a moment. "Yes. Well, the fact of the matter is, these men are known to fight amongst themselves. Every morning at the dock gates you'll see them tearing and punching their way through each other. Just to beat the other man to a job."

Buckle persisted. "But surely for two weeks they have not been working."

"Er, yes. Yes, of course." It took only an instant for Norwood to recover his composure. "But that doesn't stop them from fighting. And one of them dies. So they blame the company. You have to understand these men. They'll do anything, say anything, to further their cause. It is time for you to see the other side of the coin."

"Your side of the coin, Mr Norwood?" said Buckle, his softly spoken reply accompanied by a smile devoid of warmth. "Thank you for coming."

As George Buckle bade Norwood goodbye, three miles to the west, Charlotte Donnelly was appraising an evening gown newly arrived at one of London's most select couturiers in New Bond Street. Paulina guided her towards a mirror. "If we pin it like – this, madam. There, how does that look?"

As Charlotte nodded her approval, Lady Victoria Piggott, a close neighbour of the Donnelly's in Belgrave Square, passed by the window. Seeing Charlotte she swept into the shop. "Charlotte!" she enthused. "Just on my way to Fortnum and Mason for tea and one of their delicious cream scones."

The two women were hardly friends. Each considered the other to be insufferably superior and each was undoubtedly accurate in her assessment. Charlotte smiled briefly before returning her attention to the mirror. "What do you think, Victoria?"

Lady Victoria considered the gown and delivered a slightly wincing smile. "It's a little plain, isn't it? The sleeves. And, to be honest, I always find that style so difficult to wear," she added airily, implying that Charlotte would find it almost impossible.

Charlotte looked enquiringly towards Paulina. "Well, madam. The fashion is leaning towards the more classic style. But if you prefer, I can adjust the sleeves."

Victoria made herself comfortable in an armchair. "How is James?"

"He's – he's well."

"Tell me, Charlotte. The girls and I were talking over coffee this morning – that collar could be a touch more extravagant, don't you think?"

"Yes," conceded Charlotte. "I was about to mention it. Paulina?"

"I'll see to it, madam."

"Most of us agreed that it could not be James writing those dreadful articles in *The Times*," continued Victoria. "Not your James. Helen said, 'Charlotte would just not allow it'. And most of us agreed with her. The braiding, it's – well, one might say a touch vulgar. My housemaid, I've seen her wearing that style. Yes. Most of us agreed with her. One or two of the girls though, did insist that it was your James. Tell me it isn't true. It would so please me to go back to them and say – you were wrong, it's not Charlotte's husband."

Charlotte's voice could barely conceal her feeling of humiliation. "No, Paulina. We shall have the gown the way it was. You will have to excuse me, Victoria. The time. I must leave. I have an appointment."

Charlotte was pacing the dining-room floor when James arrived home and he had barely appeared at the doorway before she confronted him. "You have got to stop. I cannot cope with it any more. I do not intend to argue. Either you drop this pathetic obsession or – or.... You will stop and that is an end to it."

James's irritation at the mounting frequency and intensity with which the subject was being raised was not apparent and he remained relaxed. "Are you asking me, or telling me?"

"I'm, I'm telling you."

"Well, I'm sorry, Charlotte. But I won't stop. I have explained and justified my motives to you on a number of occasions and there is really nothing more I can add." Charlotte hesitated, then she rushed from the room. Suddenly James lost patience. "And how many more times are you going to storm out like a petulant child before you understand that I can't just drop it. It's not a damned hobby I've taken up."

Eleanor Marx could by no means be described as energetic by inclination and after assisting with four breakfast sessions at the Mission, she felt far from enthusiastic as she settled herself down in the committee room at the Dockers Arms to perform the daily inspection of the accounts. They made discouraging reading. Despite more than two hundred men with collecting boxes being positioned throughout East London up to the very edge of the City, the daily return was less than the value of the food tickets being issued, and with barely two hundred pounds remaining in the fund, it hardly required someone of Eleanor's intellect to appreciate that alternative sources of income had to be found.

The destination of the planned march on Sunday had been changed from Tower Hill to Hyde Park. Ben felt it was time to extend the campaign to the West End with its greater potential for donations from the public. Whether his men possessed the strength to undertake a journey of sixteen miles in the day was open to speculation. But they must try. A successful outing with the collecting boxes could keep the men and their families fed, and the strike going, for another few days. Will Thorne wandered into the room. "I've just given out the last of the food tickets for today. Had to turn men away. How much money is left?"

From the expression on her face he guessed the answer even

before it came. "Not enough," admitted Eleanor. "We can just manage until the march on Sunday. People are doing their best; local people, shopkeepers, office workers. It's touching to see them. In they come, always poor themselves, and ask Mrs Fish where the money is received for the dockers. Sometimes it's a shilling, sometimes five shillings, sometimes a pound – placed on the table proudly by the representative of the working class who has just organised a collection among his fellows. Two men arrived this morning with a bag of nothing but coppers. It amounted to nearly a pound. But it's never enough. Of course, you realise the problem? Unorganised workers not directly connected with the docks are coming out on strike and then draining our funds. Half of the men you gave tickets to were probably not dock labourers. Granted they are coming out in support, but without realising the damage they are causing. They are playing right into the hands of the employers."

Thorne shrugged his shoulders. "Ben reckons the union membership cards will arrive tomorrow. That should help with identification. Now, something else. I hear Tom McCarthy and the leaders of the Stevedores' Union are debating drawing up a general strike manifesto – a call to all workers in every trade in London to refuse to work from next Monday unless the demands of the dock labourers are met. They know funds are near exhausted and after two weeks a general strike seems to them to be the next move, the only move."

Eleanor considered for a moment and it was evident from her expression that she disapproved. "But I think it would be a grave error to make such a move."

"Yes. I have my doubts. But the overall mood is becoming one of desperation. And once the idea was put forward..."

Just then Tom McCarthy entered the room. "Ah, Tom," said Eleanor, almost the instant he appeared. "What is this about a general strike manifesto? Do you realise what will happen if such a document were to be issued?"

"Yes," enthused McCarthy. "We'd finally get what we want."

She looked at him critically. "But have you considered all the implications, the damage that could be done?"

"Better give it a go than wait for us all to be starved into defeat. If it fails, it fails."

"No," corrected Eleanor, shaking her head in disapproval. "If it fails, we all fail. For one thing it will alienate the general public and isolate the dock labourers."

McCarthy looked surprised at her words and a little exasperated. "I never reckoned on you backing down from a fight, Eleanor. You were a lot more gutsy when this thing began."

"Hey, Tom!" rebuked Thorne. "We don't need that sort of talk."

The Irishman's careless remark displeased Eleanor and she responded sharply. "Mr McCarthy. I am not backing down from anything. I am merely employing my intellect to assess any strategy devised, an approach which you and your associates have obviously disregarded. Public sympathy will be diminished by such a manifesto."

"Public sympathy?" questioned McCarthy. "But the public are with us all the way."

"Yes," said Eleanor, tapping her pencil impatiently on the table. "Because as of yet the strike has been confined to the dock labourers and trades in the East End. But this would cause a withdrawal of that support and turn public opinion against us. We would appear to be anarchist wreckers rather than a responsible union. And if we fail now, it would mean utter defeat, not only for the dock labourers, but for all the oppressed workers. A defeat that would last for ten, perhaps twenty years. Please Tom. Think about what you are suggesting. You are tired. We are all tired. None of us is thinking clearly. Now, go away both of you and leave me in peace with the accounts."

"Come on, Tom," said Thorne, placing his arm around McCarthy's shoulder. "I'll buy you a drink. There's just time before our meeting in Rotherhithe. Anyway, Ben would never sign your manifesto. So you forget it." The two men left the room and Eleanor composed herself and resumed the accounts. Will was correct, she thought. Ben would never sign.

Eleanor had been working for only a few minutes when Mrs Fish entered the room bearing a large mug of tea. From the start she had been like a mother to the committee, scurrying around, cooking soups or stews for the weary leaders as they trudged back from marches, meetings, picket duties, or the relentless relief work, and providing Tillett with the endless supply of Bovril on which he appeared to exist. She could not force them to rest and guessed Ben had not enjoyed a proper night's sleep since the strike began. But at least she could see they had food. In addition to the tea, and with due reverence, Mrs Fish carried a neatly folded copy of *The Times* – not a journal with which she had a regular acquaintance. " 'Scuse me for asking, Miss Eleanor. But there's another of them reports . . . in the paper. About the Mission this time. The good Reverend gave it to me. Be grateful if you'd read it . . . out loud like. That Mr Donnelly's words is a bit long for my liking. Page six you'll be finding it."

"Of course," smiled Eleanor. "We were wondering when the article would appear." Mrs Fish sat down and while Eleanor was reading, she nodded or shook her head at appropriate passages and sometimes smiled gently as a detail brought recognition to mind.

" 'Yesterday, in eight sittings throughout the day, the Limehouse Mission in the East End of London, supplied upwards of one thousand starving children with tea, soup, porridge, bread, cheese, and stews. From seven o'clock, a full hour before the first breakfast time, the copper-boilers in the basement of the building were full of tea and in the dining-hall, which can accommodate one hundred and fifty at a time, the windows were completely blocked with piles of bread and cheese. Outside, the broad thoroughfare was thronged with a solid mass of children, and such a congregation of hungry-looking faces, famished forms, rags and tatters, and bare limbs, could hardly be matched in the poorest quarter of any country in the world. Many of them were the families of the striking dock labourers and they gripped tightly at food tickets issued by the union. Some were accompanied by mothers similarly possessed of the precious slips of paper, and some carried infants in their arms, fearful, lest in the crush, the baby would be hurt.

" 'As the doors were opened a great cheer arose when the minister called out "No crowding, please, there's plenty for all of you". But when the first one hundred and fifty were at the tables and asked to sing *He Shall Gather The Lambs*, their lungs were so exhausted by the rush to get inside that the hallowed words faded to a whisper. Once they were seated, the entrance hall was found strewn with tattered caps, bonnets, and shoes which the children had cast off in the struggle to be one of the first group inside.

" 'Unlike in many public eating places there was no cause to complain here of the sluggishness of the servers. Reverend Adderley, the gentleman who presides over the Mission, and Miss Tillett and Miss Marx, the young ladies...' "

Suddenly Mrs Fish gasped and startled by her reaction, Eleanor stopped reading and looked up. "Oh, my word! Fancy that, Miss Eleanor. You and Annie, and the good Reverend ... all in *The Times*. Whatever next? My word, whatever next?" Eleanor smiled graciously and returned her attention to the text.

" '...the young ladies who come each day to assist, are, by constant practice, deft and active with their work. Soon, as if by magic, the tables became covered with mugs of tea and thick slices of bread and cheese. Poor children. Their hunger made them too eager. Many lips were scalded with the first sup and they ate their bread and cheese with tears streaming down their faces. They will know better tomorrow and on all succeeding days while the strike lasts, for Reverend Adderley hopes to continue these meals. Considering their usefulness, the expense can hardly be thought extravagant for the cost is barely more than a penny for each guest. That is, saving five children from starving and give them a good feed, scarcely exceeds the cost of swallowing an oyster. Perhaps the *bon vivant* of the West End who sucks down half-a-dozen by way of prelude to his dinner may, in a nightmare after such heavy feasting, be haunted by the ghosts of those thirty hungry children whom his oysters might have fed.

" 'To support the Mission, Reverend Adderley has only gifts from voluntary donors to help him. The expenses of the man-

agement are most carefully restricted to the lowest point con-
sistent with the work being well done. Anyone who sends a
sovereign to be spent on food may be sure it will be filling
around two hundred little mouths, and that two hundred little
bodies will be gladdened by the gift. Those who may be moved
to help the Reverend in his purpose need merely sign their
names at the bottom of a cheque and post it to The Limehouse
Mission, West India Dock Road, Poplar, London, E, where
their autograph will be most thankfully received.' "

Eleanor looked up and smiled. "Thanks kindly, Miss
Eleanor," beamed a delighted Mrs Fish. "I must tell Annie. All
of you in *The Times*. Fancy that!" Still glowing from excitement,
she rose from the table and carefully re-folded the newspaper.
"I'll leave you now. Must get downstairs. Oh! Almost forgot.
You heard that joke of Mr Thorne's? Very comical it is. Now,
let me think. How's it go?" Mrs Fish thought for a moment.
"What lies at the bottom of the Thames and trembles?"
Eleanor looked towards her with polite expectancy. "A nervous
wreck," said the landlady, exploding into delighted laughter.

Eleanor's response was far from enthusiastic and Mrs Fish's
expression quickly changed to one of concern. "Fancy you're
looking a touch tired, Miss Eleanor. Things going bad for the
strike?"

"They are not good, Mrs Fish. We need to raise more
money."

The landlady thought for a moment. "Well, my Matilda's
just back home. Been all round the country, she has. Doing
really fine. They all likes her. I'm sure she'd do a turn for you
. . . sort of benefit like. Maybe down the Pavilion in Whitechapel. I'll ask her. She's only downstairs." Suddenly Eleanor
felt heartened. And with good cause.

Matilda Fish was fourteen when she had begun singing for
the customers in the Dockers Arms, her captivating voice earn-
ing instant popularity in the neighbourhood. Now, five years
on and using the name Marie Lloyd, she was a national figure,
filling theatres in working-class areas throughout the country.
That very week she was performing for six consecutive nights
at the Queens Music Hall in Poplar where not a spare seat was

to be had. Mrs Fish bustled back into the room. "Yes. This Friday's fine. See the manager in Whitechapel . . . Mr Skillard. Should be alright, Matilda says."

Eleanor made some brief calculations. With a capacity of four thousand people, the Pavilion Theatre was the largest in London outside the West End, and four thousand people each paying sixpence would fund the food tickets for two days, and additional revenue from collections around the audience could double the receipts. And with the march on Sunday, the two events could support the strike for another week. She would visit Mr Skillard that afternoon. Eleanor's eyes strayed to a copy of the *East London Advertiser* left behind on the table by Thorne. It was folded open at a verse sent to the editor by an anonymous docker.

> Yes, I think we shall win in the end, guv'nor,
> but the battle's a hard one to fight,
> Though it really was time to do something,
> and most folks think we are right.
> You see we might only get fivepence
> after long hours of waiting about,
> And struggling like beasts for a job,
> yes it really was time to come out.
>
> We haven't much chance of saving
> out of the little we get,
> It makes a chap feel down-hearted
> when with hunger the little ones fret.
> But me old gal says 'Stick with yer mates, Bill,
> though me fingers are worn to the bone,
> Don't give in to a cowardly crew, Bill,
> whose hearts are far harder than stone.'
>
> I'll own up it puts up me dander
> when I think of the bosses' bitter taunt,
> That we can't hold out any length of time,
> and soon will be beaten by want.
> When they tell us that flesh and blood

must bend to the cruel laws of gain,
And refuse us an extra penny
while they lunch on cold fowl and champagne.

I've always said there were good and bad
in all of the classes alike,
We're moderate chaps, the most of us,
although we are out on strike.
But when we're told by the men in the City,
that to yield or to starve is our fate,
I'll own up the good feeling just dies away
and I hate them with a nasty hate.

Hark to the cheers for Ben Tillett,
hurrah for our brave John Burns,
Whenever his white straw hat is seen,
how eagerly everyone turns.
To gaze on their cheery, kind faces,
to meet the glance in their eyes,
We believe they'll be true to the workers' cause,
What a shout rings out to the skies.

Will I have a pipe of tobacco?
Well, thanks, I don't mind if I do,
It'll help to pass away the time,
the day does seem long to get through.
But wait, here comes a collector,
Drop a copper or two in the box,
If our pals will but help us as far as they can,
then we'll win the great strike at the docks.

Eleanor sighed and stared down at the page, not knowing whether to feel heartened or dispirited by the man's words.

The final course at the annual dinner of the London Dock Employers at the Marylebone Banqueting Hall had just been served. Addressing an audience which included The Lord

Mayor, directors of the Dock Employers, and many prominent businessmen, was the chairman, Lord Caldrick. Seated together were James and Charlotte Donnelly, Sir Alfred Pemberton, and Dr Edwin and Mrs Clarke. Lady Pemberton was ill with an attack of colic. At an adjacent table sat George Hyde with other directors of the company.

"...At this point, I must express appreciation, my own and that of my colleagues, for your support during this difficult time. As you are aware, the board has come under considerable attack these past weeks and from quarters one would least expect." Caldrick paused and surveyed the audience. "But what these people, these so-called humanitarians fail to consider, is that if we give in to all this, if we give the strikers what they demand, the working man will lose all respect – respect for the man at the top." Shouts of 'hear, hear,' came from all parts of the hall. "The future of our civilisation rests on that one word – respect. Respect for the natural order of things. And these people, these do-gooders who share our way of life, who eat the food we eat, and benefit from the work we do; these people, without it seems a moment's consideration, appear intent on destroying that way of life. And I would ask these people – is that what you really want?"

"We've got one here now," shouted Hyde. "Let him give us an answer."

From every table, heads turned towards James Donnelly while Charlotte hung hers with embarrassment. "Mr Donnelly! So glad you could join us," declared Caldrick sarcastically.

"Don't say anything, please," begged Charlotte, her eyes fixed to the table.

"Did you enjoy your meal, Mr Donnelly?" taunted Caldrick.

"Perhaps he didn't eat it," called a voice from the hall. "Perhaps he slipped it into his pockets – to take to his starving friends." The room echoed with laughter.

"Ignore them, old boy," whispered Dr Clarke. "They are most likely drunk."

Lord Caldrick continued his humiliation of James. "Because, of course, for such a caring humanitarian, it would seem the grossest hypocrisy to one minute condemn our way of life and then come here to partake of it. Do you not think so, Mr Donnelly?"

Dr Clarke placed a restraining hand on James's arm while, ashamed and bewildered, Charlotte appeared frozen in her chair. "Not so eloquent in the flesh, are you, Mr Donnelly?" mocked Hyde. "Falsehoods evidently become silent when confronted with the truth."

James stood up and stared defiantly at the audience. "Sit down," muttered Charlotte in horror, as if addressing a child.

"Ladies and gentlemen," said James decorously. "I hope you enjoy the rest of your evening. Goodnight." He strode from the hall, accompanied by hissing and the synchronised banging of dozens of fists on the tables. As he did so, Pemberton looked across at his daughter with concern.

"Ladies, gentlemen, please." It was Caldrick once more. "Let us not allow such a minor incident to spoil our evening. It would appear, however, an appropriate point at which to conclude my address. Thank you all."

Dr Clarke followed James into the street. They had been talking for only a few moments when C.M.Norwood arrived outside the banqueting hall. Alighting from his carriage, he swiftly approached the doorman and handed him a note. "See that Lord Caldrick receives this immediately. I shall await the reply." Turning, he observed James a short distance away and strode resolutely towards him. Norwood nodded curtly. "Mr Donnelly."

"Mr Norwood."

"It would appear your friends have resorted to desperate measures."

"Really!" said James. "In what way?"

"I have been advised this evening that they are now considering calling for a general strike. I wonder how you intend to report this development. Now do you see? They have no thought for the national welfare. They are quite prepared to bring the country to ruin. A suicidal gesture from men on the verge of defeat."

"It's been a pleasure talking to you, Mr Norwood," declared James. "Goodbye."

"Goodbye, Mr Donnelly." Norwood acknowledged Dr Clarke and returned to the banqueting hall. Lord Caldrick appeared at the hall doorway holding the note. Briefly he spoke to Norwood who nodded and then crossed the street to convey instructions to the driver of his carriage. The driver was Harry.

The diners were beginning to emerge into the street, several, upon seeing James, pointing, and whispering to each other. Still looking distressed, Charlotte appeared with Mrs Clarke. She ignored James and walked hurriedly the short distance to the Pemberton family carriage and waited outside. After a final consoling word with James, Dr Clarke departed with his wife. Then Hyde and Pemberton emerged from the hall, standing in conversation with Caldrick. Initially, Pemberton looked concerned at the tenor of the conversation, but soon appeared reassured. After a handshake from the two men, Pemberton walked to his carriage where Charlotte was waiting. Both climbed hurriedly inside. Shrugging his shoulders, James then followed. As the Pemberton carriage pulled slowly away, Harry cracked a whip sharply across the flank of his waiting horse, and from the hall doorway Caldrick and Norwood watched as the two vehicles receded into the darkness.

Inside Pemberton's carriage there was silence as it proceeded along Edgware Road in the direction of Marble Arch. Suddenly it veered across the highway and came to rest as it straddled the pavement. Harry had overtaken and abruptly angled his carriage across them. "There must be an accident," exclaimed Pemberton. "Go and see, James."

"What's happening?" said Charlotte anxiously.

Caringly, her father took her hand. "Please, Charlotte. Don't worry."

As James strode towards the hunched figure of Harry still positioned high in the driver's seat, two men jumped from the carriage and dragged him quickly into an unlit doorway. Charlotte gasped and reached for the window, but Pemberton held her back. "Everything is under control, my dear."

She looked searchingly at her father and grasped his hand. "Are you sure, daddy?"

"Yes. Trust me, my dear. Everything will soon be alright

[137]

again. *Drive on, Collins.*" As the carriage drew away, James saw Charlotte looking almost dispassionately at him through the window. But in the darkness of the doorway, he saw neither Harry, nor the pickaxe handle that struck him from behind.

It was almost five o'clock. Across the Thames, the dawn light had scarcely pierced the stark blackness of the Limehouse night. Along the riverbank, ghostly shapes were already on the move, searching, feeling, digging, sifting: the tiny, scraggy shapes of the mudlark children pursuing the receding tide. At one end of the bank, a small cluster was rummaging inside a derelict coal barge. "Oi, Billy. Look 'ere," shouted a small boy.

His friend ambled across. "Cor. Is 'e alive?"

"Dunno. Posh clothes ain't they?"

The two boys began searching the man's pockets as Emily clambered across the barge towards them. "What yer found? Oo's that then?" The boys ignored her. " 'Ere, 'e's the paper-man."

"Oo?"

"The paperman. Saw 'im with Mr Tillett the other day. 'E's a friend of Annie. Gave me me shoes. Leave 'im alone. Go an' get 'elp. Get Annie." The boys looked blankly at each other and neither gave any indication of sacrificing their spoils. "*Go an' get Annie.*" Submitting to sheer volume, Billy's friend shrugged his shoulders and scurried off muttering along the bank.

Billy stared ruefully at the motionless body. "Can't we look in 'is pockets?"

"No. Keep off 'im," ordered Emily, tossing her head with impatience. "Don't worry, paperman. You'll be alright. Look... I've still got 'em . . . me shoes. They's a bit big. But I still got 'em."

"Blimey," said Billy. " 'E's ill. 'E don't want you shoving your feet in 'is face."

"I'm showing 'im the shoes 'e gave me."

Billy looked doubtful. "Still fink we should go through 'is pockets. Bit of a waste otherwise."

It was ten minutes before Annie arrived, followed at a short distance by Conor, the cellar-man from the Dockers Arms. "What is it then . . . at this time of the morning?" she demanded. "What's happened?"

Emily pointed. "Down 'ere. It's the paperman. 'E's 'urt."

Annie looked puzzled. "Paperman? What paperman?"

" 'E's bin bleeding."

Annie climbed into the barge and saw the reporter lying face upwards and motionless amongst the slime and debris. "James Donnelly! My God!" She felt his hand. "Billy. Go and fetch Dr O'Neill. Tell him to meet us at the tavern."

It took Conor half an hour to carry James to the Dockers Arms. Emily traipsed behind Annie, asking questions. "Is 'e gonna be alright?"

"He's breathing."

"Is that good?"

"Better than not."

"Oo did it?"

"I don't know."

"Oo's gonna write the paper?"

"I don't know."

"Why..."

"*Emily. For God's sake!* "

With hands thrust histrionically on her hips, Emily delivered a look of indignation and stamped her foot on the ground. "I's only asking," she said, and sulked in silence during the rest of the trek to the tavern.

Conor laid James unceremoniously down onto Annie's bed. "Emily. Go and get a bowl of warm water from Mrs Fish downstairs," instructed Annie. "You know Mrs Fish, don't you? And some rags. Clean ones."

James regained consciousness a few minutes after his head wound had been bathed and bandaged by Annie. "How are you feeling?"

"I think I'm dying," he groaned, grimacing more in expectation of pain than of the reality itself, as he endeavoured to pull himself upright.

"You're not dying, Mr Donnelly."

[139]

"My head! I know how that Judy felt – when Punch thumped her with the goddam stick. How did I get here?"

"The kids. They found you on the riverbank. Who did this?"

"I didn't see. But I've a fair idea who arranged it." James looked confused. "On the riverbank? I was on the riverbank?" He made a second attempt to rise, but quickly subsided back on the bed.

Young Billy tore into the room. "Where's Dr O'Neill?" asked Annie. "Expected him ages ago."

"Not there. Couldn't find 'im nowhere."

"I don't need a doctor," said James. "It's just a graze."

Annie smiled. "I thought you said you were dying, Mr Donnelly."

"Please, please. Not Mr Donnelly. It's James. Mr Donnelly seems a touch formal under the circumstances. And perhaps I should call you Annie? I've never been comfortable with Miss Tillett." After a moment of hesitation, almost imperceptibly, Annie nodded her agreement.

Just then Ben arrived. A committee meeting was scheduled for eight o'clock and he had an assortment of preparatory work to complete. "My God! What in heaven's name happened, James?"

"Hello, Ben. A minor disagreement."

"I'd hardly call it minor. You need a doctor."

"We can't find Dr O'Neill," said Annie.

"Do me a favour, Ben. Send a message to my physician, Dr Edwin Clarke. 52 Vic..."

"Hold on, hold on." Ben pulled a note-pad and pencil from his pocket. "Right. Dr Clarke. 52..."

"Victoria Street."

"Right. And, of course, we should contact your wife."

James made a vague gesture with his arm. "No," he replied hurriedly. "I'd rather you didn't. Not just yet."

"But she should know. Surely she will be concerned as to your whereabouts?"

"I said no – thank you, Ben. I want to see Dr Clarke first. No need to worry my wife."

"Whatever you say, James," said Ben, exchanging the briefest of glances with Annie. "I'll be next door if there's anything I can do."

James half-raised his arm in acknowledgement as Ben left the room. There was a short silence. "You never mentioned you were married," she said with an air of almost excessive indifference.

"You never asked," he replied.

"How long?"

"About half a year. Look, mind if we don't talk about it."

"No," she said quickly. "Not if you don't want to. Perhaps you should rest. Oh, but first there's someone here to see you. Only she got fed up waiting, I think." Annie pointed towards Emily who had fallen asleep on the landing outside. James smiled wearily, lowered himself back onto the bed and closed his eyes.

Dr Clarke completed his examination. "There doesn't seem to be any permanent damage. But you won't be playing cricket for a while, old boy."

"Thank heavens for that," said James. "Gives me time to fathom the damn rules."

Annie looked on. "He'll live then?"

"Yes, I'm afraid so. I fear it will take more than a blow on the head to incapacitate James Donnelly for long."

James smiled. "I've been well looked after then?"

The doctor nodded approvingly. "Miss Tillett has taken excellent care of you. A fine example of a field dressing. You should consider a career in nursing, my dear. Right. I think we should get you home. I'll arrange for Charlotte..."

"No, Edwin," said James hurriedly. "I'd rather we returned to your house first. I'll explain later."

"Oh! Right. Whatever you say, old boy."

The benefit concert given by Marie Lloyd proved a success that exceeded even Eleanor's hopes. Few dockers were at the theatre, as not only could they ill-afford a ticket, or in many instances did they even possess the price of one, but as Eleanor reasoned to the committee, the seats were best taken by those in a position to contribute bounteously to the collecting boxes. There was also a third reason for their absence, as having seen Matilda Fish on numerous occasions at the Dockers Arms without charge, most of the local dockers saw little purpose in now paying sixpence to hear the same songs performed under a fancy new name. Aside from the unexplained absence of Tom McCarthy, all the committee was in the audience – as was Emily. She had persuaded John Burns, whom she had never previously met, to take her along. "I's gonna be a singer when I's big. An' yer's gotta learn somehow, ain't yer, Mister?" With the revenue from every seat precious, she spent most of the show balanced precariously on Burns's knees.

Tillett arrived late. A message had been received from the London Hospital in Whitechapel requesting strike exemption for a cargo of ice lying in a ship anchored on the increasingly congested Thames. Ben readily agreed to provide men to discharge the vessel the next day. But this only partially resolved the problem. With relations between the Dock Employers and the strikers as frozen as the cargo, Ben contacted Cardinal Manning who agreed to negotiate with the employers to seek the temporary opening of Millwall Dock.

In acknowledgement of John Burns's boater, inevitably perched on his head throughout the performance, as an encore, and to the accompaniment of four thousand voices, Marie Lloyd sang *Where Did You Get That Hat?* At the conclusion, Burns, in his exuberance, deposited Emily in his front row seat, leapt onto the stage, and gave an impromptu address to 'my hundreds of dear friends here tonight – the brave dock labourers of London.' Seemingly it escaped his memory that practically none of these 'friends' were actually present in the theatre.

Torrential rain was falling as the audience, humming and whistling, made its way home, most with their pockets and purses lighter than before. To help build their strength, Ben decided to authorise his area stewards to issue an additional food ticket in the morning to each dock labourer in advance of Sunday's march to the West End. And he prayed for an improvement in the weather.

Chapter Ten

The sun shone brilliantly that Sunday morning on perhaps the most remarkable demonstration ever seen in Britain. Press reports had told of the dockers' intention to convene in Hyde Park, but no-one could have imagined the magnitude of the procession. One hundred thousand men, eight abreast, marched from West India Dock to the Park, led by just two mounted policemen. "Let's show the folks in the West End that we're not starved yet," bawled Tillett, and at precisely ten o'clock, and with himself, John Burns and Will Thorne at its head, the vast army, which included eighteen brass bands, proceeded westward on its eight-mile trek.

The route was lined with row upon row of spectators in their thousands and as the music and rattle of collecting boxes approached, they cheered with exuberance. In addition to the illustrated displays seen on the first march, there were three hundred flapping banners and flags, including a huge Stars and Stripes borne as near to the front of the procession as they could get by a group of a hundred and fifty American sailors, truants from three cattle ships stranded in Millwall Dock. All were singing boisterously and clearly intent on enjoying themselves. One banner depicted a rich dock owner feasting in a palatial hall as the poor docker's wife munched her bread in the gutter and her husband besieged the dock gate for work. Others were aimed at the wicked landlord who was beginning to rival the employer as the villain of the piece. One had been painstakingly inscribed,

Our husbands are on strike, for the wives it ain't honey,
And we all think it right not to pay the landlord money,
Everyone's on strike, so landlords don't be offended,
The rent that's due we'll pay to you, when the strike has ended.

Windows and front doors of houses throughout the length of Commercial Road had notices stating, WE ARE ON STRIKE, LANDLORD NEED NOT CALL, and stretched across the roadway between two first-floor windows in Stepney was an improvised banner which read, NO RENT PAID TILL THE DOCKER GETS HIS TANNER.

Passing St Paul's, and the grand offices of Fleet Street, the procession moved uneasily into the West End. But as the poor had lined the drab route to the City, so, in astonishment, the rich packed the balconies and crowded the windows of the hotels and noble residences of the Strand, focusing their opera-glasses on the pageant below. 'There will be a volcano opening up in Trafalgar Square next, my dear.' Trippers on pleasure steamers on the Thames waved and blew whistles as the men filed along the Embankment and the pavements were filled with a host of applauding spectators. The collecting boxes were enjoying a rewarding time, the first occasion they had been patronised by gentlemen wearing black tail-coats, or ladies in their silk, summer frocks. A letter written to Ben Tillett by Superintendent Forster of the City Police, had astutely been communicated by Eleanor to the press. This letter had appeared in the majority of newspapers that morning.

Dear Mr Tillett,
I wish to proffer my thanks to you and your followers for your conduct during your march to Tower Hill on the 20th of August of this year. Not a single arrest was necessary and in all my

time with Her Majesty's force, I have not witnessed such an extraordinary instance of self-control on the part of suffering men with starving wives and children. It was an instance of cheerful submission to the law which is a fit subject for pride and will forever do honour to all concerned in the matter.

Consequently, when it was realised that the dockers and their supporters could march through the City and West End without a pocket being picked or a window being broken, the more well-bred London citizen felt he could follow his natural inclination and back the poor devils who were fighting with pluck, good order, and good humour, against overwhelming odds.

As the men continued along the Embankment, that same good humour was much in evidence, notwithstanding a minor blemish when for no apparent reason they heartily booed the French Embassy as they passed. When the head of the procession reached Westminster Bridge, a halt was called when a man was caught attempting to raise money on his own account with a collecting box purporting to be for the strikers' fund. When it was examined, the box was found to be without the two stamps which identified all genuine ones. Burns emptied the box of its contents before throwing it theatrically into the river, and for his own safety the impostor was swiftly removed by the police.

The men pushed on, along Whitehall and Piccadilly, the indefatigable brass bands still playing with grim determination. Passing Wellington Barracks, the guardsmen in their white shell-jackets, crowded every window as they heard the strains of *The Soldiers Of The Queen* drifting across the parade ground. At first they contented themselves with merely looking, but soon, one the soldiers waved a handkerchief from a window. At once caps were off in the procession and there was a ringing cheer. The guardsmen replied in kind and from that moment the exchange of friendly greetings between the soldiers and the men continued until the march had passed.

It took more than an hour for the vast column to file into Hyde Park within thirty minutes of the appointed time. Burns computed that assuming they had been marching at a rate of three miles an hour, this would mean the procession was something between three and four miles in length. With their drums beating and flags flying, the men moved slowly and steadily across the grass, green and fresh after rain the previous day, and in the direction of the Reformer's Tree. The scene was an inspiring one, even to the half-starved men themselves. The park seemed a mass of faces as thousands of Londoners watched the remarkable parade.

To serve as a platform, a wagon was drawn up beside the tree. The audience, both demonstrators and well-dressed and obviously well-to-do Sunday outers attracted by curiosity to the scene, was now so dense that not a blade of grass could be seen. Large numbers would be unlikely to hear the voices – even the thundering one of John Burns. At precisely three o'clock, a bugle-call gave the signal for a one minute silence in memory of Shaun Lamb, and a remarkable hush engulfed the crowd. Then the bugle sounded once more and Tillett mounted the wagon to a huge ovation. Not an East Ender moved as he stood before them, thin, shabby as themselves, his thoughtful, sensitive face and expressive eyes giving him the appearance more of a churchman than of a humble man of the docks. He surveyed the mass of upturned faces assembled before him and wondered if his men could win the struggle before their boots gave out.

"Friends. It is now three weeks since a small group of dock labourers, including poor Shaun Lamb, met together in a tavern in East London. They met and decided that fivepence an hour was not enough for a man and his wife and children. And they demanded sixpence. These men were regarded by the employers as the embodiment of everything that is weak, unorganised, and defenceless in labour – the lowest of all the workers. However, in three weeks, the dock labourer has shown the country that he intends to take a position of dignity amongst the ranks of working men." At this moment Tillett observed a Socialist Federation flag in the crowd and demanded that it be removed as he had no wish for politics to be introduced into the proceedings.

"Dockers of East London," he continued. "You are hungry men, and you have stuck together as you should. You demand sufficient wages on which to live and you are determined, with the assistance of all the people who are supporting you, to fight on to the end. The employers are resting content with the idea that the poor docker is cornered and that no-one will give him assistance. But the lie is being given to that from all quarters. From your wives and families. From the City. And from the good people of the West End. From all of them you are receiving sympathy and support to encourage you to continue until victory is won." Cheers then swelled to a roar as Tillett concluded. "Last week, C.M.Norwood claimed that starving men do not revolt. Friends, show him that men revolt because they are starving. Your victory will be a victory of bread and cheese."

As Tillett stepped down, beads of perspiration trickling from his face, the truth in his claim of widespread public support for the dockers was evidenced by the profusion of top hats and silk bonnets that were waved, along with the battered bowlers and shabby caps.

McCarthy spoke next, giving details of the negotiations, or lack of them, thus far between the leaders and the Dock Employers. Then came Thorne giving a short but effective speech. "I know most of you must be dead tired. Many of you have been on strike under very hard and difficult circumstances. I promise you that if you stand firm you will win a great victory. Our demands are just and reasonable. Wages, conditions, hours, we all know are grossly inadequate. We have protested; we have petitioned; but time after time we have been ignored by the employers. Our demands have been met with silence. We have secured no redress. And that fact alone should make everyone of you stand firm and fight in the face of whatever gets thrown at us in the days and weeks that lie ahead."

'In the days and weeks that lie ahead.' Largely unnoticed by the men, an ominous new realism had been publicly acknowledged by one of their leaders.

Thorne's words were well received but the wildest enthusiasm was reserved for John Burns, all passion and eloquence, his cane pounding the platform, his eyes blazing, his straw hat askew on his head, and his beard seeming blacker and more impenetrable than ever. With a wave of the hand, or a single expression, he could excite the crowd. "We are here today to let the rich see what hunger means. I wish everyone could have seen as I have seen, thousands of dock labourers at the gates in the morning. With their emaciated forms and sunken eyes, some of them huddled together lest they might fall from the weakness that comes from starvation. Why, I have even seen a man with nothing left in his stomach, die at the pay-box as he claimed his money. Anyone with any heart would say as I say now – I will never desert the dockers. The *Daily News* has actually suggested that Ben Tillett and I should be arrested. But no fear of Pentonville or Newgate will make us turn back until your demands are conceded. Why, if Hell itself were to open at our feet, we would unhesitatingly jump in rather than desert you. And what of this rise from fivepence to sixpence an hour? What is it? A mere pittance to those men in their plush offices, smoking their fat cigars. But it represents the lowest amount upon which a human being can live. The employers do not understand the workmen of the East End if they think they can starve you into defeat. And so I say to them now, to all of them – you will never be defeated. I move for the continuation of the strike."

The resolution was carried to wild and unanimous cheering. Collecting boxes were passed around and for nearly an hour, Tillett, Burns, Thorne and McCarthy were kept busy thanking the men who returned them so crammed with coins that many could barely be lifted. Burns sent around his hat which was returned overflowing, a large part of the contents being silver. He emptied it into the treasurer's bag and was about to return it to his head when there was a clamour for it to be circulated once more. A lady thereupon handed her umbrella to Burns who held it inverted while coins were tossed in until it could hold no more. 'Just now,' reported *The Daily Telegraph* the next day, 'the turn of a feather could send every man in London from his work.'

Two pairs of footsteps echoed from the stone walls and ceiling as C.M.Norwood strode along the dark, narrow passage. Even in summer it felt cold. A single light flickered from the lantern borne high by the guard who escorted him. The two men came to a cell door and the footsteps ceased. "I'll see him alone," said Norwood. "Leave the lantern." The guard nodded and a jangling of keys reverberated along the passageway. Norwood entered the cell and quickly the door slammed shut behind him.

For fully a minute he stared down at the poor, manacled wretch slumped motionless on the floor. But the man turned neither his head, nor gaze, to acknowledge the presence that towered menacingly above him. Finally Norwood spoke. "Do you know who I am?"

"Jack the bloody Ripper!" growled Jim Harris.

Norwood laughed condescendingly. His face was in shadow and it was impossible to see his expression. "C.M.Norwood's the name. Leader and spokesman for the Dock Employers."

"I'm busy. What do you want?"

"I assume you are aware that you are going to hang?" Norwood paused to allow Harris to respond. But he said nothing. "I have it in my power, however, to commute that sentence. I can provide you with a lawyer, and I can talk to the judge. They will in turn convince the jury and the financially influenced prosecuting lawyer that it was all an accident. A domestic squabble that ended in tragedy. It happens more often than you might imagine. And more often than not the offending party is sentenced to a paltry term in prison."

Harris thought for a moment. "And what do you want in return?"

Norwood smiled. "You may be aware that just over a week ago, a striking docker was killed. Of course, the dockers claimed that men hired by the company had killed the poor man. Fortunately, the major papers made little of the matter, there were no witnesses to the alleged crime, no evidence. So nothing will ever be proved. But something like that leaves a nasty taste in one's mouth. It does need to be cleared up, don't you agree? Some of the strikers carry pickaxe handles around with them, do they not?"

"For protection."

"Of course."

" 'Cos we're treated like animals."

"By each other I've been told."

For the first .time Harris peered upwards at Norwood through the flickering gloom. "Just tell me what you want."

"Yes. We may as well get straight to the point. As a docker – the police, the press, and the general public, will more readily accept your testimony in this instance."

Harris looked confused. "Testimony? What testimony?"

"Your first-hand account of what you saw that night. A fight between a group of frustrated dockers. And the story they felt compelled to fabricate to save their own necks." Norwood paused. But Harris remained silent and without expression. "Yes. I expected you to refuse – at first. It's not easy to turn against your colleagues. But your fellow workers are not exactly making an effort to help your present situation. Have you thought of that?"

Harris looked away. "It's nothing . . . nothing to do with them."

"Where is Mr Tillett now? Mr Burns?"

"Piss off."

"These great heroes of yours. You are a liability to them now. That's all. Someone they'd rather forget."

"I said piss off."

"You see, the problem with following, being led, arises when you're in no position to weigh up the qualities of a particular leader. A precarious position to find oneself in."

"You just don't listen, do you? I ain't gonna be no Judas."

A grim smile crept its way slowly across Norwood's face. "Have you actually considered what it means to be hanged? You may have fooled yourself into believing that you have accepted your fate. But it is almost certainly the case that you have not. Not without further information. You see, it is a most ingenious form of execution – hanging. It begins long before you step onto the scaffold. The moment the sentence is passed and you are returned to your cell. That is when it begins – in here. It all begins in here. Counting the hours, the minutes, the seconds. Staring at the bars, walking from one end of your cell to the other, tossing and turning on your bed. Because, of course, you cannot sleep. And then the final meal, each morsel of which brings you nearer to the rope, each morsel of which you chew and chew and chew and chew, but cannot taste. Because the taste in your mouth is fear. Next the priest will arrive, to give you comfort, to hear your final confession. Are you a Protestant or Roman Catholic?" Harris ignored the question and stared sullenly at the wall. "It doesn't really matter. You will become whatever the priest is, as so many others have in your situation. One man, a murderer, had spent his time with the priest cursing God and renouncing religion. But as they led him from the cell, he suddenly grew pale, his body became agitated, every limb straining as he tried to walk. It was a bitterly cold winter's morning, which made it all the more fascinating to see the beads of sweat suddenly appear on his contorted brow. I saw his hands clenching convulsively, his nails drawing blood from his palms. And then the most surprising spectacle. With an agonised cry, he suddenly grasped the crucifix around the priest's neck and began kissing the figure of Christ. The guards could not pull him away and the priest had to support the wretch all the way to the scaffold, like a mother with her sick child. When they finally managed to part the pair, he screamed like a baby would scream when pulled from its mother's breast. And like a baby, he lost control of his bodily functions and urinated into his trousers. Well, I'm sure I don't need to tell you the rest of the story." Norwood took a step closer to the prisoner; his eyes narrowed and he began to speak louder and more quickly. "The struggle as they put the hood over his head; getting him to stand in the right place; lifting him to his feet when his legs give way; *the crack of the trap door as it snaps open; the kicking of manacled legs; the final twitching of the body* . . . . and the silence."

For fully a minute the two men stared impassively at each other through the flickering gloom. Neither one spoke. The silence seemed overwhelming. Then Norwood continued in more solicitous tones. "There is no way to make it seem dignified – heroic. Every man becomes a baby. Even a brave man like yourself. It's not turned out as you expected, Jim. All your hopes shattered. Your wife forced to – work. The pressure of the strike finally getting to you. It's not your fault. None of this is your fault. And it's at times like these you need someone you can trust. Someone who can speak in your defence. A friend."

"And what about Mary?" said Harris, confused once more. "She saw it all."

"Don't worry about her."

"But she's Lamb's widow. If I lie about what happened to him, she ain't gonna be too easy on me in court."

Norwood shook his head. "It's not a problem. In fact, let me make things easier for you. She is a friend of yours, yes? Well, I can arrange for her to be given a weekly sum of money to help her in her present crisis. How does that sound?" Harris said nothing. "I realise this is difficult for you, and I have no desire to pressure you into making a hasty decision." Norwood banged on the cell door with his fist. "Why don't I leave you alone to think about it? And when you're ready, we can talk again. Just let the guard know when you want to see me. But Jim. Do try not to leave it too long. You understand? For your own sake." Norwood turned and strode swiftly from the cell while Harris remained motionless on the floor as the door slammed shut and the key turned ominously in the lock.

Dr Clarke removed the bandage from James Donnelly's head. For three days since the attack, James had lodged in Victoria Street with his friend and for the first time had disclosed the sequence of events that followed Dr Clarke's departure from the banqueting hall. "Sir Alfred? Your own father-in-law? It's hard to believe, James. Of course I knew he was far from pleased with you. But this?"

"Someone organised it, Edwin. Pemberton must have had a part. But the question is – did Charlotte?"

The doctor looked aghast. "Now steady on, old boy. That

lump on your head must have had a greater affect than I first imagined. I simply cannot believe for a moment that Charlotte would ever consent to such an outrage."

"Edwin. You know how things have deteriorated recently. And I saw her face, looking at me from the carriage. Remote, indifferent. Frankly, anything is possible."

"Alright. Assuming you are correct, and I am certain that you are not, I would recommend caution. You have been given a warning. Next time you may be less fortunate."

"Next time I'll be prepared," said James. "Would you call me a cab."

Dr Clarke looked doubtful. "But you should not venture out. You need more rest, and I strongly advise against it – whatever it is you're up to."

James smiled. "Relax, Edwin. I just want to get my things, some clothes, my notes."

"And talk to Charlotte, I suppose?"

"Sure," he said. "And talk to Charlotte."

Less than an hour later James arrived home. He removed his coat and stood in the hallway, scanning the post that had accumulated during the past few days. Charlotte's maid appeared from the dining-room. She greeted him and hung his coat meticulously in the closet.

"Is Mrs Donnelly at home, Suzanne?"

"No, sir."

"Did she leave a message?"

"Not that I know of, sir."

James noticed a metal trunk standing against the wall. "What's in that, Suzanne?"

"I don't know, sir. Shall I ask Gilbert?"

The maid withdrew and James walked across to the trunk and lifted the lid. Inside were his belongings. The butler appeared at the doorway. "Mr Donnelly, sir."

"Gilbert. What the hell is this?"

"Your effects, sir."

"I can see that. What are they doing here?"

Gilbert looked confused. "Mrs Donnelly, sir. I understood you were going on a trip. To America."

"And Mrs Donnelly told you that?"

"Yes, sir. Is there a misunderstanding?"

"No. No, there's no misunderstanding. At least," he muttered, "not any more." James grabbed his coat from the closet and strode towards the front door. "Where is Mrs Donnelly?"

"I believe she is at her father's residence, sir."

With his hands thrust deep in his trouser-pockets, it took him fifteen minutes to arrive at the home of Sir Alfred Pemberton. Banks, the doorman, stood resolutely at the entrance. "Oh. I'm sorry, sir. But I've been instructed not to allow you in."

"Is my wife here, Banks?"

"I'm afraid not, sir. Now if you'd excuse me."

Pushing his way past the doorman, he entered the hallway, calling his wife's name. Banks followed him in alarm. "Sir. Please, you're causing a scene. I must ask you..."

Charlotte appeared in the doorway of the morning-room. "It's alright, Banks. Let him in. I'll take responsibility." The doorman hesitated, then nodded and withdrew.

Charlotte and James stared momentarily at each other. "I do not want a scene," she declared firmly.

"Never do, do you, Charlotte? More the Pemberton style to have a man beaten. Far less embarrassing than a scene."

Her expression remained controlled. "I knew nothing about that."

"Assailed by some of your father's ruffians."

"They were not my father's men. He had nothing to do with it."

"Left for dead in the mud. And you and your father had nothing to do with it?" laughed James grimly. "I don't recall any sign of concern. Where do you think I've been these past days? You've made no attempt to find me, to learn if I was alive or dead. How fortunate I am to have such a loyal wife. Such an excellent example of British integrity and honour."

Although spoken quietly, Charlotte's reply to her husband was firm. "There is nothing to be gained by this outburst and I do not wish to discuss the matter further. Please leave."

A man dressed in the uniform of the British Army appeared

in the doorway of the same room from which Charlotte had emerged a few minutes before. He stood stiffly beside her. "I believe you have been requested to leave, sir."

James hesitated for a moment, disconcerted by the sudden appearance of the man. "And who might you be?"

"Major Bernard Hyde. My father is George Hyde with whom I am sure you are acquainted. Now, Mr Donnelly. You have been asked to leave. Do you understand?"

"Listen, Major Hyde," said James curtly. "If I needed help with the English language I'd consult a dictionary. I don't know why you are here or..."

"Daddy!" James hesitated as Charlotte gasped and stared uneasily in the direction of the front door. Pemberton had appeared in the hallway, together with George Hyde.

"Who let you in?" demanded Pemberton.

"He was about to leave, daddy," she said hurriedly.

James angrily faced the two men. "I thought you might like to see the result of your handiwork," and he turned his head, indicating the small covering still protecting his wound.

"Banks. Get rid of this madman," demanded Hyde, his face reddening with indignation.

"Gentlemen, gentlemen," said Pemberton. "Major Hyde. Perhaps you would escort Charlotte to the morning-room. Banks, that will be all thank you."

The three men waited for Charlotte and Major Hyde to leave the hallway. "Now look here..." said James.

"No. This is my house," declared Pemberton tersely. "*You* look here. You were warned of the consequences and you chose to ignore them. I tried my best to help you."

"Help me!" laughed James in disbelief. He pointed to the wound. "You call this helping?"

"The man's insane," said Hyde. "You have been asked to leave and I suggest you do so. *Banks.*"

James surveyed the two men with disdain. "Yes. I will go," he declared, his voice, although restrained, leaving no doubt as to his determination. "But remember, gentlemen. If, as they say, the pen be mightier than the sword, then certainly it will not be thwarted by a mere pickaxe handle, or whichever weapon your ruffians wield."

Less than an hour later George Buckle rose from his office desk. He lit a cigar and gazed out through the window at the traffic clattering endlessly along Queen Victoria Street – buses, cabs, wagons, carts, all intermingled in hopeless confusion. An overhead train rattled across the bridge on its way to Holborn. Adding to the noise, an organ-grinder outside Blackfriars Station industriously wound out the *Blue Danube* while a miserable-looking monkey chained to the top of the organ, kept time with a bell. James joined Buckle at the window. Although he had deliberated for several days over his decision, once made, he realised it had been an inevitable one. Buckle agreed. "It grieves me to accept your resignation, James. But if you are determined to throw in your lot with the dockers, then you have no alternative."

"It's something I must do," said James quietly. "These people, not just the dockers, everyone in the East End, they need and deserve help. It's not easy to explain. I think it's the warmth. The poor, they're kinder to each other than the rich. Somehow they seem bound by stronger ties of sympathy. Their hearts respond more readily to generous impulses. Of course, they have greater opportunity for helping each other. But there are no barriers of pride between them. While the rich man wraps his mantle about him and breaks his heart locked in the darkest room of the house, the poor live their lives before each other's eyes and their joys and sorrows are the common property of the entire community."

Buckle smiled. He placed his hand on James's shoulder. "Yes, James. I can hear from your words. Clearly this is something you must do. You appreciate, of course, that when they learn of your resignation, Pemberton, Caldrick, they will assume they have achieved their objective."

James nodded. "Sure. It will certainly seem like that. Like they have beaten me. But one's foes are at their most vulnerable when they relax."

Outside, crowds emerged hurriedly from the underground

station. Every man and woman seemed to be going somewhere. The two men shook hands. "It goes without saying that you have my full support, James. But you understand that now you are embarking upon this course of action, it must be without the perceived involvement of *The Times*. As I think you appreciate, both the proprietor and myself are currently being subjected to mounting pressure in respect to our stance and reporting of this affair, and from directions which, sadly, cannot continue to be ignored. We have a wider responsibility."

Buckle stabbed his pen into the inkwell on the desk and scribbled a brief note. "Here. Take this to the editor of the *East London Advertiser*. He will be pleased to employ your talents for a while, until you have considered your long-term plans. Should the need arise, I assume you can be contacted at Tillett's headquarters. And now, James, I must finalise tomorrow's edition."

The next morning anyone following the progress of the strike in *The Times*, or any other of the nation's newspapers, would have learned that workers at Peak Frean Biscuits in Mile End, the Blackwall Iron Foundry, Charrington's Brewery in Stepney, Slazenger Sports Equipment in Lewisham, the Bermondsey Tin Plate factory, and Libby's Corned Beef works in Stratford, together with delivery men at the Kings Cross Coal Depot which served all London railway stations, had voted to stop work in support of the dock labourers. It was the third of September and eighty thousand men were now on strike.

Chapter Eleven

In the House of Commons, William Gladstone, leader of the Liberal opposition, was addressing a question to Henry Matthews. "Mr Home Secretary. Would you please explain to this House, and indeed to the nation, how a small group of wretched dock labourers can bring the whole of the Port of London to a standstill? For the past three weeks vessels have been unable either to load or discharge their cargoes, and important passenger steamers are, for lack of labour, detained in port with the dates of their sailings disorganised. Tens of thousands of tons of goods are lying in the holds of ships and no-one will lift a finger to unload them. At West India Dock, row upon row of railway trucks, extending to three-quarters of a mile in length, are laden with goods which no-one will take on board the ships waiting to receive them. By the hour, the congestion becomes more formidable and soon the very economy of the country will be under threat. And yet the Dock Employers, one of the most powerful companies in London, seems incapable of resolving this situation – or even claiming access to its own property in order to perform its law-abiding trade. Can the Right Honourable gentleman explain to this House this apparent impotence on the part of the employers and, indeed, of the Government?"

For fifteen minutes the Home Secretary gave a complex and rambling reply which satisfied few who heard, or, indeed, comprehended it. The truth, however, was less complicated: it was effective picketing – undoubtedly Ben Tillett's greatest achievement thus far.

From the first day he had recognised the importance of maintaining a stranglehold over the docks as even a single breach by the employers would have inflicted a serious, if not terminal, blow to the strike. Consequently, his strategy was to exploit the single resource available to him in abundance – the men. Even in the early days of the strike, there was never a time when, for sixteen hours a day, every gate in every dock of the Port of London was not patrolled by at least a hundred dockers; and latterly the combined numbers involved each day amounted to ten thousand. And with the supporting watermen leaving their barges positioned to block river access to the docks, the stranglehold was total.

At least three times a week Tillett would visit every one of the twenty-eight dock gates in London and Tilbury to instruct and hearten the men, on each occasion issuing the same message: "No trouble lads – don't break anything, and do what the police tell you." He well understood the importance of maintaining good relations with the Metropolitan Police. Just one incident which prompted the forces of law and order to prohibit picketing would open the docks to imported labour and would have meant inevitable defeat. The employers had made some isolated attempts to induce men from outside London to penetrate the docks, but all had failed once the visitors had been addressed by pickets who vastly outnumbered them. In most instances these outsiders had not been made aware by the employers that a strike was in progress.

St Katharine's Dock, close to Tower Bridge, was the smallest and most westerly of the docks in the Port of London. Its daily complement of pickets rarely exceeded a hundred, less than ideal, but Tillett was reluctant to risk suggestions of intimidation by parading too great a body of men so close to the good folk of the City. Less than twenty-four hours after the Home

Secretary's statement in the House, the expansive figure of C.M.Norwood appeared outside St Katharine's Dock, his carriage heading a column of men who had marched from Waterloo Station after travelling by train that morning from Southampton. The strength of the column was double that of the picket line.

Wearing a top hat and frock-coat, Norwood alighted beside the dockers. "Good morning, gentlemen. Working hard, I see." He made no effort to introduce himself, but his allegiance to the Dock Employers was self-evident.

"Piss off," snarled the picket line foreman.

Norwood smiled. "Now you are all sensible men, and as such you more than likely realise that it is all over for you. The strike, I mean. Your funds are exhausted. Support is dwindling. Now, I expect you are wondering who these men are?" He waved his arm casually in the direction of the group waiting behind him. "Do not pay any attention to the current rumours being spread – hired assassins and such nonsense. No. These men are honest labourers – like yourselves. Only these men have come to work. To feed themselves, and their wives, and their er..."

Norwood hesitated, his attention drawn to the sight of a hundred and fifty or so men approaching westwards along East Smithfield, singing and revelling as they made their way towards the bawdy delights on offer in the taverns of Hackney. It was the American sailors from the three cattle ships stranded in Millwall Dock, intent on extracting as much enjoyment from their enforced stay in London as their pay would permit. Since their initial contact with the dock labourers during the march to Hyde Park, they had become firm allies, and their opportune arrival at St Katharine's Dock that morning more than redressed the numerical disparity at the gate and saw Norwood's 'honest labourers' back at Waterloo Station within the hour.

Not half a mile from the activity at St Katharine's Dock, James Donnelly and Dr Clarke were struggling up three flights of narrow stairs, dragging a huge trunk. "What in heaven's name have you got in this, James? Pemberton's body?"

"Nice thought, Edwin. Come on. Lift."

"I am lifting," gasped the doctor. "Much further and I'll be diagnosing myself a hernia. Couldn't you have found yourself quarters in a basement?" Once inside, Dr Clarke sank down on the trunk and surveyed the room. "It's a trifle small, isn't it?"

James grinned. "It's not what I've been used to these past months, that's for sure. Reminds me of Harvard. Besides, now I'm no longer on a payroll I must exercise restraint."

"The offer to stay with me is still open, James."

"I appreciate that, Edwin. But I fear your coughing and spluttering patients would be something of a distraction."

Suddenly a pile of bedding appeared in the doorway carried by a not unattractive, busty woman in her mid-fifties. It was the landlady, Mrs Blood. "Everything alright, sir?"

"Everything's fine, Mrs Blood."

"Good. 'Ere, take these. They're nice and clean; freshly washed and aired."

James smiled and bowed slightly as he accepted the bedding. "Thank you. You're very kind."

"Don't mention it, sir," fussed the woman. "I likes to see my tenants is kept 'appy. Anything you wants, just ask. I'm only downstairs." Once Mrs Blood had left the room, both men subsided into laughter although neither was precisely certain as to why.

Dr Clarke hastily composed himself. "So what is your next move, James, now that you have resigned?"

"Publicity. The dockers, they desperately need money. Caldrick just seems content to starve them into defeat. True, donations are increasing – by the day. And from all over the country. Even from Eire. But so are the numbers on strike. And Tillett's union is feeding them even though most are not dock labourers. I tell you, Edwin, unless new sources of revenue can be found – and quickly – Caldrick will succeed. Ben tells me many donations have come from members of the public who learned of the situation through my reports. So the next move is to contact my friend in America – Hearst. Maybe I can persuade him to help."

Early as it was, Eleanor Marx, alone in the committee room, had fallen asleep. A soft tap on the door had failed to disturb her and it was only after a polite cough from Mary Lamb that she awoke. "Sorry for disturbing you ma'am. The man downstairs said I could come up."

Eleanor blinked and straightened the shoulders of her blouse. "Please. I–I must apologise for my rudeness."

"No, that's alright, ma'am. You've been working. I understand."

"Do you happen to know what time it is?"

"It's a little past seven."

"In the morning?"

"Yes," said Mary apologetically. "Sorry."

"No. It's alright. I was just making sure I hadn't slept all day. Not that that would be likely to happen around here. Now, how can I help you? I'm sorry – you are?"

"Mary . . . Mary Lamb. It was my husband who . . . who got killed."

Eleanor smiled sympathetically. "Lamb. Yes, of course. Do take a seat. Well, I'm afraid, although we feel the deepest sympathy for your plight, we would like to help you, we really would. But we can't. Not to any satisfactory degree. We can give you a little money, of course..."

"No, no . . . I ain't come for money," said Mary hurriedly. "It's about Jim Harris. The man in prison . . . the one who killed his wife. I was there when it happened . . . when he killed her. And I know he don't stand no chance in court. But he's not a murderer. I've known him for years. He was drunk, see. That's all. Lost his temper. I knows it ain't right what he did, but he don't deserve to hang. She was my sister, see, and if anyone else'd done it, I wouldn't be bothering. But I just know he didn't mean to do it. It was an accident. And I know he's gonna be regretting it now. And I was wondering if you, or someone else, could do something about it? He ain't educated or nothing and he won't know what to say. But if you could help him."

"Mrs Lamb..." said Eleanor softly.

"Mary."

"Mary. We have been to see James Harris. As soon as we heard of his arrest, Mr Tillett went along to the police station. But he refuses to see anyone."

"Refuses? You sure?"

"Yes. Ben – Mr Tillett – was quite forceful in his demands to see him. But to no avail."

Mary looked confused. "You sure it wasn't the police being awkward? They can be awkward buggers at times?"

"No," said Eleanor categorically. "Mr Tillett was convinced the police had nothing to do with it. Mr Harris simply would not speak to anyone. And he is within his rights to demand that."

"He's probably feeling too guilty to talk. Like I said, he's gonna be regretting what he done."

"But in this situation, if he refused to see us, there is nothing we can do. I'm sorry I cannot be of more help."

Mary smiled weakly. "Ain't your fault. Sorry to have wasted your time."

Eleanor rose from her chair and walked towards a small cash-box standing on a desk behind her. "Are you sure you don't need any help?"

Mary shook her head. "Thanks. We'll be alright for a bit." She turned to leave, but then hesitated as she approached the doorway. "Are we gonna win?" she asked suddenly.

"I'm sorry?" said Eleanor, looking puzzled.

"The strike. Are we gonna win? Shaun said we would . . . when it all started. It took a while for him to persuade me . . . me being worried about the kids and that. But I finally saw it . . . saw what he was getting at."

Moved by the conviction in Mary's voice, Eleanor sighed and turned away. There were now less than two hundred pounds in the strike fund and with the current level of donations, she knew that within a few days the union would have no means of further supporting the men and their families. "We might not win. Not this time. But what has been achieved thus far..."

"You're tired, ain't you?" said Mary, not waiting for her to finish. "And when you're tired, sometimes you see things different. You've gotta stop and rest. I reckon we're just going through a bad patch, that's all. We'll get through it . . . and then we'll win."

Eleanor turned back. "I do not wish to dampen your spirit, but the situation at present does not look promising."

Mary sat down. "Did you know Shaun?" she asked. Eleanor gave a faint smile and shook her head. "He got scared, I know. But he wanted things to change. And the only way it's gonna change, he said, is if we get off the floor and fight back. And that's what we're doing, ain't it? And that's why I think we'll win. Like walking a tightrope. Just gotta keep your balance . . . keep going till you get to the end." Suddenly, Mary looked embarrassed and fell silent. "Sorry," she whispered and she hurried from the room.

For fully a minute Eleanor stared after her until Will Thorne wandered in through the doorway. "Morning, Eleanor. You seem deep in contemplation. Who was that – the woman I saw leaving just now?"

"Someone who believes we will win."

"Win?" exclaimed Thorne. "Obviously hasn't seen the accounts."

"I don't think that would alter her conviction."

He glanced at Eleanor with concern. "Well, she's certainly left an impression on you."

She nodded and turned towards the window, looking suddenly unsure as a wave of melancholy swept over her. "I feel somewhat ashamed – at my lack of belief."

"No, you shouldn't," rebuked Thorne firmly. "You're a realist. You face facts. And the facts are we've all but run out of money. And at the moment money is what we need."

"What I need at the moment, Will," she said, making no effort to conceal her dejection, "is that woman's faith."

There was a brief silence. It was broken by the thud of footsteps mounting the stairs in double time. They heralded the arrival of a breathless Tom McCarthy. "And a jolly good morning to you both."

"Hello, Tom," said Thorne. "What are you so happy about? Still trying to get signatures for your general strike manifesto?"

Now seated at the table, Eleanor looked up disapprovingly at the two men. "I thought that proposal had been discarded days ago. Tom, why can't you see what you are doing? We have to talk about this. All of us. Before it's too late."

"Not much point," grinned McCarthy. "It's been issued."

"*What!* " exclaimed Thorne. Eleanor turned towards McCarthy in horror.

"Yes," he announced grandly. "The manifesto, probably the most important political document since the Magna Carta, has been issued."

Eleanor's head sank slowly into her hands. "Then it's the end."

"Oh, come on now Eleanor," laughed McCarthy. "Don't be so dramatic."

"If anyone should be accused of that, Tom, it's you. Why couldn't you wait?"

"Have you spoken to Ben about this?" said Thorne.

"He's downstairs with John Burns if you want to see him." McCarthy walked to the doorway and called down. "Ben. Ben, up here a minute." He turned back and laughed. "Will you look at your faces! It's not as bad as all that. By tomorrow we'll have the bastards right where we want them."

"By tomorrow," snapped Eleanor, pointing her pencil reprovingly at McCarthy, "we will most likely be the laughing stock of the whole country."

Despite the early hour Tillett looked weary as he entered the room. "What is it, Tom? Morning, Eleanor, Will."

Eleanor wasted no time. "Ben. Has Tom spoken to you about this manifesto?"

"They think it's a bad idea," said McCarthy.

Thorne nodded. "It's too risky."

"What manifesto?" said Tillett.

McCarthy waved a sheet of paper towards him. "The one you signed."

Eleanor looked aghast and rose from the table with such

haste that her chair overbalanced and clattered to the floor. "*You signed it?*"

"No, er, yes. I signed something – last night – no – early this morning."

"And did you read it?" asked Thorne, trying to remain calm.

Ben turned towards McCarthy. "Tom, what was it?"

"Come on," challenged McCarthy. "You know what it was."

"One of Tom's stevedores came to me. I was asleep. He showed me this document and asked for my signature – a call for no work. Is that right?"

"A call for all workers," said Eleanor reading from the sheet, "of all grades and of every calling to refuse to work on Tuesday next unless the Dock Employers have, before noon on Monday, informed the union that the moderate demands of the dock labourers have been conceded. Ben. Don't tell us you didn't read it."

"I was half asleep for God's sake. Tom – *all* workers?"

"Everyone," confirmed McCarthy. "A general strike."

Tillett looked dismayed. "God, no. Where is it now?"

"It's been issued," said McCarthy defiantly. "To all newspapers and all unions."

"Jesus Christ!" groaned Thorne. "I don't believe it."

"You're not backing out now, are you, Ben?" asked McCarthy anxiously. "Yours was the most important signature."

Tillett still seemed shaken. "You bloody fool, Tom. This isn't a game."

"*You* signed it," insisted McCarthy, the word heavy with emphasis. "You can't blame me."

"We have to get it withdrawn," instructed Tillett. "Immediately."

McCarthy's face reddened with exasperation. "You can't do that. There's a lot of people put their hope in this."

"I don't give a damn," declared Tillett angrily. "Imagine if Will's gasworkers come out; the country plunged into night-time darkness; the threat to people walking in the streets. With this one document we will lose all public support."

"It's all we've got left," said McCarthy in desperation. "What else can we do?"

"You're a bloody idiot, Tom, if you think this is all we can do."

"And who's going to look a fool if you ask for it to be withdrawn?"

"I am. But that's hardly important."

McCarthy pointed theatrically across the room at Tillett. *"You* signed a document without knowing what it was. It's going to look pretty bad."

Ben ignored the remark and turned towards Eleanor. "We need to get everyone together; the committee; the leaders of the Stevedores; Gasworkers. Can you organise that?" Eleanor nodded sternly.

"Right," said Thorne. "Let's get started," and they both withdrew leaving Tillett and McCarthy alone in the room.

There was a moment of silence as the two men stared uneasily at each other. Then McCarthy spoke. "People are going to think you're losing it, Ben."

Tillett's reply was delivered quietly and without expression. "Tom. I'm very tired. But if you persist in stating the obvious – I'll break your bloody legs."

It was early evening and seated at a small desk in his new home, James Donnelly was reading a report in *The Sunday Times*, the stance of which he recognised as disturbingly close to the truth.

It is doubtful whether the great question between the dock labourers and the Dock Employers is a whit nearer settlement than three weeks ago. The men, convinced that their demands are just, and receiving from many quarters the most substantial proof that the public is of the same opinion, will not abate their demands by one fraction. Nonetheless, soon there must be a question as to their powers of endurance. For our part we are inclined to doubt whether this strike can continue for much longer. Already there are signs that the resources of the strikers are becoming exhausted and that they no longer feel themselves able to support the vast and hungry crowd which is now cast upon their hands. Every day that this strike persists, much as it may injure the mercantile community, promises to increase the strength and power of the passive resistance exercised by the Dock Employers who...

James's concentration was broken by three purposeful raps on his door. They were quickly followed by the cheerful and strident voice of Mrs Blood. "You there, Mr Donnelly? There's a lady to see you." He looked puzzled. "A very pretty young lady too, if you don't mind me saying so." The pretty young lady blushed a little as she waited.

"Just a minute, Mrs Blood." James hurriedly straightened his bed sheets before opening the door. "Annie! What are you doing here?"

He ushered her into a room still cluttered with unpacked boxes and an assortment of clothes. "I'll leave you two alone then," enthused Mrs Blood. "I'm only downstairs. Anything you wants, just call."

"Yes. Thank you, Mrs Blood," he said graciously. "You're very kind."

The landlady disappeared downstairs. "Mrs Blood?" whispered Annie, and for no apparent reason they dissolved into childish laughter.

Annie's intended opening line had momentarily deserted her and it was James who spoke. "Well," he said, still smiling. "This is an unexpected surprise. Sorry about the mess. If I'd known I'd have arranged the boxes more decoratively. Sit down somewhere. There – on the sofa."

She looked a little self-conscious. "I hope you don't mind me coming without an invitation."

"Of course I don't mind. And you've certainly got Mrs Blood intrigued."

"Ben told me you'd moved in here."

"Yes," he said, balancing himself on a trunk in the corner. "I may as well live close by if I'm going to write about this dispute."

Annie nodded. "I don't suppose your wife feels that way," she remarked almost casually.

"My wife! My wife doesn't know. Where I am, I mean. Not that she'd be too concerned, I think. Oh. I'm sorry. How rude of me. Can I offer you a drink? I'm afraid I only have brandy."

"No. No thanks. But you have one." There was a brief silence while he poured himself a drink. "You were saying?" she prompted. James looked puzzled. "Your wife?"

"Oh, yes. My wife. Well, there's not much to tell."

"I'm sorry. It's none of my business."

"No. It's alright." He raised the glass to his lips, but lowered it without drinking. "Charlotte is – well, I guess represents exactly the upper class you despise. We met a year ago – and four months later we were married. At first it was all very exciting. A beautiful wife; a large house; servants; associating with the London social circle. And then abruptly it all changed."

"What happened?"

"What happened? I met your brother and the rest of you, that's what happened."

Annie looked confused. "And meeting us ruined all that?"

"No, no," replied James quickly. "The strike has been the best thing that could have happened to me." He stopped abruptly. "Oh, I'm sorry. That was a stupid thing to say."

"No. It's – it's alright," she said hesitantly.

"I'm not certain I can fully explain it, even to myself – not just yet. A lot has happened in the past week. Let's just say circumstances have made me face up to something that, who knows, might otherwise have taken me years to recognise."

There was a moment's silence before Annie pursued the conversation. "Anyway, the reason I came was to see how you were. Oh, and I brought back your shirt. You left it – at the tavern after your attack. It's been washed and pressed, and I mended..." Her voice trailed away. She felt embarrassed and irritated by her transparent anxiety to please and looked away as James, half-smiling, glanced towards her.

"How are things going with the strike?" he asked.

"Not so good. Everyone's depressed. Eleanor says everything seems at a standstill."

She glanced at a huge painting propped haphazardly against the wall. "Do you like it?" he asked.

"It's – unusual."

She crossed the room, stooping slightly to examine it more closely. James followed her. "Albrecht Dwight. *The Last Judgement.* See how the people are being cast into Hell. They're all the ones he despised. See the Pope?"

"He's going to Hell?"

"Sure. Along with the critics. See them – with their pens."

"How do you know they're not journalists?" she asked.

James laughed at her interpretation. "They probably are. He hated journalists, as well. And the rich. See – you have something in common."

For an instant their eyes met. Hurriedly, Annie returned her attention to the painting. "And who are the others going to Hell?"

"Generals, priests, judges, industrialists. And there, at the top, the people going to heaven. Gamblers, prostitutes, thieves, drunkards. And artists, of course. Sure had a keen sense of the satirical, old Dwight."

Annie continued to stare determinedly at the picture. "I feel like I should apologise."

"What for?" he said, looking confused.

"I wasn't – I mean – I didn't really give you a chance, did I – when we first met?" Leaving him no time to reply she pointed animatedly at the painting. "Who's that?"

"I believe it's an artist he didn't get along with. Can't remember his name."

She nodded and paused for a moment. "So. I'm sorry."

"No," he acknowledged hurriedly. "You were right to be suspicious." James finished his brandy in one mouthful and placed the glass on the mantelpiece. "Can I – would you be offended if I kissed you?"

Her expression scarcely changed. "I don't know," she replied, her eyes remaining rigidly on the painting.

"I'll take the risk then," he said. His words coincided with a sharp rap on the door. It was Mrs Blood.

"It's nine o'clock, Mr Donnelly. I have your usual pot of tea . . . and a spare cup for your lady-friend."

James muttered inaudibly and opened the door. "Thank

[171]

you, Mrs Blood. You needn't have done that."

Beaming towards Annie, she deposited the tray on the table with an unseemly clatter. "It was nothing, Mr Donnelly. Anything you want. You knows you only has to ask."

Annie returned the smile and then turned towards James. "I'd best be going."

"Wait," he said, looking flustered. "Er, thank you, Mrs Blood. See you tomorrow." Humming merrily to herself, Mrs Blood bustled away, leaving the door wide open.

"I really must be going," said Annie self-consciously. "I shouldn't be here."

"It was my fault."

"No, no. I think. No. I must go. I think it best if we forget about this. I'm sorry for coming." She hurried towards the door.

"Well at least let me get you a cab."

"No," she said, half-running from the room. "I'll be alright."

James watched until she vanished from view at the landing below. "I'll see you tomorrow," he called after her, "at the tavern." Slowly he returned to his room and stood staring down at the tray and at the cup the landlady had brought for Annie. He snatched it up and filled it almost to overflowing with brandy. "Gee, thanks, Mrs Blood," he muttered. "Thanks very much."

It was almost midnight and Ben Tillett was sitting alone in the unlit committee room, downcast and frustrated. It had been a bad day: the bitter exchange with Tom McCarthy; a further refusal by the Dock Employers to agree to negotiations; the depressing reality of the union's finances. During the past few days workers at the Bryant & May factory in Bow, the Thames Cement works, the Victoria Wine distribution warehouse in Leyton, the Thomas De La Rue printing works in Ilford, and the Spratts Dog Biscuit factory in Charlton, together with dockers in Liverpool, and East London shop fitters, drainage workers, carpenters and joiners, had all voted to stop work in support of the dock labourers. It was the eighth of September and one hundred thousand men were now on strike.

Ben's head was in his hands. What had he started? And how much longer could he disguise the truth from the men? That the Dock Employers could hold out for infinitely longer than they could. He recalled what Jim Harris had said at that first meeting outside West India Dock. "Starve? We're not afraid to starve. We've been starving for years so a bit longer won't make no difference." But as Ben Tillett sat in despair that night at the lowest point of the struggle, six thousand miles away, new forces were emerging intent on influencing the balance of the strike.

Chapter Twelve

Although similar in age to James Donnelly, the journalistic career of William Randolph Hearst was appreciably more advanced than that of his Harvard room-mate. He had become owner of the ailing *San Francisco Examiner* in 1887, bought for him by his father, George, a wealthy mine owner and the incumbent senator for California. Now, two years on, Hearst's aggressive and jingoistic style had transformed the newspaper into unprecedented financial success.

He had been raised in an atmosphere of patronage for the underprivileged and his family had funded the Golden Gate Kindergarten Association and its seven hostels for disadvantaged children. Thus, it was to William Randolph Hearst that James Donnelly had turned two days previously for assistance.

LONDON DOCK LABOURERS ON STRIKE STOP THOUSANDS STARVING STOP FUNDS EXHAUSTED STOP VIOLENCE PERPETRATED AGAINST STRIKERS AND SUPPORTERS STOP MUST BRING TO ATTENTION OF AMERICA STOP FULL REPORT TO FOLLOW STOP

From his imposing office on the top floor of The Examiner Building, Hearst sat digesting Donnelly's newly arrived second and more detailed account of the situation in London. He smiled. "I knew James would become a goddam socialist if he went to England." Ten minutes later he was dictating a report to his secretary.

"In London, England, one hundred thousand men of our own race, and a corresponding number of women, and even more children, are struggling for the right to live, and are likely to perish in the fight. These poor folk, crying out for bread, are our own kinsmen and kinswomen. They are being starved into submission by employers who abuse their power. But if they are not starved they can win. The horrors of their life must therefore be exposed. It is our duty to save these people. To show them they do not fight alone and that the citizens of America and Australia are with them to the end. Full report from London now follows." Hearst turned towards his secretary. "I want that, and Donnelly's report, issued immediately to Reuters's offices in New York, Chicago, Sydney and Melbourne."

On this occasion three pairs of footsteps echoed along the dark passageway, the sound augmented by the jangle of keys as they approached the cell door. "We'll see him alone," said Norwood.

Harris made no move as the two men entered the cell. Manacles still locked his ankles and wrists, and, sullied and unkempt, he remained slumped on the rough, stone floor. "Jim. How are you?" enquired Norwood with extravagant concern. "There's someone I'd like you to meet." The second figure stepped into the meagre light cast by the lantern. "Mr Redgrave. Mr Harris has a statement to make, concerning the recent dock murder." Norwood looked down at the prisoner. "Mr Redgrave works for the *Daily News*. I'm sure he would be disposed to report the circumstances of your wife's death with sympathy."

Norwood nodded to Redgrave who removed a notebook and pencil from his pocket and took a step closer to the lantern. "Mr Harris. Did you actually witness the murder of one Shaun Lamb?" Harris said nothing. "Do you have any information concerning the murder? Was it an accident? A brawl that got out of hand?"

"Tell him what you told me, Jim," prompted Norwood.

There was a brief silence. Then Harris peered enquiringly towards Redgrave. "How's the strike going?"

The reporter hesitated and glanced at Norwood for direction. "Yes, Mr Redgrave. Tell him the latest news."

"The leaders – they issued a manifesto calling for a general strike."

"A general strike?" echoed Harris, his face suddenly alive.

"A last ditch attempt to bring the country to ruin," mocked Norwood. "Brute tactics born out of desperation."

"Desperation?" challenged Harris. "No. They've finally done it. Done what they should've done years ago." The manacles clanked as he pulled himself to his feet, elation surging through his body.

"No, no," corrected Redgrave quickly. "They held back. The manifesto has been withdrawn. The call did not go out to the people to whom it was addressed."

Harris sank to his knees. "Withdrawn? Why for God's sake?"

Redgrave paused, unsure how to respond to the sorry figure now slumped dejectedly before him. "You must understand, Mr Harris. It would have damaged the cause beyond repair. They were acting with the dockers' interests foremost in their minds. Whatever, the situation remains the same. No money, and still no response from the Dock Employers."

"And there will be no response from that quarter," sneered Norwood. "It's all over."

Harris looked around in disbelief. His eyes searched the shadows where Norwood had positioned himself in the darkest corner of the cell. "It ain't all over, you arrogant bastard. You think they've come this far just to give up?"

"They have no other choice."

"Except to keep fighting."

Norwood's expression hardened. "I don't think so. Hunger leads to despair, and despair leads to the easiest way out. A few more days and they'll be crawling back to work. One or two, at first, and then the rest. It's finished, Harris."

Redgrave nodded. "I'm afraid he's right."

"He ain't right," growled Harris defiantly.

"There is growing discontent among the dockers. An increasing lack of trust for the leaders. You can't fight hunger with rousing speeches and marches to Hyde Park." Norwood paused and smiled. "Of course, they're not all as clever as you, Jim. Not clever enough to send their wives out to work. Bring in a little extra for themselves and even..."

His words remained unfinished as Harris suddenly erupted with rage. He flung himself violently towards Norwood, but overbalanced as his manacled legs betrayed him and he slumped heavily to the floor. Norwood stared down with contempt on the desolate figure and spat his words savagely across the stone floor. "It's over. It's finished. And you are finished unless you tell Mr Redgrave what you saw that night. Do yourself a favour, Jim. You've done enough for the cause. It's time to start thinking about yourself. Three years hard labour – or the end of a rope. Which is it to be?"

Redgrave seemed confused. "Look. I don't know what's going on here..." But Norwood cut him short.

"Just do your job, Mr Redgrave," he urged menacingly. "I hope I don't need to remind you of your obligation to me?"

"Ob-obligation?" stammered Redgrave.

Harris gave a grim smile and looked up searchingly at the reporter. "So he's got you as well? What did you do?"

Redgrave remained silent. But not Norwood. "When you get to know him, Jim, Mr Redgrave is very talkative. Especially over a few drinks. And recently I've got to know him very well. Very well indeed. Built up a certain amount of trust. And he made it clear during one recent conversation, that while engaged in his work, reporting on the murder of a docker's wife, he happened to recognise the poor woman. Some extremely interesting stories were told concerning that woman. Stories which Mr Redgrave's wife and family would find quite illuminating." Redgrave turned away as Harris stared towards him in disbelief.

Almost casually, Norwood continued his humiliation of both

men. "How else do you imagine I knew details of your wife's clandestine profession? Now, you can talk to our friend here, or I can find another reporter who will take your story. Well? What is it to be?" Harris said nothing and gazed blindly at the wall. "Let's get on with it, Mr Redgrave?"

The reporter spoke nervously. "W-what did you see, Mr Harris?" Still Harris remained silent.

Norwood pulled Redgrave unceremoniously to one side. "Jim," he whispered grimly, crossing the cell to tower threateningly over the prisoner. "Will I have to recount more instances of hangings I have witnessed?"

It had been almost a week since James Donnelly visited the Dockers Arms. As he arrived, food tickets, now restricted to three for each family, were being distributed and he was shaken to see the deteriorating condition of the women and children. Most stood in gaunt-eyed, silent groups watching the packed mass of men awaiting their turn in the seemingly endless queue. One woman collapsed and was carried into the tavern to be revived by Mrs Fish and some desperately needed nourishment from the kitchen. As she stirred soup for the poor woman, the landlady wondered how much longer the dockers could hold out. Better than anyone, she knew how close to breaking point were the tired and hungry men. The only relief on an otherwise cheerless morning came when John Burns turned the corner into West India Dock Road, pulling a hand-cart laden with twelve boxes of soap, five thousand tablets in all, donated to the strike fund by Pears. Positioning himself against the wall of the tavern, for an hour he dispensed soap into the outstretched hands of the women and children. "If your face isn't clean tomorrow," he called after Emily as she dashed away rejoicing with a gift he suspected would soon be exchanged for something she found immeasurably more useful, "then I'll tan your behind."

Suddenly the strike had become front-page news and the full spectrum of the press was sending its correspondents clattering into the East End in hansom-cabs. For the first time all sections of the public, throughout Britain, were being provided with information, and, just as significantly, observation – typified by a report in the *Evening Standard* of the previous day.

Let me first describe the state of the docks and the surrounding neighbourhood. Those who know them under ordinary circumstances, but who have returned after a brief absence, will hardly recognise them now. In the street, when no meeting is going on in the immediate vicinity, a novel scene is presented. There is, practically speaking, no vehicular traffic in comparison with ordinary times. A cab progresses at a sharp trot along thoroughfares where usually the way must be picked with great care, and where, when the dock labourers are not on strike, great vans and wagons laden with merchandise block the way. But of people there is an endless supply. They stand in clusters on the pavement, listless, and listening to the observations of a casual speaker. They sit in rows with their backs to the street walls, patient, and without occupation. In effect some one hundred thousand of the poorest men in London, the men who can least afford to be out of work, are doing nothing; and in spite of the help they are receiving from outside, the sight is one of the most pitiable upon which the human eye could rest. Furthermore, not only are these men starving, but so also are those dependent upon them who hide away in cellar and attic. Doubtless all would be glad for just a portion of the food daily thrown, with never a thought, into the waste bins of the rich.

It was these concluding lines which emphasised a subtle variation now evident in the presentation of the strike by the press.

Increasingly concerned for the welfare of the people of the East End, a significant proportion of which was Catholic, Cardinal Manning issued a statement given prominence in the majority of newspapers that day.

The strike is now assuming such vast proportions as to call for a speedy settlement of the dispute to arrest, if possible, the

great distress which must follow. To this end I would suggest
the immediate appointment of an arbitrator.

Until well into the afternoon James Donnelly assisted with
distribution of the food tickets. Only then did he explain to
Annie his reasons for leaving *The Times*. "And besides," he concluded, "it's an excellent excuse to see you more often."

She looked him directly in the eye. "If you want to see me
more often, James, you can come with me now. There's eight
sacks of potatoes at the Mission need peeling."

The following morning the *East London Advertiser* announced its intention to establish a Dockers' Poverty Fund, a development also given prominence in *The Times*. Meanwhile, the
Board of the Dock Employers meeting in Dock House, was
noting with concern the progressively sympathetic stance being adopted by a broadening section of the press.

"Perhaps it would have been better for us all if there had
been a general strike," observed George Hyde. "At least then
some decision would have to be taken instead of this stalemate
situation."

"A decision *was* taken, gentlemen, right from the start."
Lord Caldrick spoke firmly and with more than a hint of irritation. "A decision to concede none of their demands."

Less convinced was Sir Stuart Wallingford. "But this impasse
is growing steadily worse. We were led to believe it would be
finished in days. That was four weeks ago. Are you aware of the
pressure the shareholders are placing upon us, not to mention
the ordinary businessmen?"

"Of course, I'm damn aware," snapped Caldrick, dropping
ash from his cigar onto the mahogany table. Hyde brushed it
fussily to the floor with his pocket handkerchief.

"They want an end to it," continued Wallingford. "Or at the
very least they want answers. Has the Home Secretary spoken
to you?" Caldrick shook his head brusquely. "I suspect you
have done well to avoid him. I encountered him briefly last
evening and he is becoming most concerned. Apparently Lord
Salisbury is of the opinion that we are walking a tightrope with
the British economy, and as the Home Secretary pointedly re-

minded me, there is no safety net."

"I don't give a damn what the Prime Minister or Home Secretary think," replied Caldrick. He drew on his cigar for a moment to allow his irritation to subside. "Yes. I am fully aware, gentlemen, of the precarious position in which we now find ourselves. Which is why I offer you a proposal to resolve this matter once and for all."

"To sit back and wait for them to starve, I suppose?" muttered Wallingford, fortunately outside the hearing of the chairman.

"It is becoming evident," continued Caldrick, "that our greatest enemy is public sympathy for the strikers. As Mr Hyde has so correctly intimated, it would have been more to our advantage if the call for a general strike had gone out. This, I believe, would have turned the public against the dockers and brought a halt to these misguided donations which serve only to prolong matters. However, I now propose that the task is left to us – the task of destroying public sympathy for these people."

"And how do you intend to achieve that?" enquired Wallingford. "Increasingly the newspapers are failing us. Soon we could reach a situation whereby no-one is on our side."

Hyde nodded. "And this morning I received a cable from my partner in New York. He tells me that news of this wretched business has now reached America."

Lord Caldrick rapped his knuckles on the table. "Gentlemen. The solution is simple. We must show the nation, and the New World if necessary, that these men are nothing more than ruffians, agitators, interested only in their own selfish needs. What I intend is that a handful of men dressed as dockers, should infiltrate one of their meeting places. Disorder will break out. There could be injuries, of course. And regrettably, as with most incidents of public disorder, the innocent will most likely suffer. One can imagine the outrage in the press against such an occurrence. Overnight the strikers would forfeit all support."

There was silence in the room as the eleven directors contended with the propriety of their chairman's proposal.

Caldrick glanced towards a lone figure seated in the corner. It was Norwood. Almost imperceptibly he nodded his agreement. Then Hyde broke the silence. "Does it not say somewhere in the Bible that it is better for one person to die for the people, than that the whole nation perish?"

There was a subdued mumbling of assent from around the table. "Gentlemen," said Lord Caldrick, "the meeting is adjourned."

In response to a message from his former editor, James Donnelly was waiting in the library at the residence of George Buckle. He was accompanied by Dr Clarke who was perusing a medical book selected from the well-filled shelves. "What nonsense," he muttered.

The door opened. "Ah, James. I do apologise," said Buckle. "I have been delayed at the office. Last minute news. There's a strike on, you know." The two men shook hands.

"Mr Buckle. It's good to see you. This is my close friend..."

"Yes. Dr Clarke. Good to see you again, doctor." He extended his hand cordially.

"You have an excellent memory, Mr Buckle."

James's eyebrows shot up. "Clearly you know each other."

"Yes," confirmed Buckle. "Lords. Last year. Middlesex and Surrey. It rained most of the day so conversation was much to the fore. Now, James. To the point. No need to concern yourself further with being unemployed. It seems you have become a rich man. This arrived at *The Times* for you today."

Buckle handed him a cablegram which he read aloud. "Your reports circulated in America and Australia. Meetings called in both countries to express support for London dockers and to discuss future action. Will keep you advised. Meantime on behalf of Hearst family, five thousand dollars transferred to London today for dockers in their fight against forces of British Imperialism. Yours, W.R.H." A smile spread rapidly across James's face. "*Five thousand dollars!*" he exclaimed. "Goddam! I can't believe it."

"This is great news," beamed Dr Clarke.

"Yes. I thought you would approve," said Buckle. "But what is all this about British Imperialism?"

James laughed. "Oh. That's typical Hearst. Doesn't have too high an opinion of British colonialism. Sees things in very simplistic terms. To him the dockers have taken on not just the Dock Employers, but the whole of the British Empire. Five thousand dollars! What a guy! Edwin, we must tell Ben straight away."

"What, now? But I have an appointment..."

"Never mind that. Thanks, Mr Buckle. This is really terrific news. Thanks very much."

As James and Dr Clarke began travelling eastward with the news, Annie, Eleanor and Mary Lamb had just washed and swept the Mission after the final meal session of an especially exacting day. Following James Donnelly's article in *The Times*, William Gladstone, accompanied by his wife and a liberal sprinkling of the press, had journeyed from the House of Commons to endorse resoundingly Reverend Adderley and his efforts to assist the dockers and their families, and at the same time grasp the opportunity to embarrass Lord Salisbury and his Conservative Government for its tacit support for the employers during the dispute. Other than a group of children playing around the entrance-hall, the room was now quiet and the three women were enjoying a brief moment of reflection before Annie left for her evening duties in the tavern and Eleanor and Mary departed to their respective homes. Mary was now working each evening at the Mission to assist the Reverend and his over-burdened staff and, although unpaid, her labours guaranteed regular meals for both herself and the children.

Mary was speaking quietly and seemed almost unaware of the two women seated beside her. "Still don't know if I made the right decision. Yesterday, I mean. When I saw Jim Harris in prison. He told me about Mr Norwood's offer to support me and the kids, and the story he'd have to tell. I told him it weren't right . . . told him it'll give us all a bad name. But that weren't the difficult part. What d'you say to a man that's been offered a way out of hanging? The cause is more important? The strike comes first? I didn't know . . . didn't know what to say. Know what I felt. But that ain't always right, is it? So many thoughts going through me head . . . still going through me head. I told him to lie. Told him to do what Mr Norwood had said. I didn't want to see the poor man hang. He looked at me and said he didn't want to be no Judas. That's all. 'I don't want to be no Judas.' 'You won't,' I said. 'You won't be no Judas.' Didn't know what else to say."

"Let's go, Mary," said Annie, touching her softly on the hand. "It's been another long day."

The tranquillity vanished with the sudden appearance of Emily in the doorway, her eyes wide with excitement. " 'Ere, Annie," she yelled, so loudly she startled the three women. "Cab outside. Fare to 'ampstead, the man said." She dashed back to the road, colliding so awkwardly with a bundle of dirty washing left by the Reverend, that one of her shoes, still a size too large despite being packed with pieces of newspaper, tumbled across the floor. Sheepishly, and with one eye on the cab, she returned to retrieve it.

The women stood and walked to the doorway. "That's for me," smiled Eleanor. "I'll see you both on – what day is it today? Tuesday. So much to remember. I'll see you both on Thursday. Tomorrow I'm meeting General Booth."

As Eleanor boarded the cab, Emily tugged sharply at Annie's skirt. "Annie."

"Umm?"

"Why's it Tuesday today?"

"Dunno. 'Cos it is, I suppose."

"So why ain't it Thursday?"

" 'Cos Tuesday's Tuesday, and Thursday's Thursday."

There was a brief pause while Emily considered the answer. "Annie."

"What?"

"If Tuesday's Tuesday, and Thursday's Thursday, what's to-morrer?"

"Wednesday."

Emily screwed up her eyes, thinking hard. "So why's tomorrer Wednesday an' not Thursday?"

"Emily. Shut up," ordered Annie sharply, "or go away."

Mary gathered Jimmy and the rest of her children from the small group playing outside the Mission. "Right. We're going home." Annie waved them goodbye as Emily skipped irritatingly around her in small circles.

" 'Ere, Annie."

"What?"

" 'Bout Wednesday..."

James and Dr Clarke were still in their cab almost a mile away as Annie and Emily began the short walk to the Dockers Arms.

Meanwhile, inside the tavern, business was uncommonly brisk. "I hopes Annie gets 'ere soon, Beth luv," puffed Mrs Fish. "Rushed off me feet, I am."

With Tillett and Burns addressing a meeting of dockers and their supporters at Tilbury, the sole member of the strike committee in the tavern was Will Thorne. He was teaching several of the American sailors the art of skittles. "No, no. It's not a bloody cannonball. Here. Like this." Thorne missed the skittles by some distance.

"Game's sure easier than we thought," observed one of the sailors with a grin.

Beth approached a likely customer who had just entered. "Wanna buy me a drink, sir?"

"Piss off," growled the man, pushing her against the bar.

"Oi. No need for that. 'Ere . . . what's wrong with your hands?" The customer was Harry.

Glancing towards two dozen or so men already assembled in the corner, Harry nodded his head. Some left immediately to linger quietly in the road outside, while others dissolved slowly around the room. "You wanna be more polite, fella," advised one of the Americans. Harry glared threateningly at the man, but said nothing and he too left the tavern.

Moments later a middle-aged docker was intercepted on the pavement as he approached the entrance. " 'Ere, mate," said Harry. "These blokes tell me you're playing around with my wife."

The docker appeared puzzled and looked at the men gathering around him. "Who, *me?*"

"Yeah, *you.* And I don't take too kindly to it."

"Nothing to do with me, mate. You got the wrong bloke. Got enough on me hands with me own missus, let alone someone else's."

Harry prodded the man forcefully in the chest. "I'm telling you not to go fooling with my wife."

"I don't know your bleedin' wife. I've just come out for a drink, that's all. Reckon you've got me mixed up with someone else."

"So you just want a drink? 'Ere . . . let me help." Harry grabbed the man, lifting him from the ground and hurling him violently through the half-open door of the tavern.

Inside, there was a moment's silence as the docker lay dazed from the ferocity of the assault. Then one of the intruders turned to a man standing next to him. " 'Ere. You lookin' at me?" Without waiting for his reply he smashed an empty ale mug over the man's head. Within seconds the fighting escalated as Harry and his associates each assailed the nearest target. Disorder quickly spilled on to the road as dozens of men became involved. Every window in the tavern was smashed, and customers and bystanders alike were caught in the violence and many lay injured and bleeding where they had been beaten to the ground.

Alerted initially by the noise, a hundred yards from the Dockers Arms and through gathering darkness, Annie suddenly became aware of the fighting. "My God!" She began running towards the tavern. Alarmed by her reaction, Emily gave chase. In their anxiety neither noticed a carriage waiting on the far side of the road, nor the hunched figure of C.M. Norwood observing the proceedings from behind a copy of the evening newspaper.

Their work complete, Harry signalled his men to withdraw and they escaped along West India Dock Road. Now only fifty yards from the tavern, Annie saw the gang advancing towards her. She turned and yelled to Emily who was a short distance behind. "Run, Emily. Back to the Mission."

Inside his carriage, Norwood had seen enough. He hit the roof with his cane and shouted to the driver. "Drive on – fast." Annie backed against the dock wall as the men approached, but before reaching her they veered into an alleyway and vanished. She continued running towards the tavern. Meanwhile, Emily had turned back and was dashing along the road in the direction of the Mission when her shoe came off. As she paused to retrieve it, Norwood's carriage sped towards her. "Don't slow down, you fool," Norwood yelled to the driver.

The wheel struck Emily as the horse galloped past. "Annie," she screamed.

As James and Dr Clarke turned the corner into West India Dock Road, their cab swerved abruptly as it all but collided with Norwood's carriage. "Good God!" exclaimed the doctor. "What's the driver doing?"

James caught a glimpse of the occupant. "Norwood! What the hell is he doing here?" Seconds later he saw a child lying in the road, and then Annie running and calling in the direction of the tiny figure. "Stop, driver. By the child." James jumped from the cab. He knelt down and took the little girl's hand. "My God! Emily."

She smiled up at him. "Hello, paperman." He gathered her gently into his arms. "Look," she whispered shakily. "Me shoe's fell off."

Dr Clarke joined them, quickly followed by Annie. "Edwin. We must get her to hospital," said James urgently. "Where is it? Annie. Show us the way."

"You still there, paperman?" murmured Emily, touching him softly and fleetingly on his cheek. James gripped her more tightly.

"Easy, James," cautioned Dr Clarke as he gently took Emily's arm. She was still smiling but had closed her eyes.

"Quickly, Edwin. What are we waiting for, for God's sake? *Edwin.*"

Sadly, the doctor shook his head. James stared down in stark disbelief at her still, innocent face. "No," he cried. "Not Emily. Not little Emily." Never had he felt such agony as he did at that moment. Annie sank to the ground. Sobbing gently, she just stared at the road. And at the single, tiny shoe that lay there.

During the previous forty-eight hours, twenty thousand Jewish tailors, the boot and shoe trade, cigarette makers, Fry's Chocolate in Walthamstow, the Singer Sewing-Machine factory in Barking, Pickfords carmen, the John Sainsbury central distribution depot in Rotherhithe, the Gaslight & Coke Company in Camden Town, and London and South-Western Railway workers, had all voted to stop work in support of the dock labourers. It was the tenth of September and one hundred and fifty thousand men were now on strike. It was the greatest withdrawal of labour ever seen. But it was neither this, nor the death of a street orphan in West India Dock Road that made the headlines of the newspapers that following morning. Nor was it, as some had intended, disorder at the headquarters of the Dockers' Union. The world had been told of how people were living and dying in the East End of London and the world had decided to do something about it.

Chapter Thirteen

It was, perhaps, more than any of the national newspapers, the *East London Advertiser* which, in five words blazoned across its front page, best captured the moment. 'The World to the Rescue' it announced. And it was scarcely an exaggeration.

Throughout the previous day news had been arriving in London of money raised and already on its way. And it was not a question of merely a few hundred pounds and the encouragement for the dockers of knowing they had the sympathy of people around the world; it was a matter of tens of thousands of pounds – support expressed in massive contributions from rich and poor, learned and uneducated; from politicians, judges, church dignitaries, and businessmen, from labourers, seamen, building workers, and shopkeepers.

In America, following extensive newspaper coverage which had created immediate sympathy for the people of the East End and indignation with the Dock Employers, mass meetings were held in New York, Chicago, Boston, and numerous other centres. Already more than fifty thousand dollars, around ten thousand pounds, had been raised and was in the process of being telegraphed to London. Such was the feeling among ordinary Americans that a donations desk installed on the concourse of Grand Central Station in New York was kept so busy that it was compelled to remain open not only during the day, but throughout the night. The surge of generosity in America was determined by an impulse of genuine and spontaneous compassion and distance seemed only to increase the impact on public opinion. William Hearst had correctly read the nation when he ignored the circumstances of the strike and concentrated instead on a single issue – exposing the plight of the people. The precise demands of the dock labourers in London meant nothing to Americans; nor did the reason for their rejection by the employers. All they knew was that a hundred thousand men, women, and children were struggling to better themselves and would starve in the attempt unless they put their hands in their pockets and purses. And that was all they cared to know.

In Australia, extracts from James Donnelly's report had been published in Brisbane, Melbourne, Sydney, and Adelaide. As a consequence of strong, well-organised unions, Australian labour was not poor and response to the words from London was unhesitating. The Wharf Labourers' Union and the Seamen's Union, each voted a donation of fifteen hundred pounds. In Sydney, a demonstration was held in the open-air in the Domain. On a brilliant spring afternoon, a crowd of thirty thousand or more cheered to the echo the resolution in support of the dockers and the sum of three thousand pounds was collected. At the Temperance Hall in Melbourne, two thousand pounds was raised at a meeting so well attended that hundreds could not gain admittance. In Brisbane and Adelaide contributions raised two thousand five hundred pounds. Banks had offered to remit donations to London without charge, the Postmaster-General had agreed to send cable messages free, and at the instigation of the Queensland Parliament, a fund was opened by the Mayor. In two days Australia, like America, had raised more than ten thousand pounds. 'The community at large,' wrote the *Sydney Morning Herald*, 'is expressing its sympathy on the side of the abused and suffering.'

In Europe, Donnelly's words had been translated into German, Dutch, Flemish, and French. In Hamburg, Rotterdam, Antwerp, and Marseilles, seamen, port workers, and the public at large were pledging support, and foreign exchange desks in the City were seeing a surge of activity. *'Liberté pour les travailleurs Anglais'* proclaimed *Le Monde*. In just two days the outside world had donated twenty-five thousand pounds to the dock labourers of the East End and all but banished the spectre of defeat through hunger.

Had James Donnelly known of the vast sums about to arrive in London, it would not have moderated his mood that morning. Caldrick and Norwood, however, were both aware, and discussing what they recognised as a disturbing reversal when Donnelly jumped from a cab in Leadenhall Street and strode into the foyer at Dock House. Pushing his way through an inner door, he entered the main office and demanded to speak to Norwood. "Mr Norwood is currently engaged – with Lord Caldrick," advised an assistant.

Donnelly's eyes searched the room. Seeing Caldrick's name shining from a brass plate on an adjacent door he strode angrily across the office. "Sir, excuse me, sir," called the assistant, rushing after him as James burst into the room.

"Donnelly! What the hell do you want?" demanded Lord Caldrick.

"I–I'm sorry, sir," stammered the assistant. "I..."

Caldrick waved dismissively at the man. "Alright, Green. Leave us. Shut the door." Caldrick walked to his desk and sat down. "Now. What is it, Donnelly?"

Struggling to control himself, James's eyes blazed across the room at Norwood who stood impassively by the window. He pointed furiously towards the towering figure. "I saw you there. Last night. After you had run down the child. I saw you."

For just an instant Norwood's composure deserted him. "You – you saw me? Where? When?" But quickly he recovered and smiled condescendingly in James's direction. "I'm sorry. I am a little confused. Who did you think you saw?"

Donnelly's eyes darted back and forth between the two men

and he spoke with undisguised bitterness in his voice. "It was you. Both of you. You set the whole thing up. The fighting – everything. Twelve people are in hospital. And one, an eight-year-old girl, is dead. An eight-year-old girl, for God's sake. A poor orphan. You *were* there, Norwood. Don't shake your head. I saw you."

Caldrick smiled. "Mr Donnelly," he proclaimed with exaggerated concern. "There must be some mistake. Mr Norwood was engaged last evening. Discussing business. I am sorry we cannot help further. If that will be all."

"No. It won't be all. You're not getting away with it – not this time."

"Getting away with it, Mr Donnelly?" said Caldrick, leaning back nonchalantly in his chair. "Getting away with what? Let me clarify the situation. When the authorities are dealing with someone of my position, the death of an eight-year-old street urchin is of no consequence. You can tell your fanciful account to whomsoever you like. No-one will believe you. And if you go as far as publishing it in *The Times*, or in whichever journal you are currently peddling your lies, if your editor is foolish enough, then I will sue you and that journal for libel."

"*You* will sue *me?*" exclaimed James incredulously.

The tone of Caldrick's voice became more severe. "I am not accustomed to playing games, Mr Donnelly. You have entered a world of money and power, and compared with your opponents, you have neither. Little boys should not mix with the big boys. It invariably results in them getting hurt. Now, I am extremely busy."

Making no effort to conceal his contempt, for a few moments James stared at the two men. He half-turned towards the door, but then spun round and punched Norwood heavily in the stomach. "Sue me for that," he said, as Norwood slumped inelegantly, and with an audible sigh, to the floor.

James proceeded from Dock House to the Dockers Arms. Halting the cab at Aldgate Station to purchase a copy of *The Times*, he was astonished to read of the support emanating from abroad. In other circumstances his mood would have been one of elation, but nonetheless the news brought a much needed revival of his spirits. Ben Tillett's reaction was more one of relief. With such generous friends it would now be unnecessary to further restrict the distribution of food tickets. This help, allied to the daily flow of donations from around the country, would keep starvation at bay for weeks.

Repairs were already underway when James arrived at the tavern. Annie and Will Thorne, his arm broken from the affray, were issuing orders to a willing cluster of volunteers, while Mrs Fish bustled to and fro thanking everyone she could find. And as they hammered and sawed that morning, all talk in the East End was of countries and cities unheard of by many of them twenty-four hours before. "James. There's a cablegram for you in the committee room," advised Ben. It was from San Francisco.

NOTHING HAS CHANGED STOP I WAS ALWAYS ONE STEP AHEAD STOP IT TOOK YOU THREE WEEKS STOP IT HAS TAKEN ME THREE DAYS STOP GLAD TO HAVE BEEN OF SERVICE STOP
                    YOURS W R H

James smiled. Hearst was right. He was invariably one step ahead of the rest. Tillett hurried purposefully into the room. "Incidentally, Ben. I almost forgot. What would you do with five thousand dollars? Doesn't seem quite so much as it did last evening, but it should keep you in Irish stew for a few days until the big money arrives."

Emily was buried at Limehouse churchyard in the afternoon. Annie wept as the tiny box was lowered slowly into the grave. For just an instant the sun pierced threatening clouds to illuminate the words James had carved painstakingly onto the lid. 'I will never forget you. Always my love. Paperman.' Still distressed from her ordeal at the tavern, poor Mrs Fish was so overcome that Eleanor felt obliged to lead her gently away, and on one occasion even Reverend Adderley who conducted the brief service found difficulty with his words.

Repairs at the Dockers Arms were not yet complete and it was closed for the day. After the final meal session at the Mission, Annie returned with James to his home. "I need to get away from the area for a few hours," she explained.

Humming cheerfully to herself, Mrs Blood was busily cleaning the front doorstep when they arrived. "Evening, Mr Donnelly, sir. Evening, Miss. Nice to see you again. Take care on the step. You don't want to be slipping on the wet." She moved to one side. "Anything you needs, just call. I'll be up with your pot of tea later, Mr Donnelly."

The room was tidier than when Annie had last visited and the painting had been hung on the wall. "Looks good there," she said, studying it for a few moments. "You didn't have to pay. For the funeral, I mean."

"No. I wanted to," said James, smiling sadly at the thought.

She continued to stare reflectively at the picture. "So, what next? I can't imagine you staying here somehow. Not exactly Buckingham Palace, is it?" She wandered across the room.

"No, I suppose not. It's been on my mind. As soon as this is over – the strike, I mean – I'll be going home, back to Boston."

Annie walked across to the painting and adjusted it slightly. "It was crooked."

"Would you like to keep it?"

"Keep what?"

"The painting. When I leave. Something to remember me by. It's too big to take back."

"I'm not sure," she said, "perhaps." Her eyes remained anchored on the picture. "Why did you want to kiss me? Last time I was here."

James looked surprised. "What sort of question is that?"

"Last time. When I came round. I've never walked three miles in my life to see someone."

"So why did you?"

It was Annie's turn to show surprise. "Why did I? So what sort of question is *that?*" She turned determinedly towards him. "I want you to kiss me."

Without speaking, James moved slowly across the room, clasped her gently into his arms and kissed her. Kissed her so passionately she could scarcely breathe.

She had already told Mrs Fish she would not be returning to the tavern that night.

The following day brought fresh promises of help. 'The money is rolling in,' reported the *East London Advertiser*, referring not only to its own fund, but to donations flowing in to various charitable organisations and newspapers, in particular *The Times* where much of the money from America and Australia, or 'Horsetrailier' as Mrs Fish insisted on calling it, was being telegraphed. At home, every church and chapel in Britain seemed to be collecting funds as men and women who would never have dreamed of financing a strike, gave generously in response to appeals from their Churchmen.

Throughout the East End the relief effort was spreading. The East London Bakery had agreed to distribute fifteen thousand loaves daily around the area; the Brooke Bond Tea Company in Whitechapel had put five thousand quarter-pound packets of tea at the disposal of the Dockers' Union; and the Salvation Army had opened a former drill-hall in Whitechapel Road to cater for ten thousand mouths a day. "I could smell the pea-soup two hundred yards away," said Ben after visiting General Booth that morning. He then directed Eleanor to advise all area committees that the value of each food ticket should be raised immediately from a penny to threepence a day. Meanwhile in south-west London, a letter was being delivered by messenger to the private residence of Cardinal Manning. It sought an immediate meeting with the Cardinal at a location of his choice and it bore eleven signatures.

Cardinal Manning was eighty-one years old. Appointed Archbishop of Westminster in 1865, ten years later he was awarded the cardinal's red hat, a colour some considered apt as in social and political affairs he was considered a radical and, by some, even a revolutionary. A patriotic Englishman, full of pride for his country and loyalty to the Queen, his sympathy with the needy and suffering was profound. 'The homes of the poor in London are often very miserable,' he had written in a letter to Lord Salisbury two years before. 'These things cannot go on, these things ought not to go on. The accumulation of wealth in the land, the piling up of wealth like mountains in the possessions of classes or individuals, cannot go on. No commonwealth can rest on such foundations. The rich can take care of themselves. But who is to speak for the poor?' While such views did not endear him to everyone in Rome or, indeed, London, his reputation was immense and even outside his own church he was widely respected.

In his reply to the Cardinal, the Prime Minister maintained, 'But your Eminence. It is socialism you are encouraging.'

'I do not know what socialism means to you, Prime Minister,' Manning wrote back. 'To me it means Christianity.'

At precisely noon on the day following the despatch of their letter, eleven of the twelve directors of the Board of Dock Employers trooped somewhat self-consciously into the drawing-room of the appropriately named Archbishop's House in Victoria. "Please sit, gentlemen," said Manning. With his hollow, penetrating, grey eyes, the Cardinal assessed each of the men in turn. He did not smile, but his tone, although formal, was not without warmth. "Thank you for coming. I'm sure you are all very busy and so perhaps we should come straight to the matter in hand. I assume that we are here to find a way of resolving this unpleasant business as quickly and as painlessly as possible." There was a murmur of confirmation from around the table. "Then may I suggest that you agree to their demands."

There was a brief silence and the eleven men looked ill at ease. George Hyde cleared his throat. "There is a problem, your Eminence. Lord Caldrick. He will, I am certain, refuse to resolve this on anything other than our terms. Or should I say, his terms."

"The very reason, no doubt, that you have embarked upon this meeting in his absence," said Manning.

Hyde nodded. "Exactly. Do you have any suggestions, Cardinal?"

Manning thought for a moment. "You could always have him murdered. No-one would suspect his colleagues."

The directors looked at each other in confusion. "I–I, with all respect, Cardinal,' spluttered Hyde. "Don't you think that is an extreme measure, to say the least?"

Manning's stern expression moderated a little. "Yes, I do. I was attempting to be humorous." The men laughed uneasily. "Do you believe Lord Caldrick would listen to the Home Secretary?"

"Yes. I am sure he would," confirmed Hyde.

"Very well. That is what I shall do."

"You will speak to the Home Secretary?"

"Have I not just implied that, Mr Hyde? Good. Then I believe that concludes our discussion, gentlemen."

"Yes, er, yes, your Eminence. Er, on behalf..."

"Mr Hyde," interrupted the cardinal, a little testily. "I am an ordinary member of the Body of Christ upon earth, and not the Queen of England. Your subservience is uncalled for and does nothing except feed my already obese pride. For my sake, the next time we meet, try to be a little less humble in my presence. Good day to you all. And may God bless you in his mercy."

Henry Matthews was the Home Secretary. He was not a decisive man and liable to persuasion by those more resolute than himself. However, once convinced, he could be singularly obstinate. He was also a Catholic – and a devout one.

It was ten o'clock on the morning of Friday the thirteenth of September, and Lord Caldrick had been summoned to the office of the Home Secretary in the House of Commons. "The facts are quite clear, Henry," insisted Caldrick. "If we give in to this..."

"Yes, yes, the facts," snapped Matthews, drumming his fingers on the desk as he considered the options that were open to him. "The facts *are* quite clear. The country is being smothered by your untimely strike. Ships have nowhere to dock, nowhere to unload. Goods are rotting even as we speak. And the economy is rotting along with them. Soon, the very survival of the government will be in question. They are only asking for sixpence an hour, damn it."

"Yes, of course. I appreciate your concern, Home Secretary," said Caldrick soothingly. "But in a few days everything will be under control once more. In a few days..."

"In a few days? You've been saying that for weeks – that you would resolve this affair quickly and cleanly. Enough is enough. I'm sick and tired of your procrastinations. From the start there has been nothing quick or clean about it. Allegations of beatings, bribery, riot mongering – and worse. And now criticism of the government is coming in daily from all sides. And over what?" snapped Matthews rhetorically. "The price of one of your damn cigars."

Lord Caldrick dropped his recently lit *Romeo y Julieta* on the floor. "But Henry. You cannot lay all this at my door," he protested, as he retrieved his cigar and made a hurried attempt with his foot to disperse the ash.

The Home Secretary looked unamused by the remark and brought his fist down on the desk with a force that surprised even himself. "I don't need to lay it anywhere. This whole bloody mess is your responsibility. And since when have I given you permission to call me Henry? An hour ago I spoke with the Prime Minister. I have now instructed the Lord Mayor and Cardinal Manning to convene a meeting of conciliation tomorrow morning at the Mansion House. You will attend that meeting and settle with the strike leaders."

"Settle – with the leaders?" echoed Caldrick, aghast at the suggestion. "But you don't seem to understand, Home Secretary. Where will it stop? They will lose all respect for their employers, for the men at the top."

"Don't lecture me on what I do or do not understand," ordered Matthews, his voice resonant with unaccustomed anger. "You will meet with these people tomorrow. And you will settle with them. On their terms."

"But Home Secretary..."

Henry Matthews rose from his desk and waved a dismissive arm in Caldrick's direction. "My decision is final."

All kinds of rumours swept through the East End that Saturday as each hour passed by without news: Tillett and Burns had been arrested; Tillett and Burns had disappeared with the funds; Tillett and Burns were dead at the bottom of Millwall Dock. By mid-afternoon, tens of thousands of men had assembled in front of West India Dock gates to await the arrival of their leaders and hear news of the final negotiations. Delayed by the discussions, it was nearly dark when suddenly there was a roar. "They're coming." In the distance a cab was seen approaching rapidly along West India Dock Road. Magically, and with almost military precision, the crowd parted, and the two men, waving and smiling, alighted outside the gate. The noise became overwhelming as the bridled emotion of the men found relief in an explosion of cheering, and several minutes elapsed before Tillett and Burns could clamber onto the roof of the cab to announce what every man present already knew.

Tillett spoke first. He looked suddenly more weary than at any period during the past weeks and contented himself with giving an unadorned statement of what had been agreed. He spoke slowly and paused for several seconds after each clause. As if reflecting their leader's mood, an unnatural silence hung over the huge crowd while he spoke. "Friends. From Monday your pay will be sixpence an hour, and eightpence an hour overtime. The minimum pay each day will be two shillings. The bonus will be calculated under the joint supervision of representatives of the company and the union. There is now sufficient work to keep you employed in the docks both day and night for weeks to come. As soon as this glut is over you will encounter a fairer system of work allocation. No longer will you fight like dogs at the chain. And finally, the company gives full recognition to the new Union of Dock Labourers. Well done, lads. Victory is yours. I now call on your show of hands whether these terms are to be accepted."

A forest of arms flew upwards and the accompanying "yes", roared in unison by a legion of voices, was of such volume that Dock House, four miles away, could well have quivered with the sound.

It took several minutes to re-establish sufficient order for Burns to address the crowd. Thousands of eyes focused greedily on his elation. They could read their own triumph in his face. "It is five long weeks since the strike began, and now, at last, it is over. You have fought this battle with a will and self-sacrifice that has secured the admiration of the whole world. You have been supported by people in Great Britain, in America, in Australia, and in Europe, and in a manner which I had not conceived possible. Tomorrow we make one final journey to Hyde Park to thank those people for their support. But truly it is you, the dock labourer of the East End who has won this victory and I honour every last one of you."

As Tillett and Burns descended circumspectly from the roof of the cab, the jubilant army pushed them inside. The horse was unharnessed and the two men dragged in triumph to the doorway of the Dockers Arms. "Suppose this means you're gonna be able to pay me up front from now on," yelled Beth to one of the dockers.

The man feigned surprise. "Up front? Thought you liked it in arrears, luv."

Meanwhile, Eleanor Marx had sought sanctuary in the committee room. With the arrival of her cab home delayed by congestion on the streets, she was constructing a reply to a telegram received earlier that evening from Cardinal Manning. During an interlude in the negotiations at the Mansion House, Ben had acquainted the Cardinal with her endeavours during the strike, both in respect to union matters and those concerning the organisation of relief, and Manning had conveyed his gratitude on behalf of all the Catholics in the East End. 'Incidentally,' he had concluded, 'I have read some of your father's book. I cannot say I agree with it all, but the essence of some of it is pure Christianity.'

'Thank you, your Eminence,' wrote Eleanor in her reply. 'My father would have been deeply honoured and offended by your words.'

It was well into the night before the doors of the Dockers Arms closed and a temporary peace fell on West India Dock

Road. Some of the revellers would have little or no rest before the start of the pilgrimage to Hyde Park. Soon, a lone figure emerged into the darkness and posted a notice on the board outside the tavern.

END OF STRIKE

All men to return to work on Monday morning.

By order of the Committee – Benjamin Tillett
General Secretary.

And the figure looked relieved.

For the last time the ragged battalion assembled. The sun only had to shine to make that Sunday a triumph – and shine it did. All through the East End, the women gathered in their thousands to cheer their husbands and sons as they marched in victory. Wives brought their babies into the streets for Tillett and Burns to kiss as they passed. The pace seemed quicker, the music louder, and the banners, flags and other contrivances of one sort or another, more numerous than before.

The American and Australian flags, wreathed in flowers, were borne aloft at the head of the procession in acknowledgement of the support rendered from afar. Just behind fluttered a banner of yellow and white crosses in honour of Cardinal Manning. Tillett, in his Sunday best, was devouring the newspapers, while Burns made notes for his final speech, and on one occasion burst through the crowd to buy a pennyworth of plums at a stall. Thorne, his arm strapped to his side, looked pale, but waved a frayed Irish tricolour pressed into his hand earlier by a proud-looking Mary Lamb. It had belonged to Shaun and she smiled brightly as she handed him the flag, something she had not managed in a long time.

The procession reached Aldgate Pump where the Metropolitan Police jurisdiction came to an end and, as previously, Superintendent Forster and the City force marched smartly toward the column to assume responsibility for law and order. On this occasion they did so to a roaring chorus of *Where Did You Get That Hat?* Then the women cleaners from Dock House appeared and tagged on, singing and dancing through the streets. Onwards marched the men to the sounds of *Clementine* and *Rule Britannia* – the latter with a passion that left no doubt of the intent of the marching dockers never, never to be slaves again. Progressing through the City, the stirring music gave way to the more rollicking strains of *For He's A Jolly Good Fellow* as the Lord Mayor and Lady Mayoress were seen on the balcony of the Mansion House, and the processionists halted, dipped their flags, and dispensed three hearty cheers. When the head of the march reached Westminster, Burns glanced at Tillett and pointed in the direction of the Houses of Parliament. "You see that, Ben," he smiled. "Some day I'll be working in there."

Meanwhile, milling around a hastily constructed platform, the numbers in the Park were mounting at an astonishing pace. James had brought Annie and Eleanor by hansom-cab and the three waited impatiently for the arrival of the men. As the head of the procession appeared through the Knightsbridge park gates, the leaders were greeted by the assembled crowd with a cheer immense both in volume and length. So too were the Australian and American flags which soon decorated the stage. Amidst the noise, Ben mounted the platform and walked across to his sister. She flung her arms extravagantly around his neck. Pride shone from her eyes. "See. I told you you could do it."

Ben smiled, savouring his sister's approval which meant so much. Momentarily, his thoughts returned to their conversation as they sat among the kittens in the Dockers Arms. It had been only five weeks before, but it seemed longer. "Yes," he said, yelling to make himself heard over the uproar that surrounded them. "Just like you said. We broke it over the bastards' backs."

Annie felt strangely confused in her elation, unsure whether to laugh or cry, shout out or stay silent. During the next few minutes she settled for all four. Smiling benignly at no-one in particular, Eleanor, all calm and elegance, resembled a youthful Queen Victoria. Other than Annie, she was the only woman on a platform becoming swamped with well-wishers. In contrast to Eleanor, James Donnelly made scant attempt to act with the sobriety befitting that of an ex-reporter of *The Times*. Beneath the huge Stars and Stripes, unaccountably billowing in full splendour despite the still conditions, he leapt up and down and waved in celebration, seemingly, to the whole of Hyde Park, while Will Thorne desperately attempted to protect both himself and particularly his arm from the exuberance of the American.

Burns spoke first. He led three cheers for all the wives, and then told the dockers that they had struck a blow at the selfishness of the employers and proved that a man had a right to live. His words were delivered in more muted fashion than usual, choosing to surrender centre stage to the final speaker.

It was four o'clock. From as far as the Serpentine and the Park Lane palings more than four hundred yards away, the eyes of around a quarter of a million people, East and West Enders together, were focused on Ben Tillett as he spoke to his men for the last time as strike leader. "I am proud of the people of London, both rich and poor, and of those throughout Britain, who have taken the side of the humble working man and assisted him in his struggle. I am proud of the generous support received from around the world, from Australia, from America, and from many countries in Europe. And I thank them with all my heart for that support. I am proud of the women who have helped us: Eleanor Marx, my own sister Annie, Mrs Fish back at the Dockers Arms, and all the wives and children who have suffered with us on the very edge of starvation. But most of all I am proud of the dock labourer. This strike has been won not by encouragement and donations, significant though they were. Nor by the oratory of the leaders. It was won by the simple determination of the dock labourer to fight for a living wage and never to be defeated. For five weeks, silence has reigned over the world's greatest port. Tomorrow we work."

The acclamation was heard at the House of Commons

nearly two miles away. Tillett turned his back on the crowd. Many, like him, were in tears; but he preferred his emotions to remain unseen. It mattered little. First Annie embraced him and she was in tears; then Burns embraced him and he was in tears; James embraced Annie and they were both in tears. Only Eleanor seemed impervious to the moment, shaking her head in astonishment at the inexplicable behaviour of the human race – and men in particular. Seeking her out on a stage now teeming with supporters, Ben clasped her hand and raised it skywards in salute. And at that moment even Eleanor found the need to produce a dainty, lace handkerchief from her handbag.

And so, in dazzling sunlight, the great strike ended in what Lord Randolph Churchill described in *The Sunday Times* as 'Tillett's victory'. For five long weeks, Tillett and Burns had organised, disciplined and controlled an army perhaps five times larger than that which assembled on the plains of Waterloo. They had caught the public imagination, and the following morning were due to be translated into wax and placed on display amid the emperors and convicts in Madame Tussaud's Museum – although not with Burns's original white straw hat. This was lost overboard as they returned from Hyde Park, when he and Tillett took a launch along the Thames to celebrate victory. "Just look at 'em," said a docker as the crowd pressed along the riverbank, cheering and waving their caps. "Anyone would think they was the Kings of England."

Chapter Fourteen

The evening sun reflected off the still water of the Serpentine. Normality had returned to Hyde Park with the marchers retreating eastward and the well-wishers and spectators alike heading home in more diverse directions. Annie and James were sitting side by side on the bank idly watching a family of evident West Enders tossing generous portions of cake to the already well-nourished ducks. "If only the kids at the Mission were that lucky," she murmured. Attracted by the fare, a pair of pure white swans glided across the water. Annie's eyes remained focused on the ducks. "When will you be returning to America?"

"I sail on Tuesday."

"Tuesday! That soon?" She looked as if she were about to say more, but then changed her mind and it was over a minute before she broke the ensuing silence. "Never been on a ship. Went rowing once, in Bristol – with Ben and the family. Didn't really like it." There was another lengthy pause. "Have you thought about staying on longer?" she asked, trying to sound casual.

James gazed down contemplatively at his hands. "Yes," he said after a while. "I've given it a great deal of thought."

"But you decided to go Tuesday."

He nodded slightly and hesitated before he replied. "Last Friday. Hearst sent me a cable. Heaven knows how, but he's secured me an offer as editor of the *Boston Post*. I can't turn down a position like that. But I must start next month." He stared down briefly at the grass before he continued. "I sail from Liverpool. The boat-train leaves Euston Station, tomorrow at midnight."

"It sounds a wonderful opportunity," she said a trifle stoically, glancing at him from the corner of her eye. "You must be very pleased."

"Yes. It's what I've always wanted. Granted the *Post* isn't exactly *The Times*, but even George Buckle had to start somewhere." He reached into his pocket and drew out a small envelope. He handed it to Annie. "Here. It's a poem. By Edgar Allan Poe. He's a poet from Boston. It's called *For Annie*. I copied it out for you – seemed appropriate."

She took the envelope and placed it hurriedly in the pocket of her dress. "I'll read it later," she said, a little self-consciously, "when you've gone." There was another lengthy silence as both struggled to capture the right words. Annie broke it abruptly. "It's getting late. We should be going back."

James nodded, but he made no effort to move from the bank. "Does it bother you?" he asked, almost challengingly. "Me leaving, I mean."

"We'll all miss you," she said quietly, gazing into the water. "You've made quite an impression on Ben. He's very fond of you."

"Yes. But what about you? Will you miss me?"

Momentarily their eyes met. Annie looked away. "Yes – yes, of course," she admitted, stumbling slightly over the words. "I – you know I will."

He took her hand. "I want you to come with me," he said quickly. "I love you and I want you to come with me."

She pulled away in annoyance. "James. Don't be stupid."

He reached again for her hand, clutching tightly as she tugged to pull free. "Listen. I mean it. I love you."

Annie looked away. "You don't. Everything that's happened

today. The excitement. You're not thinking clearly."

"No. I do. I know I do. And I want you to come with me to America," The conviction in his voice made her turn back. Their eyes met and held for a moment and what she saw in his face made her feel numb.

"James. I can't."

"You can."

"I can't. What about your wife? You're still married."

He gave a single, dismissive laugh. "That was over the day I was dumped by the river."

"No. I can't. I can't leave here. It's impossible. Who would look after the kids? America? Me! No, I can't. Look at us. We're so different. I'm not what you're used to."

He pulled her gently towards him. "But don't you see, Annie? That's what I adore about you. All the things I'm not used to. Your honesty, your energy, your humanity, your outspokenness, your hair, your eyes, your nose, your mouth, your laugh, your funny accent..."

"I don't have a funny accent," she gulped.

"Come with me. Back to Boston." James looked towards her with an intensity she had never known, and it frightened her. She stood up and his eyes followed her, trying to read her expression as she walked slowly towards the water, ripples lapping gently at the edge as a rowing-boat drifted past. For what seemed to him an eternity, she gazed into the distance. "Come with me, Annie," he repeated, a trace of anxiety entering his voice.

Staring down at the ground, she wandered back and stood unmoving beside him on the grass and from the expression on her face he guessed the answer even before it came. "I can't. I'm sorry – I just can't." Her eyes moistened. "I have the children, Ben, the Mission, my home. I can't leave, it's just..." Her words faded. She could think of nothing else to say.

"But you can, Annie," he said, becoming more insistent. "You can. Come to America."

She turned aside, brushing her eyes hurriedly on her sleeve. "Why are you doing this?" she asked, her voice growing more agitated.

"Because I want you. I want you with me."

"But you don't understand. I can't go with you. This isn't fair. No. No, I can't. I must go home. Don't follow me. I can find my own way. Please don't follow."

She ran off in the direction of the park gates. "But I need you, Annie," he called after her in despair.

For more than a minute he watched as she gradually merged with the evening strollers and finally disappeared behind the sprawling branches of a willow. James stared dejectedly at the spot where she had vanished. "But I need you," he whispered.

Annie sat motionless in her tiny room above the Dockers Arms. It was almost midnight. For a while she gazed at the painting given to her by James and then at the still-sealed envelope that concealed the poem. Finally she tore it open. The words on the page seemed to flicker gently along with the lamp.

> Now my heart it lies happily
> Bathing in many
> A dream of the truth
> And the beauty of Annie
> Drowned in a bath
> Of the tresses of Annie.
>
> Now my heart it is brighter
> Than all of the many
> Stars in the sky
> For it sparkles with Annie
> It glows with the night
> Of the love of my Annie
> With the thought of the light
> Of the eyes of my Annie.

Tears that had already been close to the surface brimmed and spilled over. So consumed was she by her emotions, she hardly noticed the page flutter face down to the floor. The church clock struck midnight. Annie wiped her tears and leaned slowly forward to gather the poem. For the first time she noticed a card pinned at the back. It was a small, blue card and the elegant gold lettering glinted at Annie in the quivering light. *Cunard Line - Royal Mail Steamers. Liverpool to Boston. Catalonia. 1 Ticket.*

It was almost dawn before Annie rose from her chair.

After a summer of almost unbroken sunshine, rain was pouring down as the cab carrying James and Dr Clarke drew alongside platform one at Euston Station. They were met by a porter. "Liverpool, sir? Train leaves in thirty minutes." The man loaded James's trunk and cases onto a trolley and with theatrical effort set off in the direction of the luggage van.

"Well, guess this is it, old pal," said James. "Thanks once again for everything. I couldn't have got this far without you."

Dr Clarke offered his hand. James laughed. "You're a stuffy Englishman to the end. Come here." Extravagantly, he flung his arms around his friend. For a moment the doctor hesitated, embarrassed, unsure how to engage his hands. Then the two men held each other. "I'll write as soon as I get settled. I'm going to miss you, Edwin. Which is more than I can say of that damn silly game of yours. Never did master the rules of cricket."

"Of course not," said Dr Clarke sternly. "Only an Englishman can do that." He broke off and beamed, as though the significance of the thought had only just occurred to him. "And I will most certainly miss you, James," he added. "The past few weeks have definitely been interesting."

"And if you ever happen to be on my side of the Atlantic..."

"I'll stay well clear of Boston, that's for sure," said the doctor in a manner that meant exactly the opposite. "Goodbye, old boy. Safe journey home."

James waved as Dr Clarke's cab drew away, its horse warily negotiating the steep upward incline to the street. As it disappeared from view, it was passed by another moving at speed in the opposite direction. He turned to board the train. "Ticket please, sir," said the guard.

There was a shout from behind. "James. James."

"Someone for you, sir?" asked the guard.

James turned to see Ben striding towards him. "Thank God!" gasped Tillett. "I was afraid I might have missed you. I've been so busy today – even more so than I had anticipated. I have come to deliver one final goodbye."

James clasped him by the hand. "I don't know what to say, Ben."

Tillett smiled. "No. I think we've all heard enough words these past few weeks. Ours has been a glorious victory, and for that, James, I am forever in your debt. Without your self-sacrifice and courage we may well have been defeated."

"No, no," said James, shaking his head. "You give me far too much credit. It was you who controlled and organised your men into – what? The greatest labour revolt in your country's history. How you achieved that I shall never know."

Ben smiled once more. "Well, in part, I am indebted to Napoleon. Let me tell you something, James, something I've told no-one until now. Last Christmas, my wife, who I've so sadly neglected these past weeks, gave me a manuscript which she was aware I had long coveted. An analysis of the campaigns of Napoleon. It took me four hours to finish the document, and the following day, all day, I walked the rain-sodden streets around the docks, hour after hour, planning a strike which would probably never take place. As if it were a military operation and I had thousands of men at my command who had to be led. I noted every dock gate where outside labour might be introduced. Decided on the best place to post pickets, and grappled in my mind with the problems of organisation and discipline. So you see I had an excellent tutor."

James smiled. "Or you are an even better prophet. Good luck with the union. I shall never forget you, Ben. You are without question one of the finest men I have ever met." The two shook hands. "Take care of Annie."

"I think she can take care of herself," laughed Ben. "Goodbye, James. Have a safe journey home." He turned and walked the short distance to his waiting cab. "Oh, I almost forgot. I have something for you, a memento, from us all in the East End." Ben opened the cab door. "I think you'll be needing a porter. No. Better make that two porters," he added, dragging out a large chest and a painting by Albrecht Dwight. A huge smile extended slowly across James's face.

"Is the young lady's fings also for the luggage van, sir?" sighed the porter.

The Times   London   Monday, September 16, 1889

The great strike is over at last. The most momentous struggle between Capital and Labour ever seen has ended in victory for the weaker side. It came to a close on Saturday, and today the men are at work and trade at the Port of London can resume. It has been a rather silly business. Almost an allegory with the part of Privilege played by the London Dock Employers and the part of the Downtrodden Underdogs by the dockers who inhabit the slums of the East End. It is still too soon to reckon what this prolonged interruption to industry has cost the nation in pounds, shillings and pence. That will come later. But there was such an absurd disproportion between ends and means: here was the commerce of the greatest port in the world being ruinously, perhaps irretrievably, damaged; here was an enormous amount of inconvenience, loss and embarrassment being injected on the mercantile centre of the Empire; here was London being exposed to the risk of famine and riot – and all for what? That some few hundreds of underpaid dock labourers might be paid a little better.

The Dock Employers do not come out of it at all well. They end by conceding all that was asked of them. They have done what the strike leaders said from the start they would eventually have to do. The demands of the strikers were reasonable enough and it was, of course, this fact which gave them the great support in public opinion without which the strike would have collapsed like a pricked balloon before it had lasted a week. For the past ten days it has seemed inevitable that the employers should yield, and if one has to yield, it is better to do so while there is yet time to retreat with the honours of war. True enough, the Directors may urge in due time that the attack upon them would never have succeeded but for the assistance rendered by outside forces. But they knew what forces they would have to reckon with from the beginning, and they might have foreseen – as Mr Tillett appears to have done – that they would hardly prosper against them. But they preferred to go on fighting a losing battle. Men of business ought to know better. A chess-player who understands the board will often resign when an indifferent player would waste hours in prolonging a hopeless fight.

We have sided almost from the start with the detractors of the Dock Employers when they say that a business which can only be maintained by reducing wages to starvation rates, is badly mismanaged. We do not see why even the lowest class of 'workers' should consent to accept a pittance barely sufficient to support life at workhouse standard, if by unification and resistance they can raise it. Mr Tillett is evidently of the same mind, and thus, his new Dock, Wharf, Riverside & General Workers' Union is a welcome development. Many others, previously abandoned as incapable of organisation, will, quite properly, be encouraged by the outcome of this strike, and like a pebble cast into a pond, its testament to the power of alliance will inevitably bring demands for the creation of new unions to protect them from practices pursued by the likes of the London Dock Employers.

And so what seemed the most desperate and forlorn of hopes has been crowned by victory. When the strike began on August 13, no-one supposed that the dockers could hold out for almost five weeks, and if they had been left to their own resources they must have long since yielded. That, the Directors knew, and that, they reckoned upon. But they forgot the outside public, or did not imagine that sympathy would take the form of subscriptions. Well, the Directors were wrong. The public did subscribe. And it was the public, first of East London with its pennies, then of the nation with its shillings and pounds, and then of the world with its assortment of coinage and dollar bills, which fought the battle alongside the dockers.

We have seen much sympathy for the poor from both the comfortable and well-to-do classes these past few days. But we should not forget that, in truth, it was the sympathy for the poor from the poor throughout the past five weeks that has actually decided this strike in favour of Mr Tillett. It was more than a fight for better wages and conditions. Unskilled and impoverished, without education or influence, the dock labourers were galvanised not by political idealism, but by a basic struggle for survival against oppressive employers, a moral uprising that roused the social conscience of the whole nation, and eventually the world. Unskilled labour for the first time in this country has had the opportunity of showing its importance to the common well-being, and this fact, now that it is appreciated both by the labourer himself and by the employer, and by those who have helped to make and mould the Empire, will make the great strike of London dock labourers memorable in the history of time.

The *East London Advertiser* put the whole thing more succinctly. 'For our part,' it said in a front page editorial, 'this newspaper has never been so proud to represent the fine people of the East End, as during these past five weeks.'

Chapter Fifteen

For the first time in three weeks Jim Harris breathed fresh air. The fresh, balmy air of an early autumn dawn. A few birds sang from a nearby sycamore and soft sunlight angled across his face.

A church bell struck the hour. It was six o'clock. A man beside him spoke. But Jim was deaf to his words. His mind was confused. Clare, Norwood, the strike. Again the man spoke. "James Harris. You have been found guilty of the crime of murder. It is now my duty to perform the sentence prescribed in law. May God have mercy on your soul."

Jim uttered a last defiant cry. "I ain't gonna be no Judas." The birds stopped singing and only the creaking of a gently swinging rope disturbed the silence. It was the seventeenth of September. No-one was left on strike.

Appendix 1

The strike of 1889 is acknowledged as second only to the General Strike in its significance to the British labour movement, generating a substantial upsurge in trade union membership – a quarter of a million within twelve months – and creating the first of the mass unions. In 1893, socialist politicians, progressive intellectuals and trades unionists, including Ben Tillett, John Burns and Will Thorne, joined together to establish the Independent Labour Party. It became the Labour Party seven years later. *The Red Flag*, the song written to commemorate the great strike of 1889, was adopted as their anthem.

Appendix 2. Biographical notes

ANNIE TILLETT - JAMES DONNELLY: Married in Boston in 1890. They had three children, all girls, the eldest of which they named Emily.

Following the acquisition by Hearst in 1895 of the ailing *New York Journal*, James Donnelly was appointed editor and within a year the newspaper attained an unprecedented circulation. In 1910 he was elected Mayor of Boston and was later narrowly defeated in the election for Governor of Massachusetts. For the remainder of his life he divided his time between politics and writing.

Annie Donnelly worked for the National Congress of Parents & Teachers Association (PTA), founded in 1897 by Phoebe Hearst, mother of William. She became its vice-president in 1919.

James Donnelly died in Boston in 1925 at the age of sixty-three. His wife died in New York three years later at the age of seventy-two.

BEN TILLETT: Remained as General Secretary of the Dock, Wharf, Riverside and General Workers' Union until 1921 when he became the prime architect in the formation of the Transport & General Workers' Union. One of the founder members of the Labour Party, he became MP for Salford in 1917 and Chairman of the Trades Union Congress in 1928.

In 1931 he retired from Westminster and public life, and died in London in 1943 at the age of eighty-three. Two thousand mourners attended a memorial service held at St Martin-in-the-Fields at Trafalgar Square. The eulogy was read by Clement Attlee, soon to become Prime Minister. 'His memory will live not so much in the minds of the wealthy few as in the hearts of the toiling masses. Ben Tillett is dead but his voice and ideals live on.'

GEORGE BUCKLE: Remained as editor of *The Times* until 1912 and his twenty-eight years in the position has never been exceeded. Subsequently became a writer and the biographer of Queen Victoria and Disraeli. Died in 1935 at the age of seventy-nine.

JOHN BURNS: Chosen as Chairman of the Trades Union Congress in 1892 and elected MP for Battersea the same year. Became the first working man to be named a British cabinet minister when appointed President of the Board of Trade in 1914. Withdrew from politics in 1918 to devote his life to his books. Died in 1943 at the age of eighty-five on the same day as Ben Tillett.

LORD CALDRICK: Resigned from the Board of the London Dock Employers in October 1889. Stood unsuccessfully as Conservative candidate in the 1892 general election and subsequently retired to the family estate in Oxfordshire. Died in 1900 at the age of sixty-four.

MARY LAMB: Following the departure of Annie Tillett, worked full-time at the Limehouse Mission. After the death of Lady Hallow in 1892, the Mission was acquired by Thomas

Barnardo and converted to an orphanage. She continued to work for the Barnardo organisation until her death in 1909.

CARDINAL MANNING: Spent the final three years of his life in seclusion, tending his beloved rose garden. Died in 1892 at the age of eighty-three, clothed, at his own behest, in the full regalia of state occasions. For three days he lay in state while a quarter of a million people filed, day and night, past his body. At his funeral, George Bernard Shaw said, 'The Cardinal was the wisest man I have ever met.'

ELEANOR MARX: Two months after the strike, she collaborated with her friend James Connell to write the words of *The Red Flag*. Became involved both professionally and personally with Edward Aveling, a scientist, actor, and leading socialist with whom she spent two years touring America, performing and giving lectures. They returned to London together where she continued to work for the disadvantaged. Distraught when she learned Aveling had secretly married a twenty-one-year-old woman, she committed suicide in 1898 by taking prussic acid. A letter addressed to Aveling lay beside her body. 'My dear. It will soon be over. My last word to you is the same that I have said during all of our nine years together – love.' She was forty-three years old.

C.M.NORWOOD: Three weeks after the strike, he collapsed from a heart attack as he dined on board a vessel anchored at Millwall Dock. He died on the quayside at the age of forty-six.

WILL THORNE: Appointed as General Secretary of the newly re-formed National Union of Gasworkers (subsequently the GMB), a position he held for forty-five years. Became MP for West Ham in 1906 and remained in Parliament until 1945 when he was made a Privy Councillor. Throughout these years he was a prominent figure within the Trades Union Congress and in 1930 was awarded a CBE. He died in 1946 at the age of eighty-eight, the last survivor of the leading protagonists of the strike of 1889.

Appendix 3

First Manifesto of the Strike Committee

DOCK LABOURERS' STRIKE August 13th, 1889.

TO THE TRADE UNIONISTS AND PEOPLE OF LONDON.

Friends and Fellow Workmen.

The dock labourers of London, the poorest, most wretched and worst paid men in London, are on strike and asking for an advance of wages of a penny per hour for day work and twopence per hour overtime. The work is of a most precarious nature, three hours being the average amount per day obtained by the men, and the system operated by the employers permits them to be driven like slaves at the bidding of men who are selected from the most brutal of their class, who underpay, overdrive, and restrict the numbers necessary to do a fair day's work. We call on all other waterside trades in London to support us by every lawful means in their power, and we will surely win if we receive that support. We appeal to the public at large for support and contributions which may be sent to **The Committee Room, The Dockers Arms, West India Dock Road, Poplar, E.** In doing so we feel sure that our efforts will be appreciated, not as disturbers or peace breakers, but as a demand from men determined to swerve not one inch from the attitude they have taken up to support the poor and lift up the down-trodden.

By order of the Strike Committee and on behalf of the men:

BENJAMIN TILLETT - JOHN BURNS - WILL THORNE - TOM McCARTHY -
ELEANOR MARX

Dock Labourers' Union

Members are requested to fall in line and to obey officers in maintaining good order.

No-Work Manifesto

MANIFESTO OF THE COMMITTEE OF THE DOCK STRIKE

September 7th, 1889.

To the Workers of London.

On Friday we were informed that the Dock Employers had again refused to meet representatives of the Dock Labourers' Union to discuss our reasonable demands. Meanwhile their obstinacy is inflicting cruel suffering upon tens of thousands of dock labourers and their families. These privations have been borne with good-temper which has excited the active support of labour throughout the country.

We have previously urged workers of trades not directly connected with the docks to remain at work and to avoid causing inconvenience to the general community. Our studied moderation has been mistaken by our ungenerous opponents for lack of courage or want of resources. We are therefore compelled to take a step which we would have wished had not been forced upon us, and which we are fully aware may be followed by the gravest consequences.

We now solemnly appeal to the workers in London of all grades and of every calling to refuse to go to work on Tuesday next unless the employers have before noon on Monday, September 9th, officially informed this committee that the moderate demands of the dock labourers have been conceded. These demands from which the men have never swerved are:- The minimum rate of pay to be sixpence an hour ordinary time and eightpence an hour overtime. No man to be employed less than four hours. The abolition of all inhumane work practices.

By order of the Strike Committee and on behalf of the men:

BENJAMIN TILLETT
TOM McCARTHY

Dock Labourers' Union

Manifesto withdrawing the No-Work Manifesto

MANIFESTO OF THE COMMITTEE OF THE DOCK STRIKE

September 9th, 1889.

Fellow Countrymen.

During the past forty-eight hours we have had convincing proof that public opinion amongst all classes declares that the demands of the dock labourers are just and reasonable, and we have been inundated with offers of assistance provided that our attack is confined to the few men who are willing to plunge the metropolis into chaos rather than admit themselves to be in the wrong. We are determined to show that we are not actuated by such miserable vanity as our opponents and that the working classes are as superior to the dock directors in true nobility of character as they are in the capacity to manage their business. We therefore hereby cancel our appeal to the workers of London to strike on Tuesday and invite them instead to strain every nerve and to make every sacrifice to supply us with the sinews of war; especially we ask the organised trades in the provinces, as well as London, to send us at once the largest contributions they can afford.

We believe that the public will respond to our call for help with a promptitude and generosity that will enable us to relieve the suffering. Meanwhile the docker starves but does not surrender.

By order of the Strike Committee and on behalf of the men:

BENJAMIN TILLETT
JOHN BURNS
WILL THORNE
TOM McCARTHY
ELEANOR MARX

Dock Labourers' Union

The Final Agreement - September 14, 1889

TERMS OF AGREEMENT

(1) The fivepence per hour be raised in the case of all labour on and after September 16 next to sixpence per hour and eightpence per hour overtime. No pay for meal times.

(2) Men called in not to be discharged with less than two shillings pay, except in regard to special short engagements in the afternoon.

(3) All bonus payments to be calculated under the supervision of representatives of the Employers and the Union.

(4) Call in procedures to be discussed by representatives of the Employers and the Union.

(5) The hours of overtime shall be from 6.00 pm and 6.00 am.

(6) The strike to be terminated and all men to return to work forthwith.

Signed on behalf of the
London Dock Employers:
C.M.NORWOOD

Signed on behalf of the
Dockers' Union:
BENJAMIN TILLETT

Witnesses:
SIR JAMES WHITEHEAD, LORD MAYOR
HENRY E. CARDINAL MANNING

Dated September 14, 1889.

LIMEHOUSE MISSION

Instituted in the year 1888

Offices: WEST INDIA DOCK ROAD, POPLAR, LONDON, E.

This Society is supported by Voluntary Contributions, and is established for the Religious, Intellectual, and Social Elevation of the Working Classes by means of gospel services held in the Mission Hall, cottage meetings held in the homes of the poor or otherwise, addresses to tramps and others in lodging-house kitchens, open air preaching, special services for children, Sunday schools, mothers' meetings, maternity societies, bible classes, house to house visitation, lectures on self-help, thrift, etc. and other social and religious subjects, entertainments, Temperance Societies, Bands of Hope, and excursions into the country.

Also for the Benevolent and Charitable purpose of relieving the sick and destitute poor by means of temporary or permanent pecuniary aid in deserving cases, daily breakfasts and Irish stew dinners to poor children, and gratuitous distribution of food, fuel, and clothing.

FUNDS ARE URGENTLY NEEDED

To develop the good work the Mission has in view, Subscriptions and Donations will be gratefully received and acknowledged by Reverend Adderley, The Limehouse Mission, West India Dock Road, Poplar, London, E. Bankers: The London & South-Western Bank, 7, Fenchurch Street, London, E.C.

Appendix 4

Verse found by the prison chaplain in the pocket of Jim Harris after he was hanged. It was delivered to Ben Tillett who ordered it framed and kept it on display in his home until he died. It was bequeathed by Tillett's family to the Transport & General Workers' Union in London.

>Six in the mornin'– and I've come for work,
>While tucked up in bed lie the boss and the clerk;
>I get to the entrance, and stand with the mob,
>One man among many who'll fight for a job;
>A chain is stretched out to serve as a gate,
>And one thousand men have to stand there and wait;
>And one thousand men, all hungry and tired,
>Stand waitin' and hopin' that they're gonna get hired;
>Waitin' and hopin' that they'll be the one
>The foreman picks out for the work to be done;
>One thousand men for a hundred-odd jobs,
>One thousand men wanting food in their gobs.
>
>An hour's gone by, and they've not made a start,
>There's fear in my guts, but hope in my heart;
>From one to two thousand the numbers have risen,
>There's regular dockers and some straight from prison;
>The casuals, the royals, the loafers, the yobs,
>And men with a trade who've just lost their jobs;
>The unemployed man fills the docker with rage,
>No newcomer pig's gonna pocket my wage!
>We're angry, and restless, some fightin' back tears,
>Then the Almighty foreman, at last he appears
>With the gangers around him, before us he stands,
>The power of life or death in his hands.
>
>The power of life or death in his hands,
>With a grin on his face the foreman just stands,
>He stands and he stares, then he walks up and down
>And the grin on his face bends into a frown;

"Now let's have some quiet and I'll tell you a joke,"
And silence falls on us like soot from the smoke.
"Now the joke, lads, is this; you're more than ten hundred,
And the amount of jobs going's not that highly numbered."
The gangers all laugh at their boss's bad joke,
But we remain silent, as silent as smoke.

'One hundred and fifty is all that we need.'
One hundred and fifty! It makes my heart bleed,
One hundred and fifty! That number's like fire
That burns through our ranks like a flame through a pyre.
"One hundred and fifty! I'm sorry, my friends,
And who works and who doesn't – on my choice depends."
On his choice depends! We know that by now,
But he likes to repeat it to make us kow-tow;
One hundred and fifty! If I'm lucky, all's well,
One hundred and fifty! There's no chance in hell;
I'm one in two thousand, the chances are slim,
Just one of two thousand all lookin' to him.

He raises his hand – like God on His throne,
To the gangers, the names or the faces are known;
With a flick of the hand, the gangers run in
And start handin' out their tickets of tin;
A ticket that means I'll work for a day,
A ticket that stands for food and for pay.

All hell breaks loose – the silence is shattered,
The weak and the sickly are beaten and battered;
If I get to the front I'll show I've got grit,
For anyone else I don't give a shit;
I shove to the ground a man in my way,
A kick to the bollocks – he's out of the fray;
The man on my back, I throw to the floor,
A kick to the head and the blood starts to pour;
I catch a wild punch – I stagger and trip,
A kick to my face splits open my lip,
I'm knocked to the ground, amid screaming and groans,
And the flesh on my face is ripped by the stones;
I try to get up – if I stay down I'm dead,
But I'm trampled by men who want daily bread.

[225]

"Now steady on lads, they know who to choose,
If you're one of the chosen, you can't really lose;
But having said that – you might change my mind
If you get to the front, a job you could find;
If you show me your guts, and show me you're strong,
A little tin ticket could be yours before long;
Now what's all the fuss, all this shouting and noise?
Just get to the front, show your face to the boys;
They'll pick out the best, the best men'll win,
So, roll up, roll up, for your ticket of tin."

I lie on the cobbles, unable to rise,
There's blood in my mouth and blood in my eyes;
The men've gone past, the tickets are given,
The tickets that get them from Hell into heaven;
I lift up my heart, and through blood and through tears,
I glimpse the men chosen going off to the piers;
But the foreman still stands in front of the chain,
And shakes his fat head at the ones who remain.
"Bad luck, lads, I know you're all disappointed,
But keep your chins up, your spirits undaunted;
If you want to stay on, there could be work later,
The wind will quite often bring in a stray freighter;
So go with my boys, if you fancy a wait,
Or I'll see you tomorrow, back here at the gate."

Some of them go, just to wait in the yard,
And waitin' all day for nothin' ain't hard,
I get to my feet, and fightin' with pain,
I make my way over and stand at the chain;
Already they've let a good hundred men through,
This time I'm gonna be one of the few.
One of the few who gets work for a day,
One of the few who takes home a day's pay.
Each hour that goes by is an hour of hope,
And hope only dies at the end of a rope.

Sources

The following publications were used for reference and research.

Books:

Adderley, Reverend the Hon. James. (1916) *In Slums and Society.*

Barnardo, Thomas J. (1888) *Night and Day.*

Black, Clementina. (1907) *Sweated Industry and the Minimum Wage.*

Booth, Charles. (1889) *Poverty. The Life and Labour of the People of London.*

Booth, William. (1890) *In Darkest England.*

Buckle, George. (1935) *The History of The Times.*

Burgess, J. (1911) *John Burns. The Rise and Fall of a Right Honourable.*

Burns, John. (1889) *The Great Strike.*

Champion, Henry Hyde. (1890) *The Great Dock Strike of 1889.*

Clegg, H.A., Fox, A. and Thompson, A.F. (1964) *A History of British Trade Unions Since 1889.*

Donovan, P.F. (1972) *Australia and the Great London Dock Strike of 1889.*

Fishman, William J. (1979) *The Streets of East London.*

Greenwood, James. (1869) *The Seven Curses of London.*

Kapp, Yvonne. (1972 & 1976) *Eleanor Marx.*

Kapp, Yvonne. (1989) *The Air of Freedom: The Birth of the New Unionism.*

Light, George. (1940) *Ben Tillett, Fighter and Pioneer.*

Mackay, Thomas. (1889) *The English Poor.*

Marcan, Peter. (1992) *An East End Album.*

Marcan, Peter. (1984) *East London. Sketches of Christian Works and Workers.*

Manning, Cardinal H.E. (1877) *Dignity and Rights of Labour.*

Marx, Eleanor; Longuet, Jenny Marx and Lafargue, Laura Marx. (1982) *The Daughters of Karl Marx.*

McCarthy, Terry. (1988) *The Great Dock Strike 1889.*

Nash, Vaughan and Smith, Llewellyn. (1889) *The Story of the Dockers' Strike.*

Purcell, E.C. (1895) *Life of Cardinal Manning.*

Radice, Giles and Lisanne. (1974) *Will Thorne, Constructive Militant.*

Political World Yearbook. 1889.
Rowntree, Seebohm. (1901) *Poverty. A Study of Town Life.*
Schreer, Jonathan. (1982) *Ben Tillett. Portrait of a Labour Leader.*
Simms, George. (1889) *How the Poor Live.*
Thorne, Will. (1925) *My Life's Battles.*
Tillett, Ben. (1910) *Brief History of the Dockers' Union.*
Tillett, Ben. (1931) *Memories and Reflections.*
Tillett, Ben. (1887) *The Dockers' Bitter Cry.*
Webb, Beatrice and Sidney. (1894) *History of Trade Unionism.*
Wisden. (1890)

Newspapers:

Daily News   *East London Advertiser*
Evening Standard   *Melbourne Bulletin*
New York Times   *Pall Mall Gazette*
San Francisco Examiner   *Star*
Sunday People   *Sydney Morning Herald*
The Daily Telegraph   *The Sunday Times*
The Times

- The front jacket delineation depicts the River Thames between Tower Hill and Woolwich, and West India and Millwall Docks on the Isle of Dogs.

- The illustration alongside each chapter heading shows the *Lady Armstrong* anchored at Millwall Dock *c.* 1885.

- The illustration on page 227 comes from the archives of the National Museum of Labour History.

Acknowledgements

Inevitably, a project like *The Price Of A Cigar* is only completed with the assistance of those who give generously of their time and resources. My gratitude goes to them all.

• Calberson International for allowing me liberal access to that godsend to all writers – a photocopy machine.

• The Guildhall, Tower Hamlets and British Museum Reference Libraries for their patience and co-operation.

• Bob Aspinall at the Museum of Docklands where I camped day after day for many weeks with flasks of tea and egg and sardine sandwiches, immersed in their admirable collection of late-nineteenth century books and manuscripts.

• Peter Marcan Publications for its series on life in East and South-East London which provided me with an invaluable written and pictorial insight into the Victorian period, on which I leaned heavily.

• Roger Farrand and Ron Lawrence for their patience and expertise in the face of the innumerable problems with which I confronted them.

• Robert Hamilton whose talents as a playwright must surely soon bring him even wider recognition.

• And finally to the instigator and inspiration behind both *The Strike Of 1889* and *The Price Of A Cigar*, the ubiquitous Steve Rogers. Producer, actor, writer, and owner of the cuddliest cat in East London, it was Steve who not only contributed significantly to the writing of this book, a development of a filmscript we wrote together, but in nine typically captivating words, persuaded me to become involved in the venture. "Let's face it. You've got nothing better to do."

Also by Peter Wood

If The Sun Doesn't Kill You, The Washing Machine Will

The true adventures of a Londoner in the Middle-Eastern state of Qatar. From the reluctant adoption of four homicidal goats named Arsenal, For, The and Cup, to the driving test which involved reversing round an obstacle course for thirty minutes; from the terrifying washing machine that took nine hours to wash one sock, to the elaborate weather forecasts about weather that never changed – Peter Wood's amazing escapades are unforgettable and cannot fail to make you laugh.

'Well written, entertaining and funny. I laughed lots.'

Chris Tarrant

'Fascinating and funny.'

Steve Wright. Radio 1

'Amazing book. Buy it.'

Radio 5

'Hilarious.'

LBC Radio

'The author has an eye for detail and sense of the absurd which makes it fun.'

The Sunday Times

'Hilarious. It's a real gem.'

Daily Express

'Devastatingly witty.'

The Independent

'Don't miss it.'

Home and Away

Published by Kyle Cathie Ltd
20 Vauxhall Bridge Road
London SW1V 2SA

ISBN 1-85626-159-X

The Author

The Price of a Cigar is Peter Wood's second book and follows the success of his widely acclaimed *If The Sun Doesn't Kill You, The Washing Machine Will.* He lives on the Isle of Dogs in London.
